PENGUIN BOOKS

AGAINST GRAVITY

Farnoosh Moshiri was born in Tehran, Iran. She received degrees from the College of Dramatic Arts of Tehran, the University of Iowa, and the University of Houston. She is the author of the novels *At the Wall of the Almighty* and *The Bathhouse* and a collection of short stories, *The Crazy Dervish and the Pomegranate Tree*. Among the many literary awards she has received are the Barthelme Memorial Fellowship, the Barbara Deming Fiction Award for Peace and Social Justice, and two consecutive Black Heron Press Awards for Social Fiction.

AGAINST GRAVITY

Farnoosh Moshiri

PENGUIN BOOKS

PENGUIN BOOKS

Published by the Penguin Group

Penguin Group (USA) Inc., 375 Hudson Street, New York, New York 10014, U.S.A.

Penguin Group (Canada), 90 Eglinton Avenue East, Suite 700, Toronto,
Ontario, Canada M4P 2Y3 (a division of Pearson Penguin Canada Inc.)

Penguin Books Ltd, 80 Strand, London WC2R 0RL, England

Penguin Ireland, 25 St Stephen's Green, Dublin 2, Ireland (a division of Penguin Books Ltd)

Penguin Group (Australia), 250 Camberwell Road, Camberwell,
Victoria 3124, Australia (a division of Pearson Australia Group Pty Ltd)

Penguin Books India Pvt Ltd, 11 Community Centre, Panchsheel Park, New Delhi - 110 017, India

Penguin Group (NZ), cnr Airborne and Rosedale Roads, Albany,
Auckland 1310, New Zealand (a division of Pearson New Zealand Ltd)

Penguin Books (South Africa) (Pty) Ltd, 24 Sturdee Avenue,
Rosebank, Johannesburg 2196, South Africa

Penguin Books Ltd, Registered Offices: 80 Strand, London WC2R 0RL, England

First published in Penguin Books 2005

1 3 5 7 9 10 8 6 4 2

Excerpt from "The Neighbor" from *The Book of Images* by Rainer Maria Rilke, translated by Edward
Snow. Translation copyright © 1991 by Edward Snow. Reprinted by permission of North Point
Press, a division of Farrar, Straus and Giroux, LLC.

Selections from *The Essential Rumi,* translated by Coleman Barks (HarperCollins Publishers).
Copyright © 1995 by Coleman Barks. Reprinted by permission of Coleman Barks.

Publisher's Note

This is a work of fiction. Names, characters, places, and incidents either are the product
of the author's imagination or are used fictitiously, and any resemblance to actual persons,
living or dead, business establishments, events, or locales is entirely coincidental.

LIBRARY OF CONGRESS CATALOGING IN PUBLICATION DATA
Moshiri, Farnoosh.
Against gravity / Farnoosh Moshiri.
p. cm.
ISBN 0 14 303568 1
I. Title.
PS3563.O88443A36 2006
813'.54—dc22   2005043375

Printed in the United States of America
Set in Granjon   Designed by Vicky Hartman

For David

Take an axe to the prison wall.
Escape.
Walk out like someone suddenly born into color.
Do it now.

RUMI

Unscrew the locks from the doors!
Unscrew the doors themselves from the jambs!

WALT WHITMAN

I'm all orders of being, circling the galaxy,
The evolutionary intelligence, the lift,
And the falling away.

RUMI

I'm a dance—play up there! The fit is whirling me fast!

WALT WHITMAN

Life is heavier than the weight of all things.

RILKE

Acknowledgments

◆

I would like to express my gratitude to Jerome Gold at Black Heron Press, who supported me when not many publishers were interested in serious literature from Iran. Also many thanks to my agent, Elizabeth Wales, who cares about my work.

AGAINST GRAVITY

MADISON

✦

God created His world in seven days; I destroyed
mine in six.

MADISON A. KIRBY

Day One

I saw her sitting on the bench of the bus stop, under the merciless sun of May, next to the dark woman with a bundle, and
I desired her. I saw her, small and lost and orphaned in this
cruel city, and I thought, Ah, if I could only lay her tiny body
flat on my hard bed and crawl on her; if I could press my
bones against her nakedness and blow my breath into her and
show her one way (the only way?) one can survive in this goddamned world; if I could teach her how one can conquer lone-
liness and worthlessness—even if for a minute or two . . . and
I know, I know . . . all the weight of the world will land on
one's shoulders after that, but so be it. So be it. That's fucking life.

I stood there in the shade of the dusty magnolia, watched her, and followed her gaze. She stared at the gorilla on top of the Transco Tower, standing tall and fat, with his arms wide open, his chest protruded, as if laughing at the city. She stared at the animal's helium-filled belly, shimmering with gold and red, the sign of one oil company or another. The gorilla lifted one foot lightly, then another, tap dancing in the hot breeze.

May is even more cruel than April in Houston, Texas. Let Mr. T. S. Eliot check this out. Magnolias open shamelessly, exposing their insides, their juices oozing, and their scent—the scent of lust and death and decay—fills every inch of the thick air. You inhale the sweet thing and you want to do something severe to someone or to yourself. You want to live and love and lust, or you yearn to cut your veins with a sharp blade in the thickness of a sunset that reflects in wide, blue windowpanes.

I stood there, ten in the morning, watching her watching the gorilla, oblivious of her daughter sitting next to her and the dark woman with the bundle on the same bench, and of course unaware of me, standing not far from her, in my gray suit, now too thick for the season, perspiring, panting a bit, because of the strong scent of the magnolias.

When I sat next to her she saw me and we both smiled. I introduced myself with the same insipid joke I've repeated all my life to mock my name. I said, "Hi, my name is Madison, but don't call me Mad!" She either didn't get it, or the humor was weak. I said, "I'm your neighbor, Mr. Thompson's tenant." She said her name was Roya and introduced her daughter—eleven or twelve years old, a bit fat, dark face, frizzled hair, and frowning—apparently a brat. She said the girl's name was Tala, meaning "gold" in Farsi. Then we talked and I realized that they'd just moved to the Thompson's garage apartment, next to Bobby Palomo's, and that they were Iranian (she said Persian), but did not come straight from Iran. They had lived in India for a while and before that somewhere else she didn't mention. I said I'd been to India too—in the late seventies—and this gave us a common subject to talk about. But I didn't remember anything decent about my India days and I couldn't talk about the dope and the wet-eyed, under-aged girls, and the long nights that I sat stoned in a small park in New Delhi, gazing at the dense woods, thinking about my dark life or rather feeling it. None of these I could share with her. But she volunteered a lot of information about herself—a political refugee, on welfare, looking desperately for a job—a single mother. She had a brother once who was executed by the Islamic regime. She had a cousin in Houston who was her sponsor, but a busy lawyer, too busy to be able to help her. She told me more than one should tell a stranger in a bus stop on a hot day in the city of smoke and cement. Much more than a man like me should ever know. She trusted my suit, I thought later, or my round glasses and my balding hair. And she was naive, unsuspicious of people and places. A foreigner. Persian.

Before her bus came we sat for a minute or two in silence, now both uncomfortable because of what the dark woman was doing. I had seen this creature's rituals before and she began right in front of our eyes. With that plastic bag on her head, the four corners tied to make something like a shower cap for herself, she began folding a pale denim jacket on her lap, then unfolding it, and again folding and again and again. Her black, spotted face—burned sometime in the past and healed in shrunken leather—beamed with satisfaction.

"She is the ghost of the city," I said and smiled.

"Is it that bad?"

"What?"

"The city?"

"It depends. It all depends."

She sighed and glanced up at the gorilla again and I looked at her pale face and large eyes, framed by black eyelashes under thick lenses. But her hair was cut brutally short, close cropped, which reminded me of a French writer whose picture I'd seen somewhere long ago and whose name had escaped me, like all the names that escaped me every day and all the books that left my memory by the dozen.

When their bus came, the girl bounced up and pulled her mother behind, unable to hide her joy that the conversation with the stranger had ended and she had her mother to herself. They ran, more like two children, the mother just slightly taller than the child. I looked at the muscles of the woman's buttocks, firm and young and shapely in tight white pants. A gazelle. Something stirred in my guts again and I wanted her the way I'd never wanted a female in my life. Now she climbed on the bus and pressed one hand on the small of her back, as if a pain had just passed through and she touched its route. She smiled at me from behind the opaque window and I smiled back.

THE HEAVY BUS jolted in large potholes and bumped up and down and creaked and cracked. My stomach was upset and I felt like vomiting. There was an odor, too. Someone behind me in the dark end of the bus carried the smell of death and decay. With my white, ironed handkerchief I covered my nose, murmured, "The Ship of Death," and gazed out the window to amuse myself.

Outside, across the street from Sears, there was a fountain with three benches around it, each one occupied by the homeless. I saw the same woman with the plastic bag on her head. How did she get here before I did? Or was she another woman with the same shower cap? A young man with shabby blond hair and a long beard sat on another bench, staring at the fountain. He had Christ's torso, bony, bloody, and injured before crucifixion.

"Have you built your ship of death, O have you?" I murmured.

Now I remembered that the book by the French woman was on my father's crowded desk at the university. The woman had large black eyes and a boys' haircut and wore a black turtleneck. Father read her, or maybe even taught her. I was too young to read it. But I'm sure I looked at the book's jacket, at those large black eyes, for long moments.

A bee passed through my chest and I grabbed my heart as if to catch it before it entered. It was the familiar pain.

Father had a wide desk in his small office. I sat on the other side and read. His dim room with a dusty window looking at the red roofs of Austin smelled of stale coffee, Scotch, and mildew of yellowing books. He graded papers with a fountain pen filled with blood-red ink and once in a while lifted his head to make a comment about the book I was looking at. I didn't doodle or draw; I read to please him. "Read the biography of the writer first, know him, then read him," he'd say, or, "This is John Donne. Look in my Oxford for the vocabulary."

When he taught a seminar, I sat in the library waiting for him. I did my homework and once in a while glanced at the tall, intimidating clock tower and watched the students coming and going and listened to the frightening sound of the big bell, too close to me, too alarming, announcing the passage of time. The daylight faded, I felt gloomy and tried to think about Mother and her delicious stew, waiting for us on the table, but even that didn't make me happy.

Home was cold and quiet and we ate in silence, because Father didn't speak with Mother and didn't encourage talking. There was no television and I was not allowed to play outside and no neighbor boy or classmate visited. I didn't do what other boys did and I couldn't have a dog. My mother was asthmatic. Once I had a goldfish, which died soon, and I didn't want another one. In my room I read and listened to Father's music, resonating in the long corridor. The tunes penetrated through the walls, reached me in a remote and dreamy way, and made me pleasantly sad. It was either a symphony or a piece for strings, and never piano, because my father didn't like piano and I thought that it was because Mother played it so well. She played piano for the church and when Father was not home.

The strings and percussion lamented and exploded and reverberated in the cold and spacious house and I interpreted the tunes in my own way and murmured to myself, "These are the footsteps of the giant. He is approaching: Boom, boom, boom," or "There is a circus in town; I'm here, watching." I whispered to myself and told stories—a lonely child's pastime.

Bending over homework in my room, I knew that Mother sat opposite Father in the cool, dim living room and her image reflected in the dark windowpane. She'd leaf through a housekeeping magazine, or if it was winter she'd knit a little sweater for me, which was only completed when the winter was over and the endless summer began. They seldom talked—Mother and Father—they only exchanged a few broken sentences until the evening ended.

Father read his favorites, Shakespeare and Marlowe, for leisure. He sipped brandy in a fat wine glass and at times smiled, or even chuckled to himself. This was when he read a line that he liked. But he didn't share any of these with Mother, nor did he ask what she read or wove. Mother and Father did not sleep in the same bed. A small oak table covered with Father's books separated them forever. I heard them saying goodnight to each other and the lights dimmed.

With me, he shared more. A heavy book in one hand, his wine glass in another, he walked the length of the long corridor and scraped his leather slippers against the shiny linoleum. He knocked on my door and said, "Son, are you doing your school work? Just listen to this for a minute; listen to the beauty of these lines. This is Titus. His daughter has been tortured and he is lamenting. Shakespeare is still young here, but listen to the language: 'When heaven doth weep, doth not the earth o'erflow? / If the winds rage, doth not the sea wax mad, / Threatening the welkin with his big-swollen face?' Now listen to this. It's like a symphony, the melody changes. 'I am the sea. Hark how her sighs doth blow. / She is the weeping welkin, I the earth.' "

When he recited, his eyes welled up and I felt an unbearable love for him. He identified with Titus, who had just lost his daughter, and as young as I was I felt the intensity of parental love. So he loved me too, as deep as Titus loved his daughter. After he left, the rest of the night I interpreted the distant tunes of the symphony under the influence of Shakespeare's lines. I said to myself, "Now the sky weeps, now the storm comes. The sea is mad. The girl is weeping."

Mother borrowed me from Father every Sunday and took me to church with her. I was an altar boy. I wore a white gown and held candles in my hands in Father McFarlin's Church of the Holy Virgin. I didn't see my father all Sunday, until supper time, when he came home after spending a long day at the library and the Faculty Club. He was a bit drunk when he came home and didn't eat much and went to bed early. A few times he took me to that club. Old professors sat around patio tables under an arbor, sipped Scotch, and exchanged campus gossip. "This is Madison, my son," Father said. "Brilliant boy. He is a little scholar. My assistant!"

But at the church I felt like a child. I played with the boys in the backyard among gray stone statues of the tall virgin and the saints and I didn't even think about serious matters. Mother held my hand tightly when we walked home. Sometimes at home, before Father returned, Mother played piano and I sat next to her warm legs and listened.

I THOUGHT ABOUT all this because the Persian girl resembled a picture on my father's book and I missed my stop. I had to walk half a mile back to Saint Luke's. Dr. Haas was waiting for me. It was getting hotter by the minute and my chest hurt and my lungs wheezed and I felt like staying in the cool bus and never getting off, never setting my foot in that hospital again. But then I thought about the small woman and told myself, I have to recover; I have to gain my health back. Who knows? Maybe, she is the one . . .

So I walked back under the burning sun and maneuvered around the piles of cement and mounds of brick on the edge of the street. Like most of the streets of Houston, there was no sidewalk, and I had to walk in a narrow pathway crowded with gigantic pipes. Cars rushed and dust rose and I covered my mouth to not inhale quicklime. I cursed like a lunatic when I stepped in a pile of brick dust and soiled my polished shoes. So by the time I threw myself inside the rotating glass door of the hospital and fell on the first leather couch to catch my breath, my mood had been ruined for the day. I pressed my chest, panting, then held my breath and listened. The bee was there, circling around my heart, trying to find a chamber to get in.

I SAT ON the edge of the bed in a paper gown, looked out the window, and thought to myself, what if God passed—by sheer accident—in his chariot, behind this window of the twenty-fourth floor of Saint Luke's Hospital, and saw me? What if He saw Madison Arlington Kirby, naked as the day he was born from his mother, sitting in a thin paper gown, waiting for the final verdict? What would He say? He'd say, "Son, the voyage of oblivion is awaiting you, build up your ship of death." He'd recite Lawrence for me.

I daydreamed and stared at my hairy legs, two sticks ending at my yellow toes, and I remembered that when I was a little boy my mother sat me like this on a tall table to trim my toenails and I cried. I was afraid of almost everything, as if my whole life with its million small threats was a monster from whom I could never escape. Why did nails grow? Why was one forced to go through the torment of a haircut? Why did doctors pierce one's skin with needles?

Where was Mother to see her naked son?

I looked out the window and waited. The bee wheezed and passed through the narrow pathways of my chest, causing me pain and worry. More worry than pain—because I could take the pain, but not the anxiety of waiting. I went mad with bad thoughts whenever I waited.

"Bad thoughts! Maddy, you think bad thoughts all the time. God loves you. You're a fine child. What are you afraid of?" Mother said.

And this was before the math exam, or the spelling bee, or the baseball game. I couldn't sleep because of the worry. And now I had to wait for the doctor to come back to the room with a piece of news for me. Bad news. I knew it. I read it in her narrow, wrinkled face, in her round, lashless eyes, those two colorless holes showing eternal wonder. I knew it when she ran the cold, deadly stethoscope all over my chest and frowned. I knew it from the way she sighed, from the way she listened to what I said about the bee and nodded. The news was bad.

I sat there and worried and looked out the window— waves of haze. On the horizon two refineries, not far from each other, swam in a white fog. Tall, dark columns, derricks and cat crackers, pierced the white clouds, but these were not real clouds, they were vapor coughed out of tall pipes. On the right side I saw the compact geometrical towers of downtown, silver and blue, taller and shorter, flat as unopened books, reflecting the crooked image of each other and mirroring the floating haze. I saw the red roofs of affluent houses on the left, and closer, the hospitals' and hotels' roofs. On top of the Marriott a swimming pool glowed like a piece of turquoise fallen from the sky. A woman, the size of a doll, bathed in the sun. I saw flattened ground, bases of gigantic structures growing out. I saw tall buildings being born out of the wombs of vacant lots, rubble that used to be people's houses and churches. The city didn't have respect for old age; it bulldozed and demolished history. It destroyed the past to build a short-living now that would never become a future. I saw moving cranes with huge hooks lifting roofs. And God never passed to see all this and I, Madison Arlington Kirby, in my white paper gown, waited and worried.

"This city is the image of doom," I told Dr. Haas.

"Why doom?"

"Look! Can't you see?"

"I know, I know. I live on top of one of these expensive towers. And we're on top of another right now. The world has changed. We are ten years away from the millennium. Capital's rule is absolute." Her German *r* rolled in her throat.

"It's doom!" I repeated.

"Don't be so negative. Look at the bright side." She didn't lift her head from the paper she held in her bony hand and didn't say where the bright side was. There were green and blue spots on her knotted fingers. Paint?

"What does the test say?"

"I think we're there."

"AIDS?"

"I'm afraid so."

"I'm going to die."

She laughed. Not a real laughter, but something sudden, dry, and short—a bullet cracking in the air. "No. There are people like you all over the world now. In many laboratories scientists are working on it. What you need to do is this: Exercise! Build up your resistance. Raise your spirit, eat well, and take your medications."

"And the bee?"

"The bee?"

"In my chest."

"It's your lungs."

"Infected?"

"Tuberculosis."

"So I'm a bag of infections, rotting with diseases."

"Listen, Madison. I'm ill, too. Hepatitis C. Did you know this? I used to work twelve hours a day. Now I'm working less than ten hours a week. I was working on the virus and got contaminated. I lost a grant for a very important project—"

"Why are you telling me this?"

"When I realized that the disease might kill me, I changed my life."

"Oh, you have a lesson for me here, huh? You're preaching."

I didn't need to become bitter with the woman, but I couldn't stop. I was all poison and wanted to spit it onto her ugly face. The goddamned German whore, the fucking anti-capitalist, who lived a bourgeois life.

"I wouldn't call it preaching," she said coldly. "What I mean is that you have to change your life. Don't withdraw. See people. Study again."

"Ha, ha!"

"Didn't you tell me you quit working on your doctoral dissertation in Austin? Start it again. Get your degree."

"Ha, ha!"

"I've enrolled in different classes. I paint."

"Good for you, Doc."

"You're not short of money, or are you?"

"Nope. I'm not poor, if that's what you mean. I have a big sum lying somewhere, getting fat, but I don't want to spend it."

"Why?"

"It's a long story, Doc. And melodramatic. I can't touch that money."

"What do you mean?"

"It's my father's inheritance."

"Spend it, Madison."

"Because I'm dying, huh?"

"Because you have to enjoy your life."

"I've never enjoyed my life and don't know how to enjoy it now that I'm being pushed out."

"No one is pushing you out, Madison."

"Yes, He is!" I shouted and spat venom at her. "He is pushing me out of life, that son of a bitch!" I pointed to the clouds of vapor.

I certainly didn't show much grace after hearing the news. I made a fool of myself and stormed out as if the poor shrunken woman was responsible for my germs. In the leather couch downstairs I sat gasping and thinking that this whole thing was not surprising news. Hadn't I been dying since I was twenty-five? Since I abandoned my widowed mother to seek refuge in the East? Didn't my death begin then? Or to be precise, on March 5, 1978—the day of the wreck?

I was working. Taking notes. Final research for the dissertation. Someone tiptoed toward my cubicle and motioned to me to come out. I left my books open on the desk and followed this man, a small clerk, a bald man whom I'd seen sitting behind the circulation counter watching the girls' legs with his mousy eyes. He told me in a whisper that there was a phone call for me. It was Father McFarlin. His old voice shook. He said that my father had been in a car accident. I said, where? He said, the Hill Country. What was he doing there? Who was with him? He didn't say more. Left it for me to find out.

So the old bastard died and I died with him. Not because he died, but because of the way he did—so cheap, so ugly, so ungraceful. I didn't want to bear the damn professor's name anymore. Kirby was my middle name. I made it into my last name and divorced the boss forever. Then I left Austin and my dissertation remained open on the desk of that cubicle in the library, half done. I had to travel. Beyond the seas. To the East. India. Turkey. China. I told Mother I'd be away from Austin for few months, but I never returned.

I WALKED ALL day aimlessly to weary myself. I strolled in the narrow, shady streets around Rice University and daydreamed. If I didn't have to die and if I had to live in Houston, this would be where I'd choose—an alley with a roof of intertwining oaks, all shade and peace and tranquility. Being here and not being here. Houses old, decent, and modest.

Cozy and inviting. Smelling of aged wood. Red brick walls, small, green backyards, tall oaks protecting them. A place to raise a family, to grow old, to become a grandfather and die a natural death on a chair near the fireplace. Now I laughed at my sentimental fantasies and resented myself for such thoughts. But I couldn't help envying the owners of the houses and feeling bitter and angry.

Never in my life had I thought about marriage or family— not even when I loved a woman and made her pregnant. Before the wreck, Father was my marriage and my family (my nourishing mother stood in his shadows) and after the wreck, I put my life on pause. I lived a temporary life, thinking that this was just a break and I'd take my manuscript back from Mother and work on it and graduate and begin to teach. I traveled through the East, lived the foggy life of an opium smoker, and returned to the States only because of a coincidence. I saw a former classmate in a teahouse in Istanbul and he told me that there were a couple of openings at the college in New York where he taught. He said he would recommend me if I were interested. I thought that New York would be a good place to get lost and I said, Sure, I'm interested. My friend didn't know how lost I was and how low I'd fallen. All he knew was the studious Madison, the Madison of the Honors List. He recommended me. After a month, the college received my transcript and my former professors' recommendation letters and invited me for an interview. Knowing that I'd impress them, I moved to New York, confidently.

For almost a year, I taught philosophy during the day and lived a wild life at night. I drank and smoked and slept in unbelievable places with unbelievable people and my contract was not renewed. Once on a long LSD trip, from which I almost didn't return, I found myself at the end of a maze, face-to-face with shapeless creatures made of the substance of night. They were the instruments of darkness and with their batlike screams warned me about something, as if there were anything more horrible than them. They had visited me in India once, but I had forgotten them. Now they were back and this was a sign. So I packed and returned to Texas, but not to Austin, where my mother was. I knew that I had hit bottom.

It was the spring of 1985 when I lived in a small room on top of a laundromat in Houston. The room shook with the vibration of a dozen washers and dryers and smelled of cheap detergent. My mother sent me money to start a life. I was willing to help myself, too. My old Greek landlord told me about the People's Aid Center, and I went to see that one-eyed, big Italian, Ric Cardinal, the saint-counselor of the Montrose area. I sought help.

The doctoral candidate in philosophy was now a night watchman of a skyscraper, a junky, a showman of AA meetings, and a paranoid bum who was visited by vague shadows and shapes. This was a good lesson in humility. It took me two years to get cleaned up and begin to debate whether it was the right time to pick up the manuscript. But then I was diagnosed with HIV and lost heart.

Then bad turned to worst. I couldn't handle the night job in the enormous building. Shadows tricked me again and followed me in the dim, empty corridors and when I wanted to catch them, they hid behind the marble columns. I flew out of the skyscraper, my heart banging in my mouth, until I was breathless. Paranoia, doctor-diagnosed. I needed rest and medication. I had to quit my job before I caused a theft or damage to the building. I didn't tell Mother that I spent three weeks in a mental hospital, and whenever she called and mentioned "my money," I told her that I didn't want to touch it, she'd better keep it in her own bank account. I became eligible for disability and my life remained on permanent pause.

What went wrong? When? When did things go wrong?

Thinking about all this, as if watching a movie of my past life, I stopped at a dime store in the Village and looked at myself in the window. But it wasn't only me looking at myself— all these masks, these old, dusty Halloween masks of years gone, stared at me from behind the finger-stained, greasy pane. I cupped my hands around my eyes to see better. It was an image out of a nightmare. All the red-cheeked, rubber-faced presidents, deformed and horrible, made faces at me and mocked me for being pushed out of a life I'd never had a chance to begin. It was as if they were saying, "We made it! We made it! You lost it, you loser!" I entered the store, not knowing why; maybe I wanted to smash all the masks and the rest of the cheap, random junk in the shop. But a hundred-year-old man, who sat on a chair, leaning against a cane, stood up shakily and approached me with stiff legs and a wide smile. I rushed out and ran for my life as if he was death personified coming to claim me. Not yet. No, I wasn't ready. There was hope. There was hope. There was a small woman with large dark eyes who could save me. Yes, she was the only one who could save me. My Persian—Roya.

• • •

AS LONG AS I could remember there had been a greasy spoon coffee shop by the name of Dot on this corner. It had the atmosphere of the old times without the pretension. When I was a night watchman I ate breakfast at Dot on the way home. A few lanky, sleepy, middle-aged waitresses in blue aprons filled my cup with coffee and served me eggs and french toast. I stared at the TV and at times glanced at their hairy thighs when they bent to pick up something from the floor.

Now I walked and walked, beginning to wonder if Dot had also been a figment of my imagination. If it was not, then where was it? The afternoon heat increased as the naked sun slipped down closer to the earth and the gulf somewhere, not far from the city, breathing out fire. With the image of a tall glass of iced tea like a mirage in my head, I kept walking until I felt dizzy and soaked in a cold sweat. The bee wheezed crazily in my chest and hit the wall of my heart. I stopped a man and asked him, "Where is Dot?" He shrugged, as if he didn't know English. I saw a bead shop and entered. An annoying doorbell announced my entrance and a woman approached me with a smile. She wore a long flowery dress and many rows of beads hung from her neck—a hippie out of place and time. Boxes surrounded her. She was packing or unpacking.

"Excuse me, where is Dot?"

"What?"

"The coffee shop next to your store."

"Oh. They demolished it a few months ago. They're building an arcade here. They're going to dump my store too. I'm moving to a new location."

"Oh." That's all I said, then glanced at the boxes and left.

"Need beads?"

"No, I don't need beads," I murmured.

In the street a yellow bulldozer crept out of a vacant lot that used to be Dot and crawled toward me. On my left, an ocean of cars roared and approached. I felt trapped in a dead end and had to decide. If I went to the right, I'd get run over by the yellow beast; if I went to the left, I'd pass out under the invading cars. So I entered the bead shop again and the bell rang. I vaguely remember that I murmured something like, "Madame, I don't feel well—" and I passed out.

I OPENED MY eyes on my bed, facing my red, round alarm clock. This old clock had been my companion for years, the only object I'd brought from the East. It had a sweet female face, Arabic numbers, and a life that was entirely in my hands. If I didn't wind it, it would die. It was ten minutes to five and I tried to remember the day. The images of the fake hippie, the crazy homeless men, and the large-eyed Persian woman mixed and mingled in my head and confused me. The dialogue with Dr. Haas played in my head to remind me that I had a terminal disease, and then I heard someone knocking on the door.

"Come in. It's open."

It was the neighbor. The boy. Bobby Palomo.

"May I come in?"

"I just said come in. Didn't I?"

"Are you okay?" He approached my bed cautiously, as if afraid.

"Why?"

"Well, the ambulance brought you home and I helped them put you in bed. They told me to tell you that you should call your doctor. That's why I'm here. To remind you. I guess you passed out in the street."

"In a bead shop."

"You need something? Food? I have lots of good stuff in my fridge. I can warm something up in a minute and bring you a fancy tray. It's restaurant food. First class. What do you say?"

"Do I look starved?"

"No, it's just—I work in a restaurant and I take home some food every night—"

"What do you have?"

"You like lasagna?"

"I guess. I don't remember the last time I had Italian food."

"I'll get you some lasagna with some fresh garden salad. I'll be back in a wink."

The bastard pitied me. Was it showing, then? The illness? The paleness? Did I smell of death? So soon? Then the woman could notice too.

A minute later I sat in my bed eating lasagna and some kind of green soup the girl had sent. Bobby sat in a chair next to my bed and said that the new neighbor, the Persian woman, saw him taking food for me and added this bowl of soup.

"Did she see the ambulance?"

"Oh, yeah—"

"Shit."

"Why?"

I didn't answer him and he just sat there and looked around.

"What are you looking at?"

"I guess you haven't had time to unpack yet. I'll help you this Sunday if you want."

"I moved here two months ago."

"But you haven't had time—I can help—"

"Why are you helping everybody, huh? I saw you sweeping the parking lot for Thompson and cutting the grass. Does he pay you?"

"He's my dad's friend. I mean was."

"Are you living here for free?"

"No, I pay my rent."

"Where is your dad?"

"Not sure."

"Mother?"

"Chicago."

"Abandoned you?"

"I'm nineteen. I can take care of myself."

"Sure you can—sure you can. Go now, I want to rest."

"Will you call your doctor?"

"What do you see in my face? Plague? Cholera?"

"I'm sorry, I didn't mean to—"

"Go kid, go. Your lasagna was good. I'll keep the rest of this green soup and I'll return the girl's bowl myself. Thanks. Now go!"

I took a long shower and all the while thought about the young woman. Her name emerged from the depth of my memory—Roya. It was as if I'd met her long ago, somewhere else, somewhere remote and strange. Now I remembered that she'd come from India and all of my long-buried memories emerged from darkness and surrounded me—the jasmine

clusters hanging over clay walls, white and purple and laven-
der, the sharp perfume of blossoms and the smell of sandalwood in the air, the occasional scream of strange birds in the
jungle, and the demons of the night, who appeared to me for
the first time in Delhi.

I stayed in a small solitary room on top of a roof in an
old widow's house in New Delhi. The house wasn't air-
conditioned, so I slept on the roof all night, wearing nothing,
under the Indian sky, which sent the waves of fire and the scent
of wild flowers down. Sleepless from the intensity of the heat
and the perfume of the plants, I went to a nearby park at the
edge of the woods. I sat on a bench for hours and looked at the
dense trees. A peacock appeared occasionally and opened his
tail feathers and remained motionless for a long time, as if pos-
ing for me. At times I heard strange screams and thought that
from within the thick woods shapeless shadows warned me.

Now this woman was coming from the same city. She had
appeared on this particular day in my life, the day of the bad
news. Could this be a coincidence? What if it was not? What
if the woman was sent for me? Wasn't this another turning
point in my life? I had only a short time to live and I had to
live it fine and full and she was here to hold me tight, to caress
me with her gentle eyes, and to stay with me until the moment
of my departure.

I left the steaming bathtub in a daze. I was confused. The
past had emerged from the bosom of the present and lived in
my throbbing cells, yearning for the future. The present
seemed unreal and the reality of death was as strong as the
urge to live and love. I smelled the intense perfume of un-

known flowers, while my windows were tightly closed. Was I going out of my mind?

All night I lay on my side, palm under cheek, looking at the face of the red clock, counting the minutes and hours. Sleep never came. My brain was so tired that it had ceased working. I was all acute senses like an animal and smelled nonexistent scents—sandalwood and curry, dust and manure and hot sweat. Then I heard the click of the old man's typewriter next door and the tick tock of the red clock; the scents of the past vanished. My eyelids pulsated with pain and a hammer hit a long nail into my scalp.

Memories came to me, but not in long, graceful chapters, nor in well-arranged sentences, edited in my mind to refinement, as was often the case. They came in a fragmented, nervous way, in the shape of broken images, meaningless and chaotic.

I was burning with fever on my narrow bed. Father sat next to me and lay his big hand on my forehead. The fever vanished. I had shivers now. Father lay his palm on my head, and his warm life entered my frozen blood. He spoke worriedly with a doctor who had come to our house. "Will he be well soon? Will he?"

He loved me, then; he loved me, I thought in delirium. He had given me life and he was worried about me and he loved me more than anyone in this world.

Now I looked up at the bell tower of the university; someone on the top was shouting. I ran out of the library and screamed, "Dad . . . Dad . . . ," and saw other people running, calling for help. I ran under the bullets and fell on the ground.

Someone pulled me down and I stayed there hunched into myself, never lifting my head up to see the man, the size of a finger, on top of the tower, shooting. Now I found myself in my father's arms. He pressed me to his chest like a baby. "Daddy, Daddy," I cried. I was a big child then. Twelve.

I sat under the piano and rubbed my body against Mother's bare calf. She pushed one foot on the pedal and sang her Irish song: "I hear a song in my deep sleep / the waters sound asleep / the moon's lonely dreams." In my tight shelter under the moving hammers I felt the evening descending and the light dimming. The darkest of all the blues had covered the sky and soon Father would come, carrying that blue light inside with him and the piano would cease playing and Mother would become silent for the rest of the night.

"MADDY, MADDY, DON'T be so Saddy!" Mother sang and soaped my back.

"No, no, no, no—not the shampoo. It burns!"

"What are you afraid of, Maddy? The cute little good-smelling bubbles?"

MOTHER HAD ANOTHER asthma attack. I heard rhythmic bangs, opened the bedroom door, and found her on the floor, squatting, rocking back and forth and each time hitting her head on the wall. A hoarse voice came out of her tight chest: "Leave! Leave, Madison. I'll be fine. Fine. My lungs are tight . . ."

I felt guilty breathing.

Father read my papers carefully and beamed with satisfaction. He went over the tiny words of praise my professors had written in the margin. I was his prodigy, on my way to becoming another him. Our fields were not the same and this was the only liberty he had given me. I impressed him when I lectured on Hegel, Nietzsche, and Heidegger. My little power was in the big books that I had read and he hadn't. I lived to please him and he loved me. I knew he loved me.

My dissertation, "Being There and Being Pushed into Nothingness: A Study of Martin Heidegger's Existentialism," was already dedicated to him:

"To Father, without whose life-giving breath I would have never been able to breathe life into these pages."

As I wrote fervently in that windowless cubicle, I imagined him holding the black hardback book, the printed manuscript, in his hands, leafing through it, looking at the dedication and the table of contents. I imagined him raising his eyes from behind his lenses and creasing his forehead, as was his habit, and nodding with a faint smile. This nod was life for me and I didn't desire more.

Then he died.

PALM OF ONE hand under my cheek, I looked out through the bare window until the morning light, still faint and reluctant, glowed between the dark branches of the thick oaks. I watched the light growing brighter, turning phosphorescent, waking the birds. They sang at once and crazily and broke the spell of my past. Now the morning, full grown, strong, and imposing, filled the room. I turned my back to the window, closed my eyes, and before falling asleep saw the image of my father. But I woke after ten minutes and sat up. I thought that if the Persian had come for me, if she was here to save me, I'd call Mother and give her the news—news of the approaching end and my happiness before the final departure. Then I thought that I should pluck a half-opened magnolia from a tree and put it in the empty bowl; I should knock on her door tomorrow and when she opens it, offer her the virgin blossom. With this plan in mind, after eleven hours of tossing and turning, I fell asleep.

Day Two

In the evening I shaved, put on some cologne, and ironed my shirt. I slicked my hair with water and combed it back to cover the near-balding top. I debated whether to wear the suit jacket. Didn't. Now I opened the window and with much effort plucked a half-open magnolia. The branch was a bit far from my reach and I hoped that no one saw me hanging out with a pair of scissors in my hand. I placed the blossom in her blue porcelain bowl and crossed the parking lot. Climbing the creaking steps, I hoped that Bobby Palomo wouldn't open his door and see me. I stood behind the door and waited before knocking. There was a conversation in the house, between mother and daughter. It must have been in their language, because I couldn't understand a word. I knocked, but no one opened. I waited. The dialogue was not friendly. There was tension under the woman's voice and the girl had a half-nagging, half-whining tone—on the verge of tears. I thought

I should return another time. The dark narrow hallway was now filled with the sharp perfume of magnolia and it made me sick. As I turned to go down the steps she opened the door. Against the sharp light she seemed transparent, as if her body was empty of organs. I almost looked for her wings and thought, Yes, she is God-sent. She is here to save me and I'm doing the right thing. I offered the bowl and mumbled a thank you. She invited me in, something she shouldn't have done. I wished I could tell her right away, "Dear girly, don't invite a stranger into your house. Neighbor or no neighbor! You're in America, my love!"

She offered me a strong hot tea, which made me perspire in that long-sleeved starched shirt. Sweat bubbled in my hair and rolled down inside my collar. Her window air conditioner was worse than mine; it rattled and shook the house without giving out cool air. The girl, the daughter, had slipped inside the bedroom, hiding, and the mother went in and out of the small kitchen, bringing more things to eat and drink.

"Sit for a second for God's sake," I said. "Why are you serving me?"

"You're my first American guest," she said. "We offer tea and sweets, then fruits. We insist that guests stay for dinner."

"Eastern rituals. I had a landlady in India who knocked on my door every evening and handed me a tray full of food."

"How are you feeling today?" she asked.

"Why?"

"You were sick."

"Oh, the lousy asthma attack. I didn't have my inhaler with me the other day—"

She didn't ask more, didn't mention the ambulance, and I

didn't explain, either. Then there was silence and I had a chance to glance around. Her desk, which was a yellow door resting on orange crates in front of the window, was covered with books and papers. I told her that I didn't know she was a student. She said she was not, but she wished she could continue her education.

"In what?"

"Literature," she said.

"What are you writing?"

"My memoir," she said and laughed shyly.

"I thought old people wrote memoirs."

"I'm not that young," she said. "But it's not really serious. Just some notes."

I asked her about her family and she told me that her parents had died in a car accident one year before the 1979 revolution. She was in the last year of high school then, but still managed to graduate. She had an older sister who was like a mother to her and then for the second time she mentioned her brother's execution. I said that my father had died in a car crash too, and I immediately regretted saying it. I shouldn't have brought up that subject and ruined my mood. More to avoid answering questions, I asked her to walk with me to the café across the street and have a light dinner with me. Neither of us had a car to go anywhere farther, I said. She agreed, but said that she had to get her daughter ready. I didn't want the daughter with us, but didn't say anything. She was in the bedroom for a long time—longer than it should take a big child to get ready—and I heard hushed and nervous conversation. At last a door banged, something fell in the bathroom sink and broke, and Roya came out, face flushed.

"We can go," she said.

"And your daughter?"

"She's not coming."

She had on the same white pants with a white T-shirt that had a hand-painted picture of a Christmas tree. The picture was out of time and place, but white was her color. With her short hair and boyish outfit, she didn't look more than eighteen. We could have been mistaken for a father and daughter.

We strolled in twilight and the moist air sat on our skin. When the breeze blew from the west, I smelled lilac on her. She had used perfume. I was short of breath, wheezed and coughed, and became embarrassed. Sweat ran down my neck and the bee spun in my body and hit the wall of my chest.

"Are you okay?"

"Oh, yes. You know; it's the asthma. The evening air bothers me."

"Then you shouldn't be walking."

"I don't drive."

"Never?"

"Never."

We sat in Café Express next to the window and while she ate a salad I recited "The Ship of Death" for her. I will never forget how her large black eyes opened wide with wonder, then became wet with tears. She stopped eating.

"I'm sorry if I made you sad. You were eating."

"Oh, please, don't apologize. I love poetry. I write some too, but not in English."

"Nowadays, death has cornered me."

"What do you mean?"

"I listen to my heart and can't imagine that this faint throbbing which has been with me for so long would ever cease."

"Why do you think about death?" she asked innocently.

"I don't think about death, my dear. I think about the benign indifference of the universe."

She didn't understand what I said; she looked puzzled. I tried to explain what I meant by "benign indifference of the universe" and, as if feeling offended, she became defensive and began to tell me that her German was better than her English and she knew a little Russian too, but her English was much better than her Russian. Then to change the subject I asked her how her past few days had been. She said she had found a job at a shirt-painting company, but this was just temporary. The employment agency was going to find her something better. She said she had a degree in comparative literature and wished she could enter a doctoral program here. I didn't mention my dissertation on Heidegger.

When she spoke more than one or two sentences her accent showed and I helped her once or twice when she got stuck pronouncing some words. But then I regretted doing so because she blushed with embarrassment. Her voice was soft and deep for her young age and she spoke slowly for fear of making a mistake.

The poor gazelle. Only a week in America.

While we sipped our coffee in silence, I gazed at her shamelessly. Her beauty was ethereal and angelic, dark and sad. There was more in her, much more than appeared on the surface. I wanted her to know that she was sent for me. She was here to save me, to stay with me during the last years of my life and console me. She was the promised happiness, a dream coming true. When she lowered her head from the burden of my gaze, black curtains of long lashes fell on her wet eyes and cast shadows on her cheeks. This was a celestial beauty.

On the way back I asked her what the meaning of her name was, and she shocked me by saying that her name, Roya, meant "dream" in Persian, "sweet dream," she corrected herself. I told her that her name suited her well, because she seemed like a sweet dream to me. In order to discourage me from intimate remarks, she told me that this was a very common name in her country and she didn't like having a common name. Before crossing the street, we stood in front of a closed clothing shop, a boutique of some sort, and we looked at the men's suits and women's accessories. I told her that I wouldn't mind possessing that black silk suit, but I didn't tell her that my secret wish was to wear it standing in front of the altar with her. Now I asked her if she liked any of the jewelry. She blushed and said that she never wore any.

"Why?"

"I'm not used to it."

"Well, let's imagine you'd wear a pair of earrings. Which pair would you choose?"

It took her a long time to look around and finally she showed me a pair of pearl earrings with three droplets hanging in a row like frozen tears. I admired her choice and told her that I'd choose those too and we laughed, imagining how I'd look wearing long pearl earrings. Then we laughed some more at our window-shopping and the fact that the suit cost twice Mr. Thompson's rent for the hot box of the garage apartments and even the earrings were worth our electricity bills put together.

In the vacant parking lot, now darkened and deserted, my stairway was on the left and hers on the right. We stood in the middle to say goodbye. I remember that the moon slipped out of the dark clouds and brightened the night and I took it as a good omen. As I bent to kiss her lips, she raised her head to watch the moon and I changed my mind and decided not to take the risk. No. Wait. Not now! Let her trust you more. We parted like old friends with warm smiles.

Day Three

Yes, I knew that soon I would die, but she was here to guard me and take care of me to the day of my departure. She was the one who had heard me among the angels and she was here to press me against her chest. But I had to help myself too. So I went to Ric Cardinal, my old friend and savior at the People's Aid Center.

If there was only one man in Houston whom I liked with a mixture of envy and admiration (envy for what he was and I could never be), that man was Ric. He saved me in 1985 when I came to this city and was confused and lost. He talked to me for endless hours, took me to doctors and shrinks and AA meetings, and encouraged me to study again. He found me a job and prevented me from sliding back. If I slid back, I'd end up under the bridge of Highway 10. He was the same with his other clients. I don't think he had much of a life for himself. His wife had deserted him long ago and he was raising a troubled teenager. I remember that half-joking, half-seriously I called him Saint Cardinal, the Saint of the Montrose Wretched.

But I quit going to PAC after I was diagnosed with HIV. I gave up on the idea of working on my doctorate, too. I remember that once, when I was very sick, I called Ric and made an appointment with him. I wanted to tell him about my failing health, but this meeting never happened. He had a family problem and didn't show up. Then I decided not to see him anymore. I moved and didn't get a phone. He couldn't find me.

Now Ric was happy to see me again. But he couldn't hide that he was shocked.

"Do I look like a bag of shit?"

"You've lost weight, Madison. Tell me. What's going on?"

"There is a bee in my blood, Ric; it circles and circles, but each time misses the entrance to my heart. The day that the bee finds its way inside, my heart will cease beating. I live only by chance, my friend, hoping that the blind bee remains lost."

"Weaving poetry again—the same old Madison. What are you trying to say?"

"AIDS."

"No."

"Yes."

There was silence for a long moment and I looked down through the wide window at the Montrose crowd. It was lunch hour rush. A tall, black faggot with short shorts, high heels, and long thighs held on to his curly blond wig as if it was falling off and tried to cross the busy street. Cars honked and heads popped out the windows.

"I'm not a faggot, Ric."

"Oh, shut up, Madison."

"I'm just being pushed out of life and it's all—all—His fault."

"Whose?"

I pointed to the window, the haze, the white summer glare, and then I covered my eyes.

What a shame! I was all in tears—from self-pity and from that goddamned feeling I always had when I saw Ric Cardinal. The man's big body gave out warmth and I felt like a child sitting on Santa's lap unable to dismount. I was only a few years younger than him, but I felt like his son. He looked like an archetypal father, a Zeus or something, but a god without the wrath.

He was looking at me now, panting slightly, as he always did. For a long moment he played with the tip of his bushy beard and then said, "How about we get out of here and go somewhere to eat? Let's go somewhere nice." He got up and paced the room, pulling his beard, as was his habit when he thought hard. I could see that he wanted to do something for me, but didn't know what. Eating was an animal instinct. He wanted to feed me.

"Let's go to Kemah. Get up, man. Let's go to the bay and get some fresh air and seafood."

Ric was mostly silent driving through the busy streets, but I chatted incessantly to make up for my disgrace in his office. I gave him a report of my life since I last saw him three years ago. I told him about the odd jobs, then disability, one dingy apartment after the other, and this last one, a garage apartment, hanging suspended in the air, in a parking lot, surrounded by walls. I talked about my temporary life among boxes that were never quite unpacked and contained objects that had lost their purpose and meaning and my life that was on pause and this was taking forever. I told him that my memory was fading away and all the books that I'd read and all the poems that I had in my head were leaving me. I told him that I was becoming an empty sack before being kicked out of this life.

Then at a red light I saw the dark woman with the bundle sitting on a bench at the bus stop folding a stack of napkins on her lap. She divided the napkins in two stacks and began folding the first. Each one she folded she hid in a pocket. Next she began the second stack. Then she made binoculars with her hands, looking through the imaginary lenses. She saw me sitting in the car and recognized me.

"This is the ghost of the city," I murmured.

"Who?"

"That homeless woman. She is everywhere. She follows me."

"Once I thought that death was following me," Ric said.

"Tell me about it."

"I was a kid, six or seven, and I thought I saw death with my grandfather in the basement." Ric paused for a long moment, deeply immersed in the past. "Grandpa had a small embalming business and I knew what he was doing down there, but I'd never seen it. I wasn't allowed there. But one day when I was playing in the street, my ball rolled to the basement window and stopped. I hunched to pick it up and I looked inside. Grandpa stood in front of a black box, working. But behind him there was a shadow on the wall—a tall, dark shadow, waiting. I got scared and ran away. A couple of days later Grandpa died and I thought that it was death that had stood behind him."

"Do you believe in God, Ric?"

"No."

"I do. But I don't think he is merciful. He is indifferent and forgetful. This dark woman is nothing to him."

"Your god is like a corporate executive or something."

"Exactly. With immense power and gigantic hands."

"Hands?"

"Because I've always imagined that if I'm falling—and I've been falling for a while now—there must be a hand with a soft, enormous palm that would hold me midway and prevent me from crashing. But now the same hand is pushing me out, Ric. I can't bear the idea of this . . . this . . . powerlessness. This fast trip toward nothing."

"You're still under the influence of Heidegger."

"I was raised a Catholic, Ric."

"Me too."

"I'm a believer, Ric."

"Didn't you work on Heidegger for years? For your doctorate?"

"So what?"

"Wasn't he an atheist?"

"Fuck Heidegger."

UNDER THE GREEN umbrella we sipped our iced tea and gazed at a white boat sailing smoothly on the blue water. The day was warm and breezy and it was good to be away from the metallic town. Ric had gained more weight in the past few years; he panted, wiped his sweat, and sweat bubbled on his forehead again.

"There are tables inside too," I said.

"Then what's the point of eating here?"

"You're right. Are you okay?"

"I'm fine. I sweat a lot. Don't worry. I need to lose this!" He grabbed the flesh of his belly in both hands and shook it. "Now tell me. What are we expecting from this disease?"

He said "we," meaning he was with me, offering his unconditional support.

"I have tuberculosis. It may become worse. And I can get any other disease in the world. Anything. I don't have an immune system, Ric. My hair is falling out. Soon I'll itch from head to foot and my stomach will bloat. I'll lose even more weight."

"Is there anything we can do to make things better? I mean—"

"There is only one thing. One person."

"What do you mean?"

"There is a girl I want to propose to."

"Propose?"

"Don't laugh at me."

"I'm not laughing. Go on."

"This woman, my neighbor—I met her a couple of days ago. She—she—"

"What about her?"

"She is poor. Educated, but poor. Peculiar situation. She is a refugee. Hasn't found her place yet. She's struggling."

"And?"

"You know that I have a sum of money with my mother. The famous inheritance. Remember? I could offer her this money."

"To marry you?"

"I could offer her this money in exchange for being with me. I don't want her to nurse me. Most probably I'll end up in a hospital, or I'll have to hire a nurse. I just want her to be with me."

"To live with you, as your wife?"

"Is this too much to ask? She'll have the money and life will become easy for her after my death. She wants to go back to school, but she can't afford it."

"Who is she?"

"A Persian."

"Oh."

"Why 'oh'?"

"I knew a few of them in college. Opinionated girls. Radicals. Of course this was in the seventies. A few years later they went back to Iran to participate in the revolution. They must be dead now. What a pity! All those dark-eyed women."

"This one is quiet."

"What do you mean?"

"Not opinionated. Angelic. Big eyes like a deer, soft voice. Kind of shy."

"But after a couple of days—?"

"I know, I know. I need more time. But I don't have it, Ric. You understand? If I become very sick, if I begin to stink, who would desire me?"

"Oh, quit this, Madison."

"All I know is fading away, Ric. All the books I've read— the poems. I'm losing my memory."

"Memory loss doesn't happen in the early stages, Madison.

Stop being negative. Tell me more. What are you planning to do? Offer her money? Isn't this offensive?"

"Is it?"

"Yup!"

Now we followed the smooth movement of the white boat. Farther in the distance, the water was darker blue and glowed with silver. What a blessing was life on this earth.

"She needs to fall in love with me."

"Yup. Girls are romantic, Madison. Even the tough ones. They're all after romance."

He was right. What could I say? And who could make anyone love anyone?

The waiter stood above our heads with an enormous tray on his shoulder. The plates were big and piled with food. Ric attacked his lobster, broke the joints, sucked the marrow, and licked the shells. He ate with absolute dedication and looked like a mythical monster, a cyclops, feasting on raw meat, juice running down his beard.

"Eat, Madison, eat!"

"I wish I had your appetite."

"That's all that's left for me."

"What do you mean?"

"Nothing. Eat!"

"How is your son?" I realized that I'd forgotten to ask him about his son.

"At the moment, he's with his mother."

"How old is he now?"

"Nineteen. He was here with me. I monitored his medication and gave him a little job at the office. But he left me."

"He'll come back home."

"I live with this feeling that any minute there will be a phone call—to rush to the hospital, or to his funeral."

"Things are that bad?"

"He has been diagnosed with schizophrenia. He was in bad shape when he left and his mother is no help. She needs help herself."

"I'm sorry, Ric."

"We'll see. What can I do, huh? Go there and grab a nineteen-year-old and bring him back by force?"

"There is nothing much you can do."

"You talk about powerlessness. See for yourself. I raised a kid and he turned out crazy. I wanted to help him, but he ran away. He is nineteen, Madison. Tell me, what can I possibly do?"

"Stay on call, Ric, like what you just said. What else can you do?"

We sat in silence for a while. Ric cleaned his teeth with a toothpick and I listened to his wheezing. He was a smoker, but because of me didn't smoke. What I liked about this man was his absolute lack of superiority. You have a problem, I'm your counselor and I'll try to help you, but I have a problem too, I'll share it with you. You talk to me. I talk to you. And he did this because this was the way he was, not the way he made an effort to be.

The boat became a white dot on the horizon and a group of noisy diners sat at the next table—young women, golden arms and shoulders bared for the caresses of the sun. I glanced at them and didn't desire a single one. They laughed loudly and flirted with the young waiter. I didn't want to sit there anymore. Ric was annoyed too. He paid the bill.

"Ric, what is your last word for me? What do you suggest?"

"About the girl?"

"Yes, my neighbor."

"Do you think she'll like you?"

"Ha, ha—"

"Do your best and don't mention the money."

SHE WOULD FALL in love with me if that ugly, unsmiling brat, that fat daughter of hers, who resembled her as much as I resembled Hercules, hadn't ruined the night. The night, I said? Oh no, my life, my short stay on this earth.

I sat for a long time on that filthy, uncomfortable couch Mr. Thompson had planted in her living room to call the mouse hole "furnished," and sweated and waited, my hand squeezing the small box in my pocket. She was in the bedroom speaking with her daughter, in their own language, explaining something in a hushed voice. Then they came out and the girl sat on the floor in front of the old TV set with her back to me and began watching something stupid with roars of recorded laughter in the intervals.

"I was preparing some dinner," she said. "Please stay."

"Oh, no. I've eaten a big meal today. A friend of mine treated me to seafood at the bay."

We talked this way while she was in and out of the kitchen and the TV was loud and the laughter made me nervous. Now she lay a tray of food in front of the girl and the girl began to eat.

"You look good in tights," I said. She was wearing black

tights, like a ballet dancer, with a long T-shirt hanging over them. It was one of the painted T-shirts, given to her for free at the job, designed with masks of tragedy and comedy and some confetti sprinkled around. Her eyeglasses were large and the thick lenses made her black eyes look even larger. "You look like a French writer," I added, remembering the image on that forgotten book.

She blushed and went to the kitchen and came back after a few long moments and sat on her desk's chair, facing me. Either she didn't know how to take a compliment, or she was very shy. It was not easy to become intimate with such a woman; she escaped each time I made a personal comment. She went in and out of the kitchen, we made small talk, and the girl ate and watched the seemingly comic show without a trace of a smile on her stony face. I couldn't find the opportunity to take the box out. Now the mother bent her knees to pick up the tray and I noticed something wooden about her back, something I had noticed the first day when she ran toward the bus. Her torso was too erect, as if an iron rod was planted in her spine.

Now she talked about her memoir again and mentioned an old man, a friend of hers, who had encouraged her to begin. Then she said that she had a small Rilke book that she read whenever she was tired of her stupid, tedious job. She talked more, moving back and forth between the memoir and Rilke and her shirt-painting job. I didn't show any interest in her memoir; in fact, I wasn't listening very well. Since she had mentioned Rilke, I was trying hard to remember a line or two to impress her, but my memory was blurred and all I recalled were Rilke's angels and nothing more. I knew that he had written a long poem or a series of poems about angels, and once I used to know a few lines by heart.

"Are you okay?"

"Why?"

"You're thinking."

"Oh, the damn poem, all of the damned poems have escaped my mind. I've lost my memory."

"Why?" she asked innocently.

"I didn't take care of it," I said and laughed.

Then instead of doing something to make her like me (as Ric Cardinal had suggested), I began to tell her all about my past drug use and my rotten lifestyle in New York. I went into detail about the bars and nightclubs, needles, and even that LSD trip in which demons followed me in a dark maze. With her large eyes that were always wet with fresh tears (they bubbled from a mysterious source within her), she watched me carefully as if measuring the shape of each word coming out of my mouth. She looked sad but stayed friendly—formal and friendly at the same time. After two visits and one dinner and a small stroll under the moonlight, she still called me by my last name.

"You're not using drugs anymore, Mr. Kirby, huh?"

"Please! Call me Madison. We're friends now."

"I'm sorry. It's hard for me to get used to first names. Back home we don't call people by their first names, unless we become very close."

"Then let's become," I said and laughed loudly, to suggest that I was joking. This was too much for her because she disappeared into the kitchen again.

"I was telling you stories about my youth. I'm not a drug

user now. Don't be afraid of me," I yelled, "I'm clean as a baby, my dear." I yelled because she was in the kitchen and I wanted her to hear me, but the girl, her brat, became irritated, bent forward, and raised the volume on the TV set. This was to let me know that I was distracting her from watching her show.

"This is too loud." Her mother came out and turned the volume down.

"I can't hear," the girl complained in English.

"We can't talk this way," the mother said.

Now the girl bounced up and dashed into the bedroom and banged the door. The whole cage of the garage apartment shook and the walls creaked as in an earthquake.

"I'm sorry," she said.

"Sorry for what? I can tell that she doesn't like me. She didn't like me from day one."

"Oh, no, Mr. Kirby—"

"Madison."

"She—she needs time to adjust. She has lost her home, you know? More than once. She cries every night and sulks about everything."

Now I made the biggest mistake of my life. I said something that changed my future (or whatever was left of it)— that short interval between a life that I hadn't lived and a death that was final, an interval to which I was trying hard to assign meaning. I led her to her destiny and took myself to my doom. Out of fake sympathy (which I'd always condemned) and a sheer lie (because I didn't care a bit if the little brat lived or died, went crazy in this wasteland, or survived), I suggested that Roya should take her to a counselor. To show that I was as concerned as a good stepdad would be, I told her that I'd recommend my friend, Ric Cardinal, who was an expert and worked with children. I even added that he was my savior and I respected him more than anyone else in this town.

Hearing this, she sat more relaxed, her stiff back softened, and she sighed a long sigh. Now like a good friend she told me a few stories (in a hushed tone) about her daughter's strange behavior since they'd set foot in America—her rudeness, disobedience, and compulsive TV watching, which she found "dangerous." She referred to certain programs that were not appropriate for a twelve-year-old that the little girl watched hungrily every night. I repeated that Ric had experience with teenagers and gave her PAC's address. When she softened and trusted me, I took the box out of my pocket and offered it to her. She changed colors and stood, ready to run away.

"What is this?"

"Nothing important. Please open it."

She opened the box, took out one earring, and held it with her thumb and forefinger as if holding a mouse by its tail.

"Oh, no!"

"Why? Didn't you say you liked it?"

"You shouldn't have done this. This is expensive and quite unnecessary—" Now she realized that she might have offended me and added, "It's beautiful, but I can't accept it."

"But why? Aren't we friends?"

"Yes, but I don't see the reason for this. Maybe it's a cultural thing. Women don't accept such gifts without—"

"Without enough intimacy? Well, it's different here, my dear." I lied, because I knew very well that here it was the same as anywhere else. You don't buy a special gift for a neighbor a few days after meeting her.

The girl called her from the bedroom and Roya put the box on the table and left. I sat and waited and the bee circled the chambers of my chest, hitting crazily against the entrance to my heart. Sweat ran down my neck and I stood and decided that if she didn't come out in a minute I would leave.

As I paced her small living room, a strange feeling overcame me. For the first time I felt a burning anger toward her that bordered on hatred. I thought that if she rejected me, I would never forgive her for denying me a small happiness and comfort that I deserved at the time of my death. Ric Cardinal was wrong, I thought, I should have mentioned the money before anything else. She wasn't an angel; she wasn't sent by God; she was a human being and I could buy her, the way thousands of women were bought and sold every day. I was mad and confused and paced in the small living room and heard the constant uproar of the artificial laughter on TV. I felt the whole world was laughing at me. Then I stood in front of her desk and looked at her papers and books. I took the small pocket Rilke and opened it. I read a line or two and couldn't understand the German words. Didn't I read German? Didn't I take five fucking German courses to be able to work on original Heidegger texts? I realized that I had lost almost everything worthy that I'd ever possessed and all that was left of me was spite. Spite. Spite. Envy and spite! I envied this woman now and felt an urge to take her papers—on which strange Persian cursive crawled like a drunk worm—and tear them and throw the pieces in the air like confetti.

She came out and passed by me and went to the kitchen.

She didn't want me here—otherwise she would say something like, "Why did you get up, Mr. Kirby?" I heard her open the refrigerator and pour something and dissolve something in a glass and all the while I waited, pacing the room. At last I went to the kitchen and stood behind her and said, "I think you want me to leave."

She was startled at first, then turned to me and said, "I'm sorry, Tala is not feeling well. I think she has a fever. The other night she had a fever too. It's more emotional than physical. I have to go to this counselor tomorrow. Thanks for your help."

"Yes," I said and left the kitchen. She followed me to the door and when I was turning the knob she handed me the box of earrings. I took it without a word and stood there looking at it. She waited with that glass of lemonade in her hand.

"Why do you keep your hair so short?" I said, as if this whole awkward situation was because of her hair.

She blushed and unconsciously ran her free hand over her hair. "Why?" she said after a pause.

"It may create misunderstanding, my dear."

"I don't understand."

"You never wear earrings, either. Are you a lesbian?"

I don't know what had gotten into me. I was spitting venom at her. I wanted to hurt her.

"I don't understand," she repeated again.

"Let your hair grow if you don't want women to approach you. You're in America now." I said this and rushed down the dark steps and almost tripped on the last one.

• • •

OUTSIDE, THE BLUE light of dusk had gathered in the narrow flowerbed along the brick wall. I stood in the middle of the lot for a long moment, not knowing where to go. I felt lonely and miserable and knew that if I went up to my room the walls would approach me from four sides and the dark shadows would appear to me. I stood and listened to the slow-paced clicks of the old man's typewriter. The crazy bastard wrote letters to sweepstakes companies hoping to win something. His room was full of junk—plastic toys, knickknacks, and useless gadgets. I stood and listened to his absurd clicks and the sky rapidly became darker. Then I turned my back to our ugly apartments and exited the parking lot.

I sat on the bench of the bus stop for hours and recited "The Ship of Death," then I repeated it when it ended. "Have you built your ship of death, O have you?" I was empty of everything except a massive pity for myself. I was swelled up with air like that stupid gorilla on top of the tower, who banged his chest and assumed importance. Who was I anyway? And in what way would my death make any difference for anyone? Who cared if today I was here and tomorrow not?

Night had fallen. The summer sky was white and the earth was black. A breeze brushed the gulf and sent the smell of salt into the city and I sat and looked up at the oaks across the street thinking that they'd soon burn and die in the merciless heat. The street was vacant now and the gray asphalt shone. Only a few cars passed by and I heard their swish and followed their taillights and counted them like a child amusing himself. Now it was silent again and I heard somewhere far away a rooster's cry tearing the night apart. This was a solitary rooster in the heart of the city and I could hardly believe that there were people who still kept roosters in their yards. My grandmother had a rooster in her yard in Llano whose alarming calls woke me at dawn every summer morning. I waited to hear more, but this untimely rooster didn't sing again and I doubted its existence. Now millions of cicadas sang in the nearby bayou and this was not my imagination. Waters were awake in this city all night and only the daytime heat put them to rest.

I sat this way for a while until the breeze swept a sour odor onto my face and the smell of rot and decay turned my stomach. This was poisonous vapor—gas and sulfur. A minute ago, I almost admired the night, the white sky, the silent waters of the many bayous, the cicadas' fuss, and now this deadly odor brought me back home. I looked for a kerchief in my pocket to cover my nose when an old beaten Dodge, once navy blue, now grayish and dented, occupied by teenagers, slowed down in front of me. All four windows were open and the stereo pumped out rap music, shattering the quiet night. A black boy stuck his head out and sang with the rapper in an angry animation, hands moving in the air, pointing to the sky, to himself, then to me.

"Tonight is your night / Your neck looks just right / Die, die, die, die, white man!" Now with a sudden gesture he turned his long arm into a machine gun, rattled with his mouth, and pierced me with hundreds of hot bullets. The bastard executed me. A cold sweat sat on my forehead and my body became hollow and numb.

"Hey, staying up tonight?" The boy, Bobby Palomo, always caught me when I was feeling the worst.

"This city is infested with worms," I said, pointing to the speeding Dodge. "Worms, worms, multiplying worms!"

"What happened?"

"Nothing. They just shot me."

"They're pretty dangerous, man," he said and laughed. "They beat up our busboy one night. They didn't even know him. I guess it was an initiation ritual. You know what I mean?"

Bobby leaned his bike against the bench and sat before I invited him. He wore a greasy apron and smelled of kitchen sink and I thought that he wasn't a waiter, he was a dishwasher or something, lying to everyone, boasting.

"How was work tonight?" I asked.

"Slow." He yawned and lit a cigarette. "Do you mind?"

"Blow your smoke away from me. I have asthma."

"I'm taking the little lady to my restaurant tomorrow," he said.

"Which little lady?"

"Our neighbor," he said. "She's working all day, painting these funny T-shirts, and she is not making anything. I guess they pay her below minimum wage. And she has a master's degree too. Did you know that?"

"That degree is worth nothing here. What do you mean by taking her to your restaurant?"

"To wait on tables."

"I don't think she can work as a waitress."

"Why? Her eyeglasses, you mean? I told her she needs a pair of contact lenses. Appearance is everything."

"She is cold and stiff. Awkward."

"I agree. She could use a little smile."

"And her accent," I said.

"Well, to tell you the truth, that's a plus in our business. Accent helps. I know a guy who has dark hair and mustache, he pretends to be Italian. He's a manager at Café Angelo. His name is Brian, but all the customers call him Bruno. He fakes an accent. It's funny."

"Everybody lies in this city. Worms, worms."

"Pah—what did you think? The real cheaters are up there!" He pointed to the top of the Transco Tower, where the gorilla stood.

"She can't be a good waitress." I wanted to talk about her. I had this urge to sit there until morning and trash her like an old village gossip. "She won't be able to handle it," I added.

"Well, let's give her a chance." He was silent for a long moment, then he said, "Hey, listen, do you know she's spent some time in prison?"

"What prison?"

"In her country. She told me that she was a political prisoner. They tortured her. They killed her brother, then let her go."

"I didn't know that."

"I thought you were friends."

"It seems she's more friends with you. She told me about her brother but not herself."

"I've got to go now," he said. "I've got to do my runs around the block."

"Now?"

"I need to exercise. I need to move."

"Are you on drugs?"

"What?"

"Taking pills? Speed?"

"I don't know what you're talking about."

"Be careful, son. I've been there too."

"I don't know what you mean."

He biked toward home and I kept sitting, wondering why I called him "son." Had I become old enough to call young men "son"? Then all of a sudden a rush of hot blood pumped into my heart and I felt feverish. The poor girl had been tortured and I'd acted like a selfish bastard. I'd insulted her only because she didn't pay enough attention to me. How could I undo what I'd done? How could I apologize and give myself another chance? But again, she had shared this important secret with a boy, with this little neighbor, and stupid me had thought that she had volunteered a lot of information to me. She had never trusted me and when she'd begun to feel a bit more relaxed, I'd ruined everything by offering her the fucking earrings and then insulting her. I hated myself, felt mad at her and jealous of Bobby Palomo; I regretted that I'd recommended Ric Cardinal and felt absolutely miserable. Was I in love? Or did I lust after her? Wasn't love just the fancy name for sex? Oh, I wanted her and needed her as I'd never needed a woman in my life. I could kiss her for hours and suck her life out. I could press my body against her and dissolve into her. Yes, I was desperately in love and in a wrong time of my life—when my hair was falling out and invisible hands pushed me out. Where was she when I was young? Where was she when I was in my sweet summer?

I SLEPT ONLY a few hours that night and woke at four o'clock in absolute horror. My chest burned and I panted, as if

I'd run a long distance. The images of a dream passed through my head and I sat on the edge of my bed, unable to move. I was a boy of eight or nine, visiting my grandmother's house in Llano. The house was even bigger than it is in reality and I saw all nine dim rooms and the bathroom with a yellow lion-clawed tub. There was a veranda opening to a garden on a hill, but the garden was wild and all kinds of trees had grown in tangled chaos. At the bottom of the hill a river ran in its stone bed. The water was transparent and glowed like silver. I saw myself running down the hilly garden, looking for my father. When I reached the river I stopped. There was a huge magnolia tree, heavy with large blossoms. I plucked as many as I could and held them in my arms. I wanted to find my father and give him the flowers. Then, for no reason, I went to the edge of the river and began to throw the blossoms in the water. But each one that landed on the water turned into a piece of excrement and this way the river's silvery water became blurred and yellow. I had contaminated the river and ruined it forever.

Looking at my thin legs hanging from the bed, I thought about this strange dream and its symbols. The river was my life. I had soiled it. Magnolia was my intense love for my father and then for Roya, and it was my first present to her. But I'd turned the heavenly blossoms into excrement. All I had done in my life—all, all . . . was human waste floating on a rushing river, turning pure water into an open sewer.

Day Four

She hid from me for a week and I didn't even see her shadow behind the window. The blinds were down. I knew that she had two jobs now—came from the painting job, changed, and went to the restaurant. As for the little girl, she was left to herself, alone. One morning I saw her going to Bobby's apartment. I spied on her and the second day I saw her again behind Bobby Palomo's window. She was a child, but was growing small buds of breasts and was capable of sex and Bobby (if not a faggot) was definitely capable of fucking her. So I thought that warning the mother like a good old friend would be just that appropriate move to restore my reputation. I waited patiently to see her. But I saw her only twice and at wrong moments. Once, early in the morning I went to the bus stop to see her, but Mr. Thompson was there and she was complaining to him about her air conditioner. When Thompson left, her bus came, she ran toward it, and ignored me. The second time I saw her with her daughter, both carrying heavy grocery bags. I couldn't talk in front of the girl. I said "hi" from my window and she said "hi" back.

Then I didn't see her for a few more days and early morning fevers prevented me from going to the bus stop. I didn't feel well these days and now I was not sure which pain was real and which imaginary. I had joint pain, fever, chills, head-splitting headaches, and I vomited at least once a day. I was ill like hell and needed to see the doctor.

After the usual exam Dr. Haas informed me that I had lost more weight, then she invited me to the hospital's smelly cafeteria. I'm not sure why this woman paid special attention to me. I was one of her ten AIDS patients and I was sure she didn't invite all of them to lunch. She bought me food—turd-shaped smelly meatloaf—which turned my stomach and we sat surrounded by people as miserable as myself. A young girl in a blue gown, with a shaven head the size and color of a cantaloupe, held an older woman's hand and they prayed with their eyes shut. An old couple sat at the opposite table and the man spoon-fed the old lady like a baby. A TV set hung on the wall, showing a soap opera. On the screen a tall, blond woman, a bit chubby for the kind of dress she wore—a shimmering gold gown—argued with a younger woman, a brunette in black. They waved their hands and shouted. The blond wiped her tears. The commotion was about a man, who appeared in the next scene, wearing a white trench coat, smoking in the rain. I was immersed in the show. The volume was not high enough to be able to hear the dialogue clearly and I had to imagine it.

"Why are you so quiet, Madison?" Marlina Haas asked.

A nurse pushed a bald child on a wheelchair and planted him next to our table. The kid was yellow and in his thin pale face a pair of large blue eyes glowed with life.

"How do you feel, Madison?" Dr. Haas asked.

"I'm willing to die, Doctor."

"Nonsense." She gulped her coffee and took a big bite of her cheesecake. "No one is willing to die."

"I am."

"I'm using your poem, Madison."

"My poem?"

"The poem you gave me once. That D. H. Lawrence poem. I'm using it."

"What do you mean, using it?"

"I'm doing a painting of it. *The Ship of Death,* that's what my painting is called."

"I didn't know you painted that well."

"I don't know how good it is, but it makes me happy."

"Good for you, Doc."

"I want you to see it some day. There is this stormy black water with people drowning in it. The ship is waiting. I'm standing on the deck."

"Why did you put yourself there? You're not dying."

"How do you know?"

"You say you're sick, but I don't think you're dying."

Marlina Haas laughed; her lipless mouth opened like a large hole. "Do I look any better than, let's say, a few months ago?"

I glanced at her reluctantly. She was less than one hundred pounds, a dried-up plum, emaciated, shrunken, and jaundiced. Clumsily, she'd covered the red spots on her cheeks with a white powder. Her eyes were circular holes, open in eternal wonder. A larger scar, fresh and crimson, like an Indian mole, sat between her eyebrows.

"So why are you so quiet? Do I look better?"

She looked worse than ever. She was Death personified and belonged on the deck of that damned ship. But in a low voice I said, "You won't die, Doctor."

"No, I won't, because I defy gravity. I'm taking dance classes. Ballet. The real thing."

"You're telling me to take ballet?"

"Why not? There is this fifty-year-old professor, this physicist who wears a leotard and stands at the barre with us. He bends and rises on his toes; he moves with the music. He's a sight!"

"He's out of his mind. I know his type—these crazy academics. I've lived with them all my life."

"I don't think he's crazy. He told me walking on a treadmill bored him to death. This way he's doing his cardiovascular while enjoying some Chopin. They have live music at the Houston Ballet."

"I'm not interested in music."

"You were talking to me about Wagner once. You impressed me with your knowledge."

"Does it mean that I listen to music?"

"Who are you angry at, Madison?" she suddenly asked. "Yourself? God? It's not that I don't understand. When I lost everything because of this untimely disease, I was angry. I couldn't find anyone or anything to be mad at. There was no one except myself. I hated myself and thought that I'd done something awful. You know what I mean?"

"But in my case, Doc, I *have* done something awful. I've contaminated my life."

"No one knew what AIDS was back then, when you shared needles. Which means you shouldn't blame yourself. The first cases of HIV were reported in 1981. And it wasn't public news. Now let me finish. When I hated myself, I decided to change my life. I began painting. I took dance classes. I hadn't touched my flute since I was in high school. I began to play again. I joined group therapy. We talk."

"Oh, Doctor. Please!"

"Do you want to join us?"

"You're a bunch of professionals with a streak of bad luck

in your privileged lives. Who am I? Huh? A former night watchman. A marginal person. A bum. And now I'm being pushed out. That's it. No, thanks, Doc. I don't need group therapy and I don't dance." I spat all this out and stood up to leave.

"No one asked you to dance, Madison. You cannot dance."

"No, Doc. I cannot. And I hate music. But I did something for myself last week. You want to hear it?"

"Sit down and tell me." She plucked at my sleeve to make me sit.

"It's not worth sitting. It's not really a story. Nothing like you see up there." I pointed at the TV screen. "I screwed up the possibility of a relationship."

"Oh—" She covered her mouth like a little girl.

"Yes, oh. Indeed, oh. I've always been like this, Doc. I don't know how to treat women. I say something that hurts their feelings and turns them off. You want to hear a side story? When I was in grad school, I had a real girlfriend for the first time. I mean a steady one. Her name was Cindy. She became pregnant and we were both confused for a couple of months. Until she went and got rid of the baby and I went to visit her in the hospital. I was sensitive enough to buy her some flowers. I sat there by her bed, held her hand, and told her that I was happy that we'd got rid of the problem, that we were alone again. That was the last thing I ever told her because she didn't want to see me anymore. I turned her off somehow. Now this woman—my neighbor—I bought her a present and went to her place to give it to her. When she rejected my gift, I called her a lesbo and stormed out."

"Madison, you were angry at something."

"Angry at that unsmiling, suspicious-looking brat of hers who clings to her mother like a leech. Angry at the woman's books and her stupid memoir on that ridiculous door sitting on orange crates. Angry at her beauty, her innocence, her muscled thighs—yeah, I was angry. See you later, Doc." I left and on my way stood close to the hanging TV for a second. The young man in the white trench coat and the young woman in black were kissing in the rain. The plump blond woman watched them from an upstairs window, wiping her tears.

"Don't you realize they're feeding you shit? They feed you shit from morning to night," I said loudly to the people and left.

I DECIDED TO see Roya and apologize. So I went to her place later that day and knocked. I could hear Vivaldi's *Four Seasons* playing on a cheap portable stereo. The little brat opened the door without asking who it was or looking through the peephole. Through the wide-open door I saw my Persian in her black tights, head on the floor, legs up in the air, against the wall. She looked like a sharp arrow sent by gods, piercing the ground. She saw me from her upside-down position and jumped on her legs like a cat.

"I'm so sorry to bother you—"

"It's okay. I'm exercising—for my back." She stood in the frame of the door, slightly panting. She didn't invite me in.

"I need to talk to you for a second."

"Can we talk some other time?" she asked. She was definitely cold. Cold as a corpse. Dead and gone.

"It's important and it's not about me." I said this to relieve her.

"Okay. Could you wait for me downstairs? I'll come down in a minute. We can talk in the parking lot."

She didn't want me in her apartment anymore and this was as clear as daylight. I went down and stood in the middle of the hot lot like an idiot. The afternoon sun was strong and my head was bare.

She came down and we walked toward the bus shelter. The woman with the bundle sat on the bench looking through the binoculars of her fingers, murmuring something under her breath. We sat next to her. The merciless heat of June brought the rotten stench of death out of the woman's flesh. This was the worst setting for my purpose. But how could I change my damn fate?

"It's hot here. Can we go in?"

"Please tell me what you want to talk about. I have only a short time to get ready for my second job."

"I wanted to talk to you about your daughter. Did you see the counselor?"

"Yes. But what is it you want to say?"

"I saw her in Bobby Palomo's apartment. It's not good. You get me? How old is she? Twelve? Thirteen?"

"Twelve." She paused. "She was in Bobby's apartment?"

"Yes. At least twice."

"Thank you." She got up.

"I'm very much concerned about you and your daughter. This is America. You get me? It seems that you trust everybody."

"Bobby is a good boy. I rely on my gut feelings a lot." When she said, "gut feelings," she put the flat of her palm on her belly. "Something tells me that Bobby is a good boy. He helps us. I'm sure they chat or play."

"Play? Bobby is twenty years old!"

"I know. I'm not saying it's all right. I'll talk to Tala. But I'm sure it's nothing like what you imagine."

She began walking toward home and I followed her like a dog, panting. Now she thought I had dirty thoughts about her daughter. She had a gut feeling that Bobby was good and I was bad. How else could I interpret this coldness?

"I just felt that I should tell you."

"Thanks," she said coldly.

"I'm sorry about that night."

"Which night?" She stopped in the middle of the burning parking lot.

"The earrings and all—"

"Oh. It's not that I don't wear earrings. I'm dealing with so many problems right now. We have a hard life. No time for earrings." She said this and entered the building.

"I know. I know." I said this before she closed the screen door on me. "It was a bad time. Can you forget?"

"Forget what?"

"What I said about your hair. I was a bit upset."

She laughed behind the screen door, banged it, and ran up the steps. I couldn't see her from where I was. The afternoon was too bright and I saw black spots in front of my eyes; I had to go home before I passed out.

NOW EACH DAY I dreaded the coming night. Days passed more easily, because I spent them at the hospital, cafés, and bus stops. In the long afternoons I took short naps in my bedroom, but at night I was frightened of the house. Shadows and shapes danced around and between the unpacked boxes, and I knew that they were my old enemies who appeared at each turning point of my life. I sat sleepless on my bed looking at the dusty kitchen table covered with unwashed dishes, medicine bottles, and yellowing newspapers. I murmured that morbid poem in delirium.

Then a day came when the moon covered the sun and the sky darkened as if it were doomsday. I sat next to the dark woman and we watched the pale disc, the sun-moon, for hours. She whispered meaningless words and talked to the sun and the moon that were one and neither and I kept her company. I was used to her stench—the odor of death.

The days after the eclipse I sat on the same bench and watched the silent radiance of the sun and dreaded another eclipse. I knew that it wouldn't happen again in my lifetime but I couldn't stop the choking fear. Bobby Palomo joined me most of the nights. We chatted and strolled toward the apartments. He urged me to get some sleep and went to run around the block. I didn't accuse him of drug use anymore. He was anorexic, I decided. He wanted to burn the fat he didn't have.

He told me more about Roya. She had been a gymnast before she was arrested. Her back was injured when they hung her in that jail and she could never do gymnastics again. These days, he said, she was suffering from back pain again.

"Did you say they hung her?" I asked.

"Upside down," Bobby said. "From her feet. Her ligaments are pulled."

I didn't mention Bobby's visits with Tala. I didn't really

care what went on between the kids. I even secretly wished he'd do something stupid and put himself and the mother and the girl in big trouble so that I could tell the woman, "Didn't I warn you?"

And they did something stupid, but not what I was thinking. More horrible? Less? It depends on the interpretation of the incident. It happened on the Fourth of July, but before that I talked to my cold angel one more time, and that was when I poured everything out on the table (literally on my dusty table). But let me start from the beginning of that endless day.

Day Five

A tall, bald doctor entered the room, introduced himself, and informed me that my doctor was hospitalized. After the examination, I rushed to find Marlina Haas. I'm not sure why I felt the way I did. Maybe because I'd never acknowledged her illness. Maybe because I'd been unkind to her, ungrateful; or simply because she was my only caretaker. Who cared for me in this world except this jaundiced woman? What if she should die? What if she should leave me orphaned in the short life left for me?

I found her room on the thirteenth floor and the nurses didn't let me in. I insisted. They said she was sleeping. I said that I just wanted to leave a note next to her bed—I was her patient. They looked at my yellow face and let me in.

She was sleeping soundly on a narrow bed, a hose running into her nose, her twig-like arms resting on her sides, ending at wide, thick-veined hands. Her knuckles were large and knotted, her nails short and dried up—a working man's hands. I gazed at her for a long moment and thought that she was dying. I didn't want the bald doctor to see me. I wanted Marlina back. Now I had this urge to touch her head where pink scalp showed. I saw specks of paint on her short hair—blue and red. This meant that she had been taken to the hospital when she was painting. I looked at her chapped lips, half open in wonder, and the dried blood that smeared at the corner of her mouth. Could I kiss that bloody spot? I gazed at the fresh, open blisters spattering her face. I sighed and murmured, "The voyage of oblivion awaits you, Marlina, so build your ship of death, oh, build it!"

I glanced out the window and saw the window of another hospital. A woman wearing a black scarf bent over someone's bed. She either sprinkled water on the person or threw white petals. Jasmine? Then she lay her head on the body and didn't rise again. Now with an unusual clarity, as if under the influence of a drug, I saw myself in 1978 sitting in my small cubicle in the library of the University of Texas, reading Heidegger. I recalled the philosopher's long-forgotten words. *"Dasein,"* I repeated. Being there. Being-in-the-world. I am, therefore I think. And anxiety comes when one realizes that anything one does has already been defined for him in advance by "The One." And then, "Fallen-ness" comes and that's when one cannot bear the possibility of the "Nothing," of being pushed out of life, out of being.

A short, bald man, a librarian, knocked on the window and called me out. From the library I went to the scene of the accident, where my father's car had fallen down a cliff. They had cleared the bodies, but the car was there. Bodies, I say, because he was not alone. They'd found a naked girl—not a woman, not a secretary or a middle-aged clerk, but a girl, and not a mature graduate student, but a young girl, a freshman out of high school—they'd found an underaged freshman in his car, wearing almost nothing. The old rat was having a secret affair with a girl-child.

I took my mother to the morgue that evening and we sat watching him in his coffin until all the candles burnt. His face looked innocent, like when he had recited Shakespeare for me with tears in his eyes. Mother wept calmly and steadily in her white handkerchief.

Fallen. Fallen-ness. Pushed out of life. My life. Father. Dad. Oh, Dad, what had I done to you? Huh? What?

I sobbed for my long-dead father and for myself, then took the small box of earrings out of my pocket and left it on Marlina's pillow with a little note: "Get well and dance, Doc! And paint the whole world!"

THE REST OF the day I walked aimlessly around the Houston streets. I walked like a madman in the heat of June when even the homeless sought shelter and poor dark maids held umbrellas over their heads. I walked until the sun slipped behind tall glass towers. I was a mourner all over again, as if it was yesterday that I had lost my father. I recalled his image in the open coffin and Marlina's on the narrow bed and tears gathered in my eyes. I sat on a bench to watch the falling sun.

There are certain locations in Houston where swallows gather in the hundreds, soar above treetops, sit on them, fly in different directions, almost collide with each other, then vanish. Before you know it, they appear again in the hundreds. Bell Park on Montrose Avenue is one of these mysterious spots. I thought either these birds were playing, or they were lost. Sometimes they sat on a treetop, absolutely motionless, as if thinking, as if having a silent conference, then flew away. Then I remembered "The Conference of the Birds" by Attar of Nayshabour, a Persian Sufi poet I had read many years ago. I tried to remember the story, but I couldn't. I left the darkening park, fearing the shadows that approached me.

On the bus going home, I decided to talk with Roya and tell her the truth. I practiced the sentences in my head over and over to pick the best one: "Look, I'm dying, stay with me for a little while," or "I won't bother you for long, stay with me," or "Roya, I can relieve you of all this work. You can get your degree. Just stay with me for a short time. I'm dying." I noticed that in each phrase I repeated, "Stay with me," and "I'm dying." This pleading tone disgusted me. I needed to think more. When I saw the sign of Saint Ann's Catholic Church from the window, I got off. I needed to speak to God.

I hadn't been in a church since I was a child and I felt awkward. The chapel was empty. It didn't feel like a holy place. I could hear the uproar of laughter from a classroom behind the wall. In the school yard children played and screamed with joy. I knelt and prayed. I stared at the wounded body of Christ on the cross and murmured in delirium, "O Lord. You're granting me my deserved death. A dying that will come slow, but soon, and will extinguish my life—an empty life, insignificant, on hold. What am I, my Lord? But a husk, a leaf? The great death will lift me, but it won't take me that high."

I wept and didn't mention Roya.

In an early evening nap I dreamed of her for the first time. She uncovered me and lay on top of me. She was there to offer me solace. God had sent her to me. There was no doubt. She kissed my face and neck, then rubbed my body to warm me up. I was a cold corpse and she touched me with her benevolent hands. Now she put her mouth on my mouth and blew her breath into my body. I breathed with her and we breathed together in a rhythm that led to ecstasy. I moaned and she moaned, little breathy moans, and this way I was not scared anymore. I awoke and found myself surrounded by the shapes and shadows. They were visiting me again. I rushed out of the house.

I sat on the bench of the bus stop and waited. Going home from the restaurant she would pass by me. I was in flames; my evening fever had risen up. I sat and sat and sat but she didn't come. At midnight, Bobby Palomo pedaled toward me.

"Hey, Madison, how do you feel tonight?"

"Not good. Fever."

"Did you take anything? Your medication?"

He had grown into the habit of acting like a son, seeing me as an old father.

"Yes."

"Is it worse?"

"What?"

"Your fever?"

"Yes."

"I'm sorry." He lay his bike against the bench and sat. He took a cigarette out but didn't light it."

"Where is she?" I said.

"Who?"

"Roya."

"Didn't I tell you? They fired her. My manager, this bastard Tony, fired her a few days ago. But, fortunately, she found another job. They've opened a sidewalk café downtown. One of our waitresses took her there."

"Downtown?"

"Yeah. A real cool place. Right in front of the Alley Theater. If I didn't make such good money here, I'd go there too. But the customers know me here and tip me well."

"How does she get home from downtown?"

"I don't know. Haven't thought about it."

"What about her girl?"

"Oh, you know? One good thing about this café is that she can take the girl with her. She sits there in a corner, I guess. It's a sidewalk, it's not really a restaurant."

"A sidewalk."

"Yeah. Hey, Madison, you're really hooked on her, huh?"

"Hooked?"

"So to speak. Don't be offended."

"What else has she told you?"

"About what?"

"Anything about me?"

"No."

"You're lying."

"Come on. Why would I lie to you? Why would she say anything about you?"

"Does she know that I'm ill?"

"She hasn't mentioned it. But I guess everybody knows."

"Everybody?"

"It's okay, buddy. Cheer up. You'll get better and feel fine."

"Shut up!"

"You're in a bad mood, man. Need some food?" He pointed to a plastic bag hanging on the handlebar of his bike.

"No, I don't need food. Go!"

"Don't you want to walk home with me?"

"No. Not tonight."

"It's kind of late."

"Go, boy. Go!"

She came past midnight. An old Chevy dropped her off and a young man behind the wheel said something and she laughed. A loud burst. The man yelled, "See you tomorrow, Lola!" She laughed again and said, "Roya, not Lola! See you tomorrow, Carlos." Her daughter was not with her (the poor bastard was alone again—the wretched brat). She didn't look at the bench and passed. She wore a short black skirt and a white shirt and walked awkwardly, almost limping. She was afraid of the night, and wanted to walk faster, but she couldn't. I followed her. She reached the screen door and I approached her before she opened it.

"Isn't it a bit too late for a young lady to come home?"

"Ah!" She gasped and grabbed her chest. I'd startled her. "Is that you, Mr. Kirby?"

"I was taking my night walk."

"I work, you know?" she explained. "I work at the Sidewalk Café."

"The sidewalk? What an appropriate place!"

I was spitting venom again. She must have blushed in the dark. She pulled the screen door to enter.

"Did I offend you again?"

"It's late, Mr. Kirby. I have to go up. Tala is alone."

"The girl is sleeping now. I need to talk to you."

"About her?"

"No, about me."

"I'm sorry. I have a backache, Mr. Kirby—"

"Madison. Madison." I repeated my name loudly like a madman.

"It's late," she said desperately. "My back hurts."

"Come with me."

"Where?"

"To my apartment. I just want to talk to you. We can't talk in this goddamned parking lot."

Now she let go of the doorknob and looked at me in the weak light of a yellow bulb on the wall. There was no moon in the sky. I'm not sure what she read in my face. She wasn't wearing her eyeglasses and her large black eyes gave out sparks, as if a pair of stars twinkled in the dark.

"Are you scared of me?"

"I've been scared of some people in my past life. But I'm not scared of you."

"Then come with me. I won't hurt you." I said this in a calm tone.

"I believe you," she said and followed me.

She had seen the death in my eyes.

I TRIED HARD not to repeat those pleading words, but what I said became the same refrain.

"I'm dying. Stay with me!"

I had pulled up a chair for her at the chaos of the kitchen

table and she sat erect, squeezing her purse on her lap, looking at me.

"I don't have much time left," I added.

She looked around the apartment for the first time and then gazed at the table.

"This chaos shows how I feel. I haven't been able to unpack since I moved here a few months ago."

"I'm sorry," she managed to say under her breath.

"Why should you work so hard?"

"Pardon me?" she said, as if she didn't hear me well.

"You're so talented. You know languages. You have degrees. You need to go back to school."

"How? I need to work."

"I have twenty thousand—it's with my mother. I can make you my heir. You know the word? *Heir?* With an *h,* not an *a*." Now I was delirious, saying meaningless things, offending her over and over again. "I'll die soon and this money will be yours."

"I don't understand."

"If you stay with me. To the hour of my death."

She went pale in the face and stood. She was shocked. She managed to walk to the door.

"Roya!" I called her name for the first time and uttering it made my voice quiver.

She turned and looked at me with the saddest eyes in the world. But she remained silent.

"We'll get married, but not for a long time. Because I will die."

"I wish I could, Madison."

Finally she called me by my first name. Then she left.

I ran to the door and shouted, "I know, this is not very romantic—and it sounds like a deal—" But she had already
gone and was crossing the parking lot to her place.

"I love you!" I whispered into the dark, empty corridor.

WHAT WOULD ANOTHER woman do? The same as she
did? Wouldn't that woman say something different? Something awful, or something kind? Who would leave so silently?
So sadly? Removing herself from my life like an angel, like
someone who knew I was dying even before I told her, like
someone who was mourning me all the while.

Day Six

God created His world in seven days and I destroyed mine in
six. I talked to this woman only six times in my life—first, I
lusted after her, then I fell in love with her and esteemed her
as an angel, next, I resented her; I loved her again and begged
her to stay with me, and when she rejected me, I hated her. A
week after the night of the proposal (ha, ha!), I decided to kill
her. Now that she had rejected me so coldly and cruelly, she
had to accompany me in my final journey. She would become
my fellow traveler on that ominous ship. I would push her out
of life the way He was pushing me. But let me start from the
beginning.

After she removed herself quietly from my life, my fever
rose and I spent the whole night speaking deliriously to myself, to the red clock, to God and the increasing shapes that

crowded my apartment. When the old man next door clicked on his typewriter, I threw whatever came into my hand at the wall to shut him up and when he didn't shut up, I pounded on his door and threatened that I'd kill him with my bare hands. Fever, anger, and fear of the approaching shadows were choking me. I was desperate.

And something the size of a hand grenade was about to explode in my heart. I was sure that this was the bee that had grown enormous and had finally gotten inside my heart. Toward the morning I threw up and passed out for half an hour on the bathroom floor, then I called 911 and the ambulance came at dawn. I checked myself into the hospital and the bald doctor told me that I had to stay seven days for various tests. I stayed in a bed near a window with a view of the sky and, in a half-conscious state, gazed at the ash-gray clouds. Soon summer rain hit the window and gloom covered the world.

I philosophized in delirium to pass the time. I told myself between attacks of devastating stomach cramps that if God didn't exist, then everything was permissible. If we were beings-toward-death, as Heidegger suggested, and we had to face Nothing, and death was our most unique possibility, and there was no One there to save us, then our entire relationship with this world would transform. We could do anything to prove our existence. We could take responsibility for our death and why not for another person's? Would we disturb the order of the universe? But hadn't it been disturbed since day one? Genghis Khan, Alexander, Napoleon, and Hitler took millions of lives and defined a new meaning for their relationship with this world. They acted God-like, while they were beings-toward-death. They didn't want to fall, I concluded, like worthless leaves or empty husks; they died heroically in battles and stayed responsible and dignified to the end. Couldn't I die heroically? Couldn't I give my life meaning in the last moments?

Bobby Palomo came to visit me. Like an old nanny, he brought some food in a plastic bag. He sat and for the first time I saw his face in daylight. His eyes were restless and a purple shadow colored his sockets. He never seemed healthy to me. He barely slept and I could hear him every night taking his bike up and down the steps, riding around the block after his famous runs.

Now he took the food out of the plastic bag and told me that he had checked with the nurses and they said I could eat anything I wanted. He helped me sit and lean against the pillows and while I tried to eat a few bites of meatball, he reported about the neighborhood. He said that the university had accepted Roya's transcripts and they had let her in the Ph.D. program. She was so excited that she had bought her books and was studying for the fall semester. As to how she would pay the tuition, PAC was planning to give her a scholarship.

"PAC?" I asked.

"People's Aid Center," he explained. "In Montrose."

"I know where PAC is. But how?"

"How what?"

"It was I who told her about PAC—for her crazy girl. She must have pleaded for money."

"She said people like her over there."

"People?"

"The social workers, I mean."

"There is a lesbo there by the name of Maya. She must have liked her and decided to spend PAC's money on her. Steven Will has just married and Ric Cardinal is too old for her."

The minute I said this something told me that I was lying. It was Ric Cardinal who had become fascinated with her. And it was I who had led her to this man.

Then I became irritable and told Bobby to leave me alone. This was enough. The bitch had rejected my offer and begged PAC for her tuition.

Later that day, Marlina Haas called my room and with her thin, girlish voice (the only female aspect of her entity) invited me to her place for supper. She said she had been home for four days now and she felt much better and would go back to work soon. Why didn't I join her for a sandwich tomorrow night, after checking out of the hospital? Then she paused and said that she wanted to unveil the panel for me—*The Ship of Death*. She didn't mention the earrings.

The next day I was released and Bobby, who had already checked with the hospital, was there to take me home. He helped me pack my bag and escorted me to the taxi. I didn't know what to say. This boy was embarrassing me with his excessive attention. I told him that I appreciated his help but I didn't feel like going home at all. I'd been lying down for seven days and I wanted to go somewhere and stroll and after that I was invited to my doctor's place. I asked him to drop me somewhere downtown. I'd be fine.

In the backseat of the taxi, the boy took a silk tie out of his pocket and handed it to me. He said his father had left him a few items he didn't use—ties, a couple of suits, boxes of cigars, and so on. He said I could use this tie; it matched my suit. I accepted his offer and wore the expensive red tie. I'd been invited for dinner after all.

I walked aimlessly toward the end of downtown where they had erected a university on top of a hill by the bayou. The sky was cloudy again and a strong breeze blew from the top of the skyscrapers and brought some relief. But I felt a slight twitching above my left eye. This had started a few days ago and wouldn't go away. I also felt muscular contortions inside my head. But I kept walking toward that university and watching people. It was around seven, offices were closed now, and only lawyers and their secretaries, the ones who worked overtime, passed on the streets in their suits. The summer school students walked by with their bags on their shoulders, and occasionally a spectacled professor trudged toward the university's tower. Had I not put my life on hold when I did, I could be one of these balding professors, with an attaché case full of knowledge for the ignorant youth.

Then I reached an intersection and stood for the cars to pass and this was when my fate was sealed.

They had gathered under the sign "God Listens." The billboard stood on tall legs and on its white surface the sign showed bold and black. One of the men sat on a bucket, the other on the curb, and the third spread his legs out on the asphalt, leaning against the soot-covered wall. People passed by them and didn't see them. The men were invisible. Suddenly the one on the bucket, the older one, stood up, took a tape measure out of his pocket, and began to measure his body. He did this carefully, like a tailor intending to make a suit for himself. He measured the length of his arms, then his legs, first from inside his thighs to the ground, then from his waist down. He measured the thickness of his waist and neck and even his thin wrists. After each measuring he chuckled to himself and shook his head, as if pleased. Now the one who sat on the curb stood up. He was a black man in his thirties; he climbed on the bucket and began to play a trumpet without having one in his hands. He blew into his fists and the muffled sound of the trumpet filled the air and rose above the roar of the cars. After he finished his piece there were a few seconds of silence. His friends applauded and I clapped too. Now the three of them began to walk. I had seen the third one a few times before—he was naked to the waist with dirty blond hair sweeping his shoulders. This was the man who resembled Christ.

They turned onto Louisiana Street and I followed them as if hypnotized, not knowing that they were taking me one step closer to my fate. Had I not seen them that day, or had I not followed them half-consciously, the rest of the events would never have happened. There was a small park across the street from the Alley Theater; the men entered and sat on the grass, facing the café on the opposite sidewalk. I sat a few steps behind them, leaning against a tree, half-hiding behind another tree. The waiters and waitresses were setting the tables and Roya was one of them.

The trio of ragged men watched her climb the theater's steps in her tight black skirt, and I watched with them. They gazed at her muscled calves in black panty hose and the quiver of her breasts in her white silk shirt when she rushed down the steps with a tray, and I gazed with them. They studied her every movement and I did the same. Now I noticed that her daughter was sitting in a corner table with Ric Cardinal and another woman, a redhead I didn't know. The woman wrote something in a notebook and once in a while talked to a waiter, commenting on something. Ric and the brat talked. The girl had a huge ice cream in front of her with cherries on top. I'd never seen her talk to anyone, let alone smile. Now Ric said something and she laughed. Roya came to the table and stood, one hand pressing her back, where I knew it hurt, and Ric ran his eyes all over her, from head to foot as if taking her clothes off with his crooked eyes. The redhead said something and Roya sat down. They talked and I could hear the burst of laughter now and then. Then I saw how the seduction began. It was a scene out of *Paradise Lost,* but ironically it was my paradise that was going down the drain.

I saw the whole show and the men who were with me saw it too and their mouths watered. Roya took a cherry from the top of her daughter's ice cream and put it in her own mouth, then took another and offered it to Ric. The cherry was between her thumb and forefinger and she would have put it between the man's lips had the redheaded woman not stared at them. Ric took the cherry and put it in his mouth. They were more intimate than a period of two weeks should allow. When the redhead, who was obviously the manager of the place, got up and went inside, the three of them remained at the table and shared the ice cream. The cherries kept coming and going from hands to mouths and they laughed like a happy family.

This was a fucking family *I* had created.

When the darky with the imaginary trumpet went across the street and begged to be allowed to play, there was a little commotion at first, because the redhead didn't want a home-

less man in her café. But as expected, Saint Cardinal inter-
fered and let the man play. Roya stood there next to the darky
and he played his sad fake song that sounded real. Ric stood
behind Roya, who was only up to his chest. Their bodies almost rubbed. Now the damn Italian lay his hand on Roya's
neck, where short baby hair grew on her olive skin. He kept
his hand there for a second maybe, but this was enough for
me. No doubt they were more than friends.

When the crazy nigger ended his pathetic solo I knew that
I had to kill the woman.

IN THE BUS, going toward Marlina's place, I philosophized
again. Now that you're being pushed out of life, now that
you're a living-toward-death and your unique possibility is
Nothing, assume power and change your relationship with
the world. The world is like putty in your hand, shape it!
Didn't you shape a relationship by leading the woman to the
man? Break it now; push her out. What will you lose? Your
life? Ha, ha!

My longtime hero, Ric Cardinal, became an enemy in a few
minutes because he had betrayed me by taking my woman
away from me. Didn't I tell him I was in love with my Persian
neighbor? Didn't he know that this was the woman? I'm sure
the first day that she went to his office, she told him who had
sent her. I felt cuckolded like a man who finds his wife in his
friend's bed or, worse, in his own bed with his friend. And Ric
knew that I was dying. So, I was nothing to him, absolutely
nothing. Ric was as fake as everyone else and all these years he
was a worm in the world of worms. He was only another mul-

tiplying parasite and I was such a simpleton that I had thought he was a saint!

I muttered venomous words and walked fast and furious toward Marlina's glass tower. She resided in one of the twin skyscrapers of Greenway Plaza. I thought of my doctor as a rich, ugly whore when the automatic door slid open in front of me. The goddamned glass elevator sprinkled out Mozart and the red carpet of the hallway gave out the scent of jasmine. "Rich, fucking worms," I murmured as I passed each door, and felt a choking anger when Marlina Haas greeted me.

She was not in her long, loose-fitting white gown, but in a short, cream-colored skirt and a sleeveless blouse. I noticed her bare feet first—large and bony and wide like a man's feet. She had used powder on her face, but clumsily—patches of white showed on her dry skin and the red blisters were not fully covered. When I saw the pearl earrings hanging next to her sallow cheeks, a shudder ran through my body and the hair rose on my arms. I dropped my head so as not to stare.

"Why don't you come in?"

I stepped in and looked around. On an oval glass dining table two red candles burned. Between them a single white lily stood in a tall blue vase. On the opposite wall there were two unframed paintings. The first one was a deep blue landscape of a forest burning; the amputated tree trunks glowed with orange and blended into blue. The next panel was yellow and silver, translucent light reflected on the surface of a river, which passed through orange fields. It was as if the burned trees of the first panel had grown again and they were now saplings. In the distance the pure blue of the horizon merged into the yellow of the vast sky. Here and there twigs and trunks of long-dead trees remained. This was a new universe born out of the old.

"Are these yours?"

"Yes. *Death* is the first one, *Transfiguration,* the second. Inspired by Straus."

This exceeded my expectation. I was impressed but tried not to show it.

"I like this place," I said and looked around. "Wealth well used."

"I'm not wealthy, Madison. I'm well-to-do and I've earned it. Worked to death." She laughed and added, "Literally!"

We walked on the polished wooden floor and lounged on a white leather couch. Another such couch and a few armchairs surrounded a small oval glass table, on top of which another lily stood in a blue vase. Everything was a replica of something else, but in a different size.

"Would you like to listen to music while I'm bringing some drinks?"

"Sure," I said.

"The CDs are over there."

She left and I got up and went toward the spiral CD stand, more to rescue myself from the unpleasant comfort of the white couch. I didn't want to sit there. She had a good collection of classical music all arranged chronologically, like in a library—Baroque to contemporary. Now I'm not sure why I picked a Wagner. *Tristan and Isolde* highlights.

Marlina came back with a tray and put it on the table. "You picked one?" and, before I could say anything, she took the CD from me and went toward the stereo.

"I haven't listened to Wagner for ages," she said. "These days I listen to Berlioz's *Fantastique* when I paint. I don't know why. I must be in a good mood."

"Can we sit on regular chairs?" I asked.

"Oh, of course. Do you want to sit by the window? We can watch the sunset in the glass wall of that building. How about that?"

We pulled two straight chairs from the dining table and sat facing the tall window. A mirror image of Marlina's tower, blue and translucent, reflected the gray clouds and the red glow of sunset. Wagner began. Strings pulled human agony to the edges of the universe and suddenly it became clear for me why I had quit listening to music. It tormented me.

"I live in a clean glass cage," she said. "Unreal world. This world suits me better," she added. "I moved here a few months ago, away from the real world. I tried to create a space for myself, to live leisurely, in case I die."

"I've done the opposite."

"How?"

"I moved to this ugly garage apartment a few months ago when my illness got worse and I haven't unpacked yet."

"What do you mean?"

"I live in chaos. My things are in boxes. I'm living the life of a man between two journeys. Why unpack?"

"Oh, Madison. You may very well live longer than you think. Unpack!" She said this and handed me a tall glass of iced tea. "As your doctor, I know that you don't drink alcohol."

"True."

We sipped iced tea. We listened to Wagner.

"Well, where is the ship?"

"It's over there. I have to unveil it for you. I have covered it."

"To create suspense and surprise?"

"Oh, Madison, no. I didn't intend to surprise you. Maybe I shouldn't have covered it. I thought when they show a painting for the first time, they do this. I must be wrong. They do this for statues in the middle of a plaza. You see what an amateur I am?"

She was definitely insecure about her art and she sounded like a high school girl, justifying something. She has never married, I thought. She might still be a virgin. A spinster with an old, decaying cunt.

We went to the other side of the room, where it was dim; the curtain was drawn. She pulled it open and then uncovered the panel. She stood there next to me looking at me to see my reaction. I had her in my hands. She was putty in my palm.

"Well?"

"I'm not an art critic. What do you want me to say?"

"What do you think? I didn't paint this for art critics. This is for us."

"Us?"

"For the dying."

"Is that me? In the black waters, drowning? I can recognize my glasses." I laughed dryly.

"I'm up there to save you." She pointed to a woman in a black robe standing on the deck, but not quite standing, because her feet were off the floor; she was levitating.

"That's you—Death?"

She laughed—a girlish laugh—and went to the window and dropped herself on the chair. She looked exhausted.

"Who are these people with cute little wings, sitting on a cloud?" I asked this with a sarcasm that bit even me. I liked the painting, but I felt an urge to hurt her.

"They're my parents and other victims."

"Victims?"

"Hitler gassed my parents."

"You're a Jew?"

"No. Communists, homosexuals, and Gypsies were gassed too."

"Well, since I'm sure your parents were not homosexuals or Gypsies, then—"

"They were red."

"Commies, huh?"

"Right. Commies, as you Americans say."

A chilling silence fell. I paced the length of the room and the heels of my shoes stamped the floor in a repetitious knock, as if marking the seconds. Outside the clouds darkened and thunder cracked. I went to my chair and sat and looked at the reflection of daylight dimming. Marlina's eyes were closed. I looked at her bony face and lashless eyes.

"Everything is a reflection here," I said. "You don't see any of the real world. Plato would love this."

She didn't say anything. Was she asleep?

All of a sudden a summer shower, a monsoon rain, poured and hit the windowpanes. A few thunderbolts exploded and a blinding light reflected in the blue panels. Marlina opened her eyes and smiled. She closed her eyes again.

Strange, I thought. What was she suggesting, closing her eyes like this? Why did she invite me here? Does she want me to touch her? A shudder passed under my skin again. I looked

at the pearl drops against her face and Roya's image appeared.
The café must be closing now. It's raining. Ric Cardinal is taking off his jacket, covering Roya's shoulders. He takes them in
his car. The three of them in a car together.

A fucking family.

Now Isolde lamented and I ran my eyes over Marlina's
body. Her upper belly was protruded, like starved children's
in Biafra. She had crossed her bare legs. Long, yellow hair
covered her skin. I remembered Roya's legs in her tights, her
muscled calves, her young flesh. Oh, how awkward this was.
How awkwardly sexless. A man and a woman in one. Neither. And a girl at the same time. Her voice, her sudden
laughter, her shyness, all went against her appearance. I could
close my eyes and touch this hermaphrodite; I could lay my
hand on her cheek and play with the cold pearls, dreaming of
the other one, my Persian.

Was she a virgin?

Now light vanished from the world and the room remained dark. The candles, burning on the dining table,
dimmed, then whizzed and died. I glanced at *The Ship of
Death* in the last rays of light and looked at the black waters,
then I looked at the woman, asleep or dead. A stream ran on
the long windowpane.

Could I in ten years create such a work? Could I even draw
a stick figure? I was worthless. I had done nothing. I was
being pushed out of life before I had left a mark. What had I
done in my life? What had I created or achieved? Where was
my panel? My book? My child? Something of me, remaining
on earth? I was raised as an attachment of my father and nothing else. Not an important attachment for that matter, an in-

significant one. An earlobe, a pinky, an attachment he could cut and live without. That's why he betrayed me and abandoned me.

Isolde screamed with joy, joy at Tristan's approaching ship. I couldn't take it anymore. I stood above Marlina's head and thought that I could touch her now. I could touch her and hurt her. I could smash her thin, hollow bones. I was capable of destruction. Her thin neck would fit in my palm. I could grab her neck like a chicken's and crack it. Snap! "My parents and other victims!" I mimicked her in rage and glanced at the commies on the cloud. She was a damn communist who lived like a bourgeois whore and I could kill her only for this hypocrisy. She was fake, too, like Ric Cardinal, like all of them.

As if feeling a negative current above her head, she opened her eyes. "It's dark," she said.

"I'm leaving."

"Sandwiches!" She tried to rise up. "I've made sandwiches."

"I don't have any appetite."

"There is something here you don't like, Madison. Is it my painting?"

"Rain," I said. "It's rain I don't like. Forgive my rudeness. I must go."

Now I'm not sure why I bent over her and picked her limp bony hand and held it for a long moment. I kissed it gently like a prince; then I left.

"There is an umbrella on the coat tree," she said.

I left without the umbrella and closed the door quietly. As the glass elevator smoothly sank, I heard Isolde's voice vanishing in the dark island surrounded by all the waters of the world. "I'm drowning. I'm sinking. What bliss!"

I COULD'VE BUILT a pyramid with the effort it took me to cling to reason. But reason like sweet bells jangled out of time. I remembered my Shakespeare in sudden sparks and Heidegger hunched in the corner of my brain like a cunning devil. At night, every night, I talked loudly with my demons—Heidegger, the shadows, and the red, round clock, which ticked and told me that the time was ripe.

On the Fourth of July, I began to throw away my things. I called it a clean-up operation, moving toward liberation. The thought of murder pumped adrenaline in my blood, but I had to wait until I saw a sign. Fate knocked on my door again. Now I had no doubt that everything was predestined. I didn't have a weapon and fate put one in my palm.

It was Bobby Palomo at the door saying that old Thompson and his wife were having a barbecue down there in the parking lot and all the tenants were invited. I said I was cleaning my house. Maybe I'd go, maybe not. He said he was happy for me that I was cleaning my place at last and he'd help if I wanted. I said no I didn't want help and dismissed him.

I began in a trance. It was as if everything was far away and long deceased. The objects with memories attached to them were remote. The memories belonged to someone else. Someone I knew once, but not anymore. With a garbage bag I walked around the room. The most important things were out of boxes and I needed to discard them. I began with Mother's picture on top of the refrigerator. I brought it close to my eyes. This was a Polaroid photo that a neighbor had taken of her. It must have been one Sunday morning when she had dressed up for church. She sent this in 1985 when I came to Houston. She stood in front of the church door, hands clasped, smiling, squinting. Her once beautiful body was shapeless, the sexless body of an aging woman. A puff of white hair showed above her meaty face. She never colored her hair when the grays grew in. Did I love her? Did I ever love this woman? When I was little, I did—when I hid next to her legs under the piano and listened. When I watched her worriedly in the grip of an asthma attack and was tormented with guilt. She rocked herself and wheezed, rocked and wheezed. But that was a thousand years ago. After the accident I stopped loving her. I resented her perfect sense of contentment, her needlessness, her peace in her small life, her life with small things. I envied that peace and that narrow window she had managed to open to life—a window through which every-thing looked just fine. I had wished many times that I could also narrow my window, to blind myself, to conceal the world that stretched forever from all sides. I'd wished to be able to stare ahead, straight in front of me, through a slight crack of a window that showed order and peace. Mother found this long ago in a run-down Austin suburb and I resented her for that. I resented her for reacting the way she did to the accident—submission, forgiveness, resignation, passivity. She retired in her dim room like a nun. She was only forty-five then, young and beautiful, with massive auburn hair, and the full, shapely figure of an earth mother. But she wore black and sat in front of that narrow window of hers and looked at a small patch of the world. Had she gone out of her mind, screamed, cursed, broken, burned, taken a lover before her husband's corpse was buried, to get even with him, had she gone mad, I would have remained sane and loved her still. I'd stay to protect her. I'd never leave the house, would never get lost in the world. I'd be saved. This woman's strange sanity in the face of horror destroyed me.

To the garbage bag of oblivion I send thee, Mother. So long!

I dropped the picture in the trash bag and then did the same with my other belongings. The key chains, cigarette boxes, knives, cups, this and that dirty, rusty, sun-washed, weather-beaten object that I'd kept just because each was attached to a place, a person, an incident. I shoved in what was overflowing from the cartons and taped them. The clean-up operation was over. But something pulsated somewhere in the dark room. The red alarm clock. I picked it up, debated for a second, then put it in my chest pocket. The little thing's heart beat in harmony with the pulse of my heart. This was time. Life. I decided to keep it until death would take us apart.

At dusk, when fireworks exploded downtown and the once-a-year patriotic nation got drunk on cheap beer and blasted firecrackers and shot bullets in the air, I went down and found the parking lot crowded with neighbors, all low-life people like myself. The Thompsons were feeding us tonight. The stingy old man owned an air-conditioning repair business across the street but let the poor tenants boil in the hothouses of mousehole garage apartments. Now his old witch of a wife with rollers on her flaming red head forked meat and sausage and dumped them on paper plates with a spoonful of mashed potatoes she'd made. I only knew Bobby Palomo and the crazy old Gary Whitefield, who typed absurd letters and wrecked my nerves every night. The rest were neighbors from another cluster of run-down apartments next to ours. All a bunch of losers like myself. Roya and the kid were not here. But they soon drove up in Ric Cardinal's old Toyota.

Ric parked and the three of them came out together like a happy fucking family. When Ric saw me he acted surprised, even shocked.

"Hey buddy, what're you doing here?"

"I live here."

"You do?"

Oh, villain, I thought; you smiling, fucking villain, you're pretending you don't know that I live here and you don't know who this woman is.

"Good to see you, Madison. Why didn't you come to see me after that lunch together?"

"I was in and out of the hospital."

"I'm sorry, Madison. You didn't leave me your address or phone number."

"I don't have a phone."

"How's your health now?" He asked this in his concerned counselor's voice.

"Pretty good, pretty good," I said coldly and walked away. I didn't want to talk to the bastard so I joined the other neighbors.

From the corner of my eye I watched Roya in her white pants and sleeveless black blouse, a can of beer in her hand, talking to old Mrs. Thompson. She wasn't wearing her eyeglasses, which meant she was trying to look more attractive. Then I noticed that the boy, Bobby, and the brat, Tala, laughed and ran upstairs. The fireworks blasted crazily and every head turned toward the sky. From some roofs in other neighborhoods real bullets were shot but one cracked right above our heads, in Bobby Palomo's apartment. His windowpane shattered and pieces of glass fell down. Roya screamed and called her daughter and I rushed up the steps with old Thompson and Ric. We found Bobby flat on the floor, blood gushing out from under his head. The little girl stood above Bobby holding a gun in her hand. Something told me that this gun was meant for me and I had to be quick and take it now or never.

But Ric stepped in front of me and sat on the floor, facing the girl. He raised his hand to get the gun. But she didn't give it to him.

"Go check on Bobby," I told Ric. "I know how to get the gun from this little girl."

I pushed Ric toward Thompson and two other men who were examining Bobby. The bullet had scratched his left ear and hit the bathroom door. The boy was laughing and saying that he was fine, but there was a big noise in his head.

"Hand me the gun!" I looked into the girl's eyes and ordered her in a tone meant to chill her blood. She handed me the gun and dropped herself in her mother's arms and sobbed.

It was a revolver; I slipped it in my pocket and stood up. Everybody was talking at the same time and Bobby kept saying, "I'm fine, I'm fine. It's just a scratch."

Someone wrapped a towel around his head and no one called the police.

"Kids!" Mrs. Thompson said and wiped her tears. "They were trying to shoot a bullet in the air. To celebrate the Fourth of July!"

"I'll take him to the hospital," Ric Cardinal said and left with Bobby. Then everybody cleared the apartment and went back to the icebox full of cold beer.

Roya remained on the floor, her girl buried in her arms. Now she was the Madonna with large dark eyes full of tears, pressing the child's head against her chest. This wasn't the last time that I saw her, but this image lived in me for a long time.

"I'm leaving," I said and knelt down in front of her.

She looked up and didn't say anything.

"I'm leaving for good, I mean. I'm going away."

She remained silent.

"Away from you," I said. But I was lying. I knew that I would follow her like a shadow until the day that I'd see a sign. And that day we'd leave together.

She remained stony and silent, as cold as an angel of God. I stretched my hand and with the tip of the forefinger gently touched a pearl-shaped teardrop cooling on her cheek. This was where I had kissed her in my imagination during long sleepless nights. I stood up and left, my hand pressing the gun in my pocket.

I didn't go up to my apartment. Old Mr. Thompson would tell Bobby to take the boxes and garbage bags out to the dumpster. I walked toward the street and passed the windows of the closed stores. That boutique in front of which we once stood displayed another pair of pearl earrings. I looked at them for a while, then sped up toward downtown. I felt light and free. In the land of the pretty objects I had only a few belongings: an old suit, a gun, and a clock ticking somewhere in my chest pocket. I didn't have much to lose. An old man, a street person, wearing the flag of America like a robe, passed by me and saluted; a flock of white doves flew toward him and sat on his head and shoulders. Above my head, in the sky, thousands of stars blasted in unimaginable shapes.

"Madison!" I whispered my own name, "Mad, mad, Madison! Farewell, sweet prince, farewell!"

✦ ✦ ✦

In her vast room she moves barefoot, from the stereo to the canvas and from the canvas to the window to watch the beginning of sunset in the blue glass wall. Now she moves on her toes in front of the dimming panel. This is a gray roaring sea darkened in the evening shadows. She walks lightly, vibrates like quicksilver, rises, dances almost, so that she stays alive, so that she doesn't fall. She works in motions, in rhythms, as if she is the heart of the whole world, the heart of the dark picture she creates. Now with a sudden impulse she drops the brush and picks up a flute. She faces the reflection of the red glow in the twin high-rises and begins to kiss the mouth of her instrument. She kisses and tongues and blows her breath, first shakily, then with confidence. The notes she had learned so well as a young girl fly back to her and enter the narrow body of the flute and the flute sighs and cries and gives birth to a familiar melody. She smiles and plays, her bony fingers run up and down, her hot breath fills the instrument. She plays until daylight vanishes from all the glass panels of the city and darkness paints the surfaces black. When she sees her image in the windowpane, alone in this glass room, close to the black, empty sky, she stops. Now in this absolute silence she hears murmurs and whispers. She turns in panic and glances at the The Ship of Death. *She hears women weeping and men shouting for help. She hears steady pulsation—heartbeats approaching, an immense heat entering her body. Her veins stretch and swell and burst like small firecrackers and under her skin blood splashes in starry shapes. She hears the deafening pulse, the rhythm of death. She falls and her flute rolls on the wooden floor, hollow and lifeless, empty of all dance tunes.* The Ship of Death *drowns in the sea of tar.*

◆ ◆ ◆

How absurd is a yellow door that functions as everything but a door? It becomes a desk, then a bed, and later . . . who knows? A lid to a coffin? There is a solar eclipse outside and the world is dark. They say the moon has covered the sun and the sun is gray and cold and the day is not a day anymore, it's a long dusk. Her daughter hears this on TV in the other room and reports. But she cannot see the sunless sky; she cannot move today. She is lying on the yellow door. The windows are covered with boards and the boards are nailed in a crisscross way and the room is dark. Not that the eclipse is anything exciting or uplifting, but it's a once-in-a-lifetime experience. She has missed once-in-a-lifetime experiences before and has regretted for a while, then forgotten. Like when one of the girls in the prison hanged herself from the shower and all the women rushed to see and she couldn't move her limbs. She knew the girl—a virgin, who was afraid of rape and had killed herself before the guards could touch her. She could rush and see her hanging from the shower, she could see it and record it in her head forever, but she couldn't move. She knew the girl.

What if she is not feeling as bad as she thinks? What if she can move herself, slide off the yellow door, get on her feet, and see the eclipse? Her daughter could be kinder, couldn't she? She could come in and whisper into her ear, "Mother, do you want to see the sky?"

Oh, how she misses someone's kindness, anyone's—a warm hand on her cold forehead, a soft voice whispering to her, a mother, a sister, a daughter pulling the blanket up to her chin, a father, a brother, a lover murmuring into her ear, "You'll be fine, Roya, you'll be alright. Now let me lift you up and take you to the balcony. It's a full eclipse, you shouldn't miss it. It's a once-in-a-lifetime experience."

ROYA

✦

And when you're gone to return to me some day,
I'll let my hair grow long for you.

ROYA SARAABI

Why did Tala have fevers every night? Why did her young, tender body burn? I rubbed alcohol on her golden skin and sang to her: "Sleep, sleep my little tulip, the leopard is crying in the mountains. Sleep, sleep my little hyacinth, the nightingale is singing on top of the tree—" This was a rhymed Persian lullaby and normally had a soothing, sedating effect, but before I reached the third flower and the third animal, she cried and called Bobby's name. When she was delirious she thought that she had killed Bobby Palomo and when I assured her that Bobby was fine, spending the summer with his mother in Chicago, she felt better, but now, burning in fever, she demanded the story. She didn't like fairy tales or stories from books. She wanted the tale of our own life.

I insisted that now we should read from books and enjoy

stories that are invented by others. I told her that I'd bought her *The Wizard of Oz,* a book American children read much earlier in their lives and she could still enjoy, but she threw the book away and urged me to tell her "our story." So I began.

ONCE UPON A time, in our old country, the guards took your uncle and me to this old prison—the Bathhouse. Your Uncle Hamid was a revolutionary, but I was just a little girl who had read some books to find out what the revolution was. The guards killed your uncle but I was lucky to be released—by accident, of course. My sister, your Auntie Mali, enrolled me in the College of Modern Languages, a private school. I couldn't enter the public universities, because of the religious exams. I had to give up the idea of studying medicine, something I'd been dreaming about all my childhood. I already knew English and a little French thanks to my expensive Catholic school education, so the College of Modern Languages seemed to be the right choice.

On the first day of classes I met your father, a twenty-year-old shy boy who stood in the yard, leaned against the wall, and chain-smoked. It was I who approached him. We liked each other and wanted to be friends, like many young people around the world. But we couldn't. Under the new laws, men and women couldn't talk to each other in public. The guards would stop them and ask for identification. If they were not brother and sister, first cousins, or husband and wife, they would be arrested. If we talked in the college they'd call us to the office and warn us. After three warnings we were told we'd be expelled. Mali suggested that we get married, to be free to be friends. So we married and lived together in my parents' house with Mali. But three months before our first anniversary, your father was called to the front. There was a bloody war in the Persian Gulf and all the youth were recruited. Your father was killed in the first week of the war. He was only twenty-one. The news of his death came sooner than his first letter. You were born a few months later and this is the reason for your name: you were my unique treasure and your skin glowed golden, so I named you Tala—gold.

When I graduated the guards began to arrest people again. They called those who had been released a few years earlier for interrogation. They harassed families of those who'd already been executed. Mali was alarmed. She knew that if they arrested me again, they'd take you with me, and we wouldn't survive. The prisons were worse than they'd been a few years before and there were rumors that they tortured mothers in front of their children and then trained the children as future guards. Mali knew some people who had left the country illegally and she wanted us, you and I, to leave as well. She wanted us to be safe, to live a normal life and not to feel fear and insecurity all the time. She sold our house and paid drug dealers, who now were smuggling people out of the country, and we all traveled to a faraway town on the eastern border. You were only three.

Zabol was a small town, which had one square and four streets. In the house of the smuggler we met two women. One of them was a doctor by the name of Simin. She had been in prison before and her husband had been executed and now the guards were searching for her. The other woman was

Pari, a teacher, who had been fired from her job because she had taught what she should not have. During our stay in the smuggler's place, waiting for our journey to happen, we became friends with the women and they fell in love with you because you were sweet, pretty, and smart. You knew what we were doing in this remote town and you had promised not to speak when we crossed the border in the dark night.

It's true that the desert was a minefield. A man on a horse led us in the dark and we followed on foot. The three of us walked on thorn bushes and in a short time our shoes were torn to pieces. You were sleeping soundly on my back. I had sedated you, not because I didn't trust you when you said you wouldn't talk, but because I didn't want you to see the dark night and the sight of three women leaving their homeland behind. I didn't want you to see how we fell on the dust, how we bled on the thorns, and how we blindly followed a turbaned man who could rape and kill us or betray us to the guards.

But in twenty-five minutes we reached the other side of a wide ditch. The turbaned man shot a bullet in the air and a jeep appeared with a soldier in it. When the soldier shook our hands and said, "Welcome, comrades!" we realized that we were in Afghanistan.

At dawn we reached a ruined town, a war-infested ghost town by the name of Nimrooz, which means midday. The Red Army officers interrogated us and we explained why we had to leave our country. The Soviet officers were impressed by our stories but they said we had to stay in this empty school until the airplane arrived to take us to the capital.

For two weeks there was no sign of the airplane and we

stayed in one room of this half-ruined school, which was like a desert prison. The soldiers brought us canned food and drinking water in a bucket every day and we had to use a ditch outside the room as a toilet. The heat was intolerable and the insects were large and strange. At noon, unable to stand the heat, we used our drinking water and poured it on our heads to cool off. You and Pari developed a strange skin disease, which the Red Army doctor had never seen before. Your thighs were red and swollen and itched so badly you couldn't sleep. But you never cried or complained. You played with whatever was around—a piece of brick, someone's slipper, the dust, and the insects. But your body was inflamed and you scratched yourself all night and whispered to me that there were worms crawling under your skin.

At night we sat outside our room under a sky full of millions of stars. The smells of dry earth and cold wind that had swept the mountain tops were soothing. This was how the deprived people of Nimrooz forgot the eternal midday heat of their town before the fire descended on them again at dawn. We enjoyed our canned food and told stories. Then the wind blew harder and sand rose in the air and we found sand in our mouths, inside our ears, and on our skin. The Russians brought us a transistor radio and we listened to the music of other lands and we felt lonely and sad for not recognizing the tunes. Our land and her songs were lost.

At last the army plane came and took us to Kabul. We'd been in the desert for three weeks—one week in Zabol and two weeks in the half-ruined "Midday." We were all ill, suffering from dysentery, skin diseases, and fever. I'd been bleeding for two weeks now and it wouldn't stop. They took us to a hospital and we were grateful to be able to rest in clean sheets.

After we recovered they took us to the camps. The camps were numbered and we were in Camp One, government housing with six apartments. They gave us a one-bedroom apartment and set up beds for us in the only bedroom, like in a dormitory. You were happy and carefree and you liked your new life, your new aunts, and many little friends who filled the dirt-covered street in front of the project apartments every afternoon. You rushed out to play and it was safe. No cars passed by and armed Red Army guards paced back and forth or sat in the tanks, protecting the area.

And even when it was not safe, when from the mountains that surrounded the city rockets flew and exploded nearby, or an apartment in the next camp was blasted and we heard that people were killed, even when there was no power and there were missiles in the sky, you laughed and clapped and ran to the window to watch what you called the fireworks.

A guarded bus took you to kindergarten every day and they gave me a job at the radio station as a translator. Simin worked in the women's hospital and Pari taught in the camps' elementary school. We were a family. You had three mothers and no father. But you were happy. We all cooked, and although shopping was not an easy chore (we had to walk in the sticky mud to find a few dingy stores), you ate good food every day.

We lived this way for four years and now you were seven.

One day Pari had a toothache. I took her to the army hospital, where we all had to go when we needed a doctor. I left her there in the waiting room and went to work. But Pari didn't come back home. At night an official came to our apartment and reported that she was dead. How could one die from a toothache? we asked. He shook his head and said that sometimes these incidents happened in Kabul. Enemies had surrounded the city and they had infiltrated the staff of the hospital too. Someone must have injected Pari with something. She was a "martyr," the man said.

Kabul is an ancient city that looks like a bowl, walled in by rows and rows of impassable mountains. Winter wind howls and lashes everything in its way. For Pari's funeral all the residents of all the camps walked a long distance against the wind to the Hill of the Martyrs. On top of this hill the revolutionaries were buried. They put Pari's shrouded body in that dark hole and we stood long enough under the cold rain to see that she was covered with dust.

Nothing was the same after Pari's death. Our family was broken. Simin stayed at the hospital most of the nights and didn't come home. She had been very close to Pari and couldn't see her empty space. Soon the authorities told us that we had to leave the country, because now our case was handled by the UN and soon we'd have Red Cross passports as political refugees. We had to find a country and move out of Afghanistan. Some people had relatives in Europe and left first. A few people chose to go to India—we were among them. We thought we'd be close enough to our country and when the crazy government toppled, we could return.

Your Auntie Simin didn't believe that the government would topple soon, so she went to Sweden, where she had a sister. She could be a doctor anywhere in the world, she said. We packed and with an airplane, in a surprisingly short time, flew to New Delhi. You cried for the first time because you wanted to stay in Kabul. Camp One and its dirt road and that little shared apartment were home for you. You were used to missiles and bombs; you liked dust-wind and the chains of the yellow mountains that concealed dangerous gunmen.

INDIA WAS AS beautiful as inside an aquarium. But in New Delhi no one offered me a job or free housing. A fellow traveler introduced us to his cousin, an Iranian student, who knew about a room somewhere. This room already had tenants—a young couple—but they were jobless refugees and wanted to share their room with someone. Our friend's cousin explained that this was called a servant's room, attached to the back of the house, where the yard and kitchen were located.

So we moved to a servant's room and this was the beginning of summer. The city was like a hothouse, the light was blinding and the heat numbing. We had come from cold Kabul; we were not used to heat.

But you were happy again. I enrolled you in a funny summer school that was in a yard. The students all sat under trees, studying. The monkeys and parrots quarreled on top of the branches or laughed at the poor children who had to work hard. Soon, India mesmerized you. You found friends at school and in the neighborhood and played with them in the alley until dark.

Your Auntie Mali sent us money because I didn't have a job. She was still a head nurse in a big hospital and had a good salary. She wanted me to go to graduate school and as usual I listened to her. I had learned German and a little Russian in

Kabul, so counting my native Farsi, English, and French, now I knew five languages.

This way four more years passed and now you were almost twelve. I finished my degree and there was no job for me except a few hours of teaching in a high school. Our two roommates had left and our expenses were heavy. And how long could we live in the servant's room? I was getting older and now I had six strands of gray hair on my temples, three on each side. In India there was no future for me.

It was around this time when Cousin Bijan wrote us a letter and suggested that we move to the U.S. He would become our sponsor. I was surprised, because I didn't have any contact with my cousin. I knew that he was a lawyer in Houston, but had never thought about asking him for anything. Mali was the one who had asked for help. Cousin Bijan told us to go the U.S. Embassy and ask for political asylum. The lady who interviewed us at the embassy listened to our story from the very beginning to the end, then excused herself and left the room. When she came back her eyes were wet. She had gone outside to cry. She signed the papers and we were allowed to travel to the U.S. Who knows? Maybe if the embassy official had not been a softhearted woman, we would never have gotten a permit to emigrate.

As much as we loved India with its jasmine blossoms, happy monkeys on top of the lampposts, peacocks crying in the dense woods, and golden temples full of secrets and scents, we couldn't stay there any longer. It was time to move on. And we moved. The Red Cross loaned us money for plane tickets and Cousin Bijan lent us five hundred dollars to rent a place and this is the end of our story. We are here now, in America.

• • •

MY TALE FOR Tala was a simple narrative of the events. I didn't mention my dark thoughts—despair, dread of the unknown future, and the constant presence of death, real or imagined, in my dreams and wakefulness. Madness at times. So I had to move fast in the story and hide from my daughter that more than once I had wished for death or disappearance.

I experienced the dark waves of despair in the first winter in Kabul when I had to walk three miles against the whipping wind to the radio station. I left early in the morning, just after the curfew was removed, and a cold fog enveloped me and hid me from the gunmen in the mountains. I covered myself in a woolen hat and a long shawl that protected most of my face. Then the wind blew, sharp and dry, and I walked against it in unfamiliar deserted streets. Heavy tanks sat ominously in each intersection and bombs exploded in the folds of the mountains. In those gloomy mornings I looked around with detachment and disbelief and wondered what I was doing there and what had happened to me and why.

My job was joyless and mechanical. I had to translate the text of foreign news into Farsi and this was all I did for eight hours in a cold office with a tiny kerosene heater that struggled to burn in the corner of the room. I shared this windowless office with a polite middle-aged gentleman who had the same job as mine with the difference that he translated the news into Pashtu, the other official language of Afghanistan.

Mr. Kheibar lifted his sheepskin hat in the morning to greet me and lifted it in the afternoon to say good-bye. In our few tea breaks, when an old janitor brought us a pot of hot green tea and two glasses on a tray, we sat very close to the heater, warmed our hands, and exchanged a few words and carried on a formal conversation. He was a refined, sophisticated gentleman, a member of the Communist Party who had university degrees from Russia. But he was sad and quiet. Only after a few months, when we became closer, did he trust me and confess that his older son had joined the Ashraar (the fundamentalist Muslim terrorists). He was in the mountains and Mr. Kheibar feared that one day he would come down and murder him and his family.

"I live in fear, Roya Jaan [dear], fear from my own flesh and blood."

At home my roommates were lively and I was grateful for that. Pari was thirty and Simin, thirty-two; neither had children and soon they adopted Tala. They entertained her and helped her with kindergarten homework (there were serious homework assignments for four-year-olds in the Russian system). My child was not a burden on me and most of the time she preferred to spend time with Pari, who told her long fairy tales in unending installments.

Pari was a child-woman who didn't know what sorrow was. I often envied her bursts of laughter, her energy for chatting, and her singing and humming. In the shower she sang louder, in the kitchen while cooking she hummed, and I was astonished that she could read a book and hum a song at the same time. She graded her students' little notebooks every night in front of the TV, which besides the news had only one program—a variety show of singers that lasted all through the evening. Pari watched it to the end, graded, and sang the songs.

Simin was the serious one. She had been married only for

a year when her husband was executed. She had been released by chance and accident and had fled before the second wave of arrests. Simin was a gynecologist and spent most of her hours in a small clinic outside Kabul. If she came home at night, she led us in serious political discussion and analyzed the situation of the world. She was a monument of positive thinking and—in a different way than Pari—despair was alien to her. While Pari called herself a "progressive," Simin claimed to be a Marxist-Feminist, a revolutionary.

Without these women I wouldn't have survived the gloom of the camp, the chain of the mountains outside the window, and the nights of darkness and curfew. During such nights we heard the dialogue of the bullets and our candles died when the house shook after a missile landed nearby. Without them I wouldn't have survived homesickness, but even with them I was disoriented and melancholy and fantasized about escape, disappearance, or death.

The camps were on the outskirts of Kabul and we were not allowed to go to town without permission. Kidnapping and assassinations had happened before and since we were refugees, or, as the authorities put it, "Mihmaan" (guests), our lives were in danger as much as the lives of the members of the ruling party and their Soviet advisers. Once in a while these advisers were kidnapped and skinned alive. Getting permission to go to town for shopping or sightseeing meant that a large group would travel in a bus with several bodyguards. We had done this before and I didn't enjoy such visits to town.

After a few months of confinement, on a bright windy autumn morning, I decided to go to town in disguise. My hair had been cropped short since my time in prison and if I wore slacks and a windbreaker, a woolen hat, and dark sunglasses, I could easily pass for a young man. So I sat in the wobbling bus that drove the passengers to the center of Kabul and my heart banged behind the plastic jacket. But when the driver turned to me and said, "Hey, beche [boy], this is the bazaar, get off!" I felt pleasantly secure.

I walked for hours aimlessly in a half-dream state in crowded, muddy streets among men and women and animals. I passed through the maze of bazaars where open sewers ran between narrow alleys and the smell of sheepskin and sharp spices filled the air. I crossed a bridge that separated the present world from the past and stepped into the medieval East. Here there was a market that had remained intact since Rumi's time. I stopped at many vendors' displays and bought dried fruits from one, a brass bracelet from the other, a used woolen sweater from the next, and a small, awkward doll made of cotton and old fabric for Tala.

I walked deeper and deeper into the heart of the crowd and thought, What if I didn't go back? What if I stayed until dark and spent the night in that ancient caravansary where turbaned men reside? But how about the next day? How about the rest of my life? Thinking about the impossibility of escape into a different life, I rushed back, crossed the bridge, and climbed onto the bus at twilight with a heavy sack of meat, fruits, and secondhand clothing. This last item was the most precious gift for my roommates.

At home, Simin and Pari reproached me for risking my life and I promised not to repeat the adventurous trip again. But I knew that I'd slip into my boy's clothes a few months later.

My other option for temporary escape was the eye clinic.

When the authorities asked who needed an eye exam, I was the first one to board the bus. We traveled for an hour to the remote eye clinic and the driver dropped us off with plans to return in three hours. We all entered the clinic, but I hid among the crowd of patients and exited from the back door. There was a thick wood behind the clinic. I had come all this way to get lost among the trees.

I entered the colony of the dense ash trees (I never dared to step farther into it) and sat on a trunk for three hours. What did I do in the course of these long hours? Nothing. I looked at the leaves and patches of clouds that moved fast above my head and the insects and the birds that sat near me. What went on in my head was never clear. What I felt was a strong urge to stay in the dark woods alone forever, and this feeling was not bitter and did not make me sad. I emerged out of the woods happier but unwilling to speak the rest of the day.

These adventures happened only once in a long while. Our normal days were always the same. We woke up and went to work and came back and ate and slept, or ate, read, and slept, or talked and slept and then another day and then the next. The days had no identity; they were all the same. Many times I planned to resume my gymnastic exercises, but I didn't. Many times I decided to write regularly in my journal, but I didn't. I had no motivation. No hope.

Fridays were different. This was the weekend. Water was not rationed and we did a huge laundry in the bathtub. We hung the wet clothes and sheets on the two balconies and tied ropes throughout rooms and hung more clothes in the kitchen. Then we cooked and baked and in the evening took the meal to another refugee's apartment (more and more of them were escaping Iran), or in haste gathered the laundry and prepared the living room for the guests to come.

It was during these Friday evening visits that I sat fully invisible, as if I were smaller than Tala, gazing and listening. These men and women, who had crossed the same border as we had, were the best brains of my land, after all. They had been forced into self-exile. I was among political leaders, writers, artists, and historians. But it's not that all they did was debate politics and analyze events. They recited poetry, sang and danced, and consumed vodka and got drunk. Like prisoners, they told tales of their adventurous lives, especially the accounts of dangerous crossings. They were as human as anyone could be.

I looked around the room with a vague yearning that I'd never felt before. Who among these men would love me for what I was? No one. The mature men were all married and the "boys" approached the "girls." (I could hear their secret murmurs from the dark balconies.) I was a widow with a small child and, to make it even worse, I was not an attractive seductress. My appearance was plain and boyish. I was short and had the flat chest of a gymnast. My lips were chapped because of the winds and my face was pale; I never used makeup. I could neither impress anyone with my knowledge and eloquence, the way Simin did, nor charm people with my anecdotes and songs, like Pari. I felt that I was uprooted and misplaced from home before I'd had a chance to form a solid identity. I knew languages, true, but this didn't make me proud. I wished I had known only my native tongue, but in a refined way, like these poets and writers. I wrote small, ordinary poems and incomplete, immature sketches, only for myself, and hid them among my clothes, and the idea of publishing a book in the future was a dream as impossible as becoming attractive or eloquent. My twenties were passing by in exile and isolation and I didn't know who I was, who I would become, and who would ever love me.

Soon life wrote a scenario for me full of dark humor and sad irony. I came out of this experience confused about the nature of man and love, but clear about the route of my own life. I didn't gain any self-esteem about my female identity, but felt clear and confident about my goals.

A half-blind old man fell in love with me. It was serious, comical, and pathetic at the same time. I resented him at first, then tolerated him, and at last became friends with him. The memory of this friendship will remain in my mind as long as I'm alive.

EVERYONE CALLED HIM "the Professor." He was a scholar who had fled for his life after publishing his last and seventh book, an account of the failed revolution in our country and the betrayal of the religious leaders. As a celebrity he couldn't hide his real identity and enjoyed the respect and attention of the youth who helped him with his daily life—edited his manuscript, washed his clothes, and cooked for him. The Professor had a mop of thick white hair and a short stocky body that was unusually young and muscular. He was not bent with age and spoke in a calm and pleasant voice that belonged to a younger man. But all this didn't make him look attractive. His eyes were weak and he had to use a cane. Watching him knock his cane on the cement of the sidewalk, like a blind man, walking from one apartment to another, one unmistakably recognized a very old man. But was there a youth hiding in him? Or was he wise and insane at the same time?

Reading had become my only pleasure, one thing I looked forward to after the tedious and dry job of translating the news (always of wars and other calamities). So I searched for books in everyone's houses. With the permission of these friends, I studied their bookshelves, borrowed a few books, and read them hungrily.

One Friday evening, the weekly gathering was at the Professor's house. He lived with two younger men who had volunteered to help him and keep him company (obviously they were his bodyguards as well). I asked one of the men, a robust athlete who ran around the camp all the time, if I could look at their books. He said the books all belonged to the Professor and he didn't mind if I looked at them, but if I wanted to borrow one I should ask him. So he let me into the Professor's study—a small room with a crowded desk facing the door and a bookshelf covering the length of a wall. There were many books I could borrow and read, but first I looked at the Professor's volumes. I picked one and this was not history or sociology (what he wrote). It was called *The Autobiography of My Former Self*. I began to leaf through it and skimmed the first chapter. The prose was graceful, but a bit lofty and pretentious, typical of how the writers of the older generation wrote.

"I've written only one such book. The rest of my works are scholarly. This was published a few months ago. It covers all of my life, well—up to this new exile!"

He was standing behind me—very close to my body—and

I could feel his hot breath on my neck. He was very short, my height.

"I'm sorry, Professor. I couldn't find you—I got permission—"

"It's okay, my dear. You can take this home and read it. You'll know me better. Book One ends when I lost my wife. I was fifty then. I've been living alone for more than thirty years now, a lifetime."

He sighed and took my hand and pulled me down on a small sofa. We sat and he kept holding my hand.

"I've been looking at you, studying you—" he said. "How different you are!"

My free hand unconsciously went to my short hair. How bad were his eyes? Had he seen the details of my face from a distance in our weekly gatherings?

"In what way different?" I asked.

"In every way. Your quietness. The depth of your soul. Your absence. As if you're not here with us. You're always somewhere better."

I laughed, because I knew where I often was; it was not a better place.

"Roya—" he murmured. "I meant to write to you many times, and I wrote and tore the letters—"

"About what?"

"About my love—"

I bounced up from the sofa and pulled my hand away, which he had still been holding. I placed myself at a safe distance at the other end of the room, next to the window, in case I needed to escape.

"I'm disgusting," he sighed. "Old and disgusting. You dream of young men, don't you?"

"I need to find my daughter. Please don't feel offended. I'm not thinking about these matters at all." I sounded childish—a child who lies to an old, wise man. I had gazed at and measured every single man in the community, but had no hope that any of them would approach me. But now this old man, who could be my grandfather, was confessing his love to me. Was he insane?

As I reached the doorknob to flee, he blocked my way and embraced me.

"All I want is an embrace. Tight like this."

The situation was bizarre. We were both short and he was stocky and I was very thin and he held me against his smelly suit. His young comrades hadn't cleaned his suit and it smelled of old food, sweat, and something sour, like an old man's puke. The snow of dandruff had covered his shoulders and his hair smelled of grease. I pulled myself out of his grip and fled.

Before we left the house, he limped toward the door and handed me the book, *The Autobiography* . . . At home I threw the book on the couch and went to bed, but at one-thirty in the morning, unable to sleep, I crept out of the room and turned on a flashlight that I used for late-night reading. Wrapped in a blanket on the couch, I devoured the book until morning.

He had lived a kind of life that I'd read about only in novels. Raised as the only child of a mother, without a father. They lived in poverty. He joined the revolutionaries in Iran at the peak of the Proletarian Revolution in Russia (that's how

ancient he was!). He was imprisoned. Most of his comrades
were executed by the old Shah. He was the youngest and was
released. He fled to Europe. Studied. Returned with a different name and identity. Married, taught at the university, and
wrote books. He was arrested again in 1953 after the American coup d'état brought the monarchy back to Iran. He spent
ten years in prison, was freed, fled again, and returned to Iran
in 1979. This time he thought "his revolution" was finally
happening. But he was wrong. The clergy took power, his
books were banned and burned, and he had to escape before
the guards arrested him and put him against the wall. He was
an old hero, a monument who was out of his mind now,
falling in love with a twenty-three-year-old.

Then his letters came. They were full of romantic nature
imagery in which I was a little bird or a rose blossom or a soft
breeze. He embraced me or plucked me and I caressed him
and so on. I kept these letters in my suitcase next to my poems
and didn't say a word to my roommates. Pari would burst into
loud laughter and make jokes about me, and Simin would
crease her forehead and debate whether we should ignore the
old man or talk to him. So whenever we sat with friends, I tolerated the professor's piercing gaze from behind his thick
lenses. Until the day that the vicious morning winds did their
job and I fell ill, first with a cold and then with pneumonia
that lasted a month. This was my second winter in Kabul.

I was lonely and miserable, lying on my narrow bed all
day burning with fever and looking at the window. The first
snow was falling, thick and solid, sitting on the roofs. Most of
the afternoons Tala and the other children were on top of the
next building's roof making snowmen. I watched them with

blurry eyes. In the evening friends came to visit me with soup, oranges, lemons, or whatever they had found for me in the market. But my regular visitor was the Professor, who came with his books and sat at my bedside and read to me like a grandfather. He didn't say a word about "love" and I was grateful.

One day, delirious with fever, I confessed that I wrote sometimes and since childhood I'd had two dreams—one to become a physician and the other to write a book. The government took the first dream from me, but the second grew stronger when I lost the first. I told him that every night when I closed my eyes to sleep I imagined the shape of my book, its jacket, and my name on it. I didn't want fame, all I wanted was a book so that I would remain in this world, so that I wouldn't die after my death.

"Write it!" he said calmly.

"But I don't have the slightest idea."

He thought, or pretended that he was thinking, then said, "Find what is in you!"

"What do you mean?"

"Find a memory, anything that has happened to you and you can never forget."

"The prison—" I murmured.

"Then write about it. Write about your prison time. Make it a book."

Next time he brought me two books—*The Diary of Anne Frank* and *My Childhood* by Maxim Gorky.

I kept telling myself that I was not ready to begin, but I thought about writing obsessively. Then it happened that in one of my adventurous trips downtown, I bought a large, hardback notebook from an ancient stationery store in the bazaar. This was an accounting pad, but I pressed it against my chest and imagined it was filled with my cursive writing.

In the second year of our exile I began to write every day and I took it as seriously as Simin took her patients, or Pari took her small students. Now I knew what I wanted in my life and how I could achieve it. Why hadn't I thought about this before? Why did I need someone to push me to begin? Later, my old friend gave me more directions. He advised me to write a daily journal as well and record my days in this camp, because sometime in the future this journal would become my second book.

Gradually a friendship developed between us that I'd never experienced before. With Simin and Pari, and in the past with my husband—who had been my good friend—I'd never talked about literature. With the Professor, it was different; our conversations (which became a permanent tape in my brain's archive) inspired me and gave me ideas for writing. We read books and analyzed them and I listened to his comments on my poems and sketches. He never embraced me again but never stopped gazing into my eyes from behind thick lenses that magnified his eyes like a frog's. He held my hand now and then and I let him.

During the three years that we were friends, he taught me Russian and we read and wrote together. I edited his manuscript and helped him type it. We translated a small selection of Rilke's poetry together from German to Farsi and published it under a fake name—a combination of our names. We were inseparable. Literary partners. But when I felt the heat of his love, when our arms rubbed and his body shivered, when he gazed at me while working or closed his eyes when I read a poem, I often thought about this awkward love and tried to understand it. Was it possible at all? Did he really desire me?

IN THE WINTER of 1986, our last winter in Kabul, Pari died. One night she moaned until morning and suffered from her toothache. At dawn I took her to the hospital. This was a military hospital and since we hadn't notified the authorities ahead, there was no car to take us. Wrapped in woolen shawls, we walked through empty streets. She held her chin and cried and I held her arm and whispered encouraging words, promising her that in a few hours her pain would be over and we'd all celebrate tonight with pastries and that bottle of French wine I'd bought from the black market in the bazaar. There was no taxi, no bus, and no other vehicle except the Russian tanks filled with soldiers, sitting at each intersection.

Finally we reached the hospital but now we had to stand at the end of a long line of soldiers for our turn. A military dentist, an old colonel, pulled teeth in a small room and soldiers came out with tears in their eyes, spitting blood. The dense air of the lobby was filled with the smell of alcohol, blood, snow, and dust from the soldiers' unwashed uniforms. Pari insisted that I should go to work now; she'd wait for her turn, or maybe someone would have mercy on her and let her go in soon.

I left and this was the last time that I saw her.

When I came back from work in the afternoon, I found Tala sitting on the front steps crying. Pari was the one who always arrived first and opened the door for her. Tala had waited a long time and she was afraid that none of us would ever come home. Pari didn't show up in the evening either and when Simin came back from the hospital late at night we called our emergency number to seek help from the authority in charge of our camp—Comrade Mahmood.

MAHMOOD WAS A tall, mustachioed man in a black suit and red tie. A hammer-and-sickle pin glittered on his collar. He came at midnight and told us that Pari was dead. "She was martyred," he said and bent his head in grief.

Simin and I put Tala to bed (she had woken up at twelve and was now dozing off in my arms). We sat at the kitchen table and lit a candle. It was curfew so we had no electricity. We sat silently for a long time, listening to the distant sound of bullets in the mountain. Neither of us could cry.

"She could've been kidnapped, raped, and skinned alive. She died quietly," Simin said in a remote voice. "I think they injected air into her vein."

I didn't know what to say. I was not in that dark kitchen. I had confused the present with the past and was in my cell in the Bathhouse and someone was telling me in a whisper that a girl had hanged herself in the shower.

"You hear me?" Simin said. "She died instantly."

"Yes."

"This was an assassination. We have to arrange her funeral tomorrow."

She was cool and strong, a leader.

• • •

A FEW MONTHS later, all the Iranian refugees were moved out of Afghanistan with Red Cross passports, but the Professor didn't want to leave. He said that he was not willing to change his country anymore. He was comfortable and happy in Camp One.

We parted in the small airport. The Professor extended his hand to shake mine, but I embraced him tightly and held him for a long time. He cried then and covered his face with a big, white handkerchief. He said he would get permission to travel to India and visit us, but I knew that I wouldn't see him again. This was April 1986 and I remember that as our airplane took off, I looked at my friend's short body and his mass of disheveled white hair whipping in the wind. He kept waving his handkerchief for me until he became a dot and then nothing.

MR. VARMA, WHOSE servant's room we occupied, had a position in the Ministry of Foreign Affairs. He was a kind, sickly man, who coughed hard and long every morning and woke us up with a variety of gurgling sounds. He was especially kind to me and now I had no doubt that I was a favorite of the old! He knocked on the door that separated the master's and servant's quarters and when I opened it, he peeped his small, gray head in and said, "Pretty lady, how are you today?" He invited the diplomats to his house and often insisted that Tala and I join the party.

I always excused myself from the Varmas' parties and told the kind man that I had to work. I was working on my memoir religiously with the voice of my old friend echoing in my head, "Write it! Make it a book!" But the writing was dry and lifeless and read like a cold report. It felt more like telling someone else's story with a detached narrative. But I insisted on pursuing "the project" out of loyalty to my friend. In order to concentrate, I sat every night in a storage room, which was the size of a coffin and was filled with the odor of our roommates' sex.

This couple had escaped the country only to make love. They occupied the storage room every night and moaned and panted and embarrassed us and our landlords, who were on the other side of the wall. I had warned them to control themselves when my daughter was awake but this was not very easy for them. Tala and I heard tiny, controlled bird sounds coming out of the closet—I blushed and Tala covered her mouth and giggled while doing her homework.

At night I sat in the same storage room and squeezed out the juice of my prison memories. The whole thing seemed absurd. Who was I writing for? Who would publish this book? I didn't have any contact or know anyone who would be interested in this prison memoir. To make everything worse, halfway through the book, I realized that even if I finished the book, no one could read it in Farsi. Why didn't I write the book in French or German? So the whole exercise was a self-deception, but nevertheless I took it as seriously as someone would take a project under contract. It was all for my sanity. From the prison of the present I tried to escape to the prison of the past.

One evening, the love-crazy couple, unable to find a ride to the amusement park—where they spent most of the evenings playing like children until late—were home and restless.

Since they never read or carried on a mature conversation, or occupied themselves with anything other than sex or play, it was obvious that they needed to use the storage room. Tala was restless too and the atmosphere was tense and I couldn't read or write. So when Mr. Varma invited us to a gathering, I accepted his invitation.

Tala and I dressed, passed the servant's border, and entered the master's house. It was refreshing to be on the other side of the class line. In the cool yard, the fans turned around and the boy-servant carried trays of hors d'oeuvres. The party was a casual one and foreigners arrived in their khakis and shorts. Indian ladies' colorful, transparent saris were a feast for my tired eyes.

When Jean-Marc arrived, my little girl noticed him first. She said, "Look at that handsome man. He looks like a movie star."

The man was tall and square-shouldered and his dark yellow hair glowed like golden silk under Mr. Varma's fluorescent lights. He was alone—no woman had accompanied him. He noticed our gazes and nodded. I smiled back. But we were not introduced that night. He stayed with a group of English diplomats and I heard him talking with a thick French accent about theater productions in London. My companion at the party was Mrs. Varma's older sister—a crippled lady, who sat between the frame of her walker and kept calling me "charming girl." She lectured me about the merits of a vegetarian diet and gave me recipes I could never prepare. She didn't let me get up and walk around and meet other people, and of course I was too polite to desert her.

A few days after the party, when as usual I was walking

with Tala to school, I saw the Frenchman standing behind the iron gate of his yard. He was in a blue silk robe, picking up the newspaper. We slowed down, he noticed us and raised his head and smiled.

"You live in this neighborhood?"

"Yes."

"You're not Indian; then where are you from?"

"How can you tell I'm not Indian?"

"Your hair. Indian girls never cut it this short."

We were on the opposite sides of his barred gate, both speaking in accented English. I was not confident enough to switch to my rusty French. He said that his wife and daughter were in Paris for the summer and he was alone with a male servant. He invited us for a meal that night and we accepted.

Even if Jean-Marc hadn't said that he and his wife were arranging a divorce, I'd have begun the affair. This was our third month in India and I was on the verge of madness again. Now that I was free to go anywhere and walk in any street without danger, the brutal heat didn't allow me. This wasn't just heat, it was hellfire on earth. I was confined in the servant's room with an old window air conditioner that, if it stopped, I would die. I had no job, only the slow and lingering hours of the endless day to think about my recent losses. Now my old pains were cured by the new ones. Not only did I miss Simin, Pari, the Professor, and every single camp friend, I missed the city itself—the bazaar, the ancient bridge, and my ash trees behind the eye clinic. Kabul had become my second home and had been taken from me like the first.

Jean-Marc saved my long, deadly afternoons, when the heat became intolerable and the young couple made love noises in the storage room. When he came back from the embassy to rest I walked to his house, holding an umbrella over my head to not melt. His Indian servant opened the door and I entered the cool, spacious house. He sat in his study behind his enormous desk, reading and sipping gin and tonic. The fax machine made rattling noises and I walked barefoot on the cool tiles and roamed around, drifting in and out of dreams with Chopin Nocturnes that dripped from the hidden speakers in every corner of the house. He insisted that I should open the refrigerator and eat whatever I wanted and take some home for Tala. He knew we didn't have much to eat. I nibbled on a sausage or munched a pickle and wrapped some to take home.

When he got tired of his leisure reading—the American magazines, soft porn, or art reviews—he yawned and approached me sluggishly. I knew that he was coming toward me and my heart banged hard against my chest. With a lock of golden hair slipping down and covering one of his dark green eyes, he stood close to me and gazed at me. I came up to his chest. He held me tightly in his arms and murmured, "How beautiful you are! How angelic!"

Was I really beautiful, or was this part of the love game? If it was real, why had the interrogator in the Bathhouse called me "ugly little brat"? Why during the four years in Kabul had only a very old man desired me?

Then Jean-Marc lifted me up with ease and carried me upstairs. In a bright spacious bedroom he lay me gently on the bed. There was a wide window next to the bed behind which a branch of a tamarind tree tapped rhythmically against the pane. He kissed me and assured me that he had not slept with

his wife in this bed for almost a year. As a proof of this he
showed me another bedroom and said that his wife slept here
if she ever happened to be in town. She was with her own
lover, he said. He showed me his daughter's room too, connected to his—a pink room with gadgets and accessories of a
spoiled teenage girl.

I made love for the first time at age twenty-six (what I did
a few times clumsily with my young husband was not lovemaking). I had finally experienced the thing, but Jean-Marc
insisted that I hadn't and I didn't know what real pleasure
was. He believed that as the result of that bizarre rape in the
prison, I'd become frigid and I needed to recover. He was patient with me and tried to satisfy me. But I was content to be
held and protected. He explained what orgasm was and how
some of his women had experienced it more than once in the
course of lovemaking. I smiled and told him that all I wanted
was to be held tightly in his arms.

After love, we ate in a dim dining room, where the male
servant, who acted deaf and dumb, served us authentic
French food. Then Jean-Marc left me to work in his study for
a couple of hours and went back to work. He admired my dis-
cipline and told me that the way I took my writing seriously,
I'd become something in future. It felt good to hear the praise
and the memoir flowed more easily. In his absence I worked
while the Chopin tunes dripped around me softly like rain-
drops. Now and then I took a break and leafed through the
books that covered two walls of his room. When the time
came to pick up Tala from school, the dumb servant led me
quietly to the door and closed it behind me. Tala and I walked
home reluctantly, hoping that the crazy young couple had al-

ready gone to the amusement park. After spending the afternoon hours at Jean-Marc's, the servant's room and that storage
office looked like scenes from a bad dream.

I could have lived this way the rest of my life—be loved,
make love, and read and write. But less than three months
later, in the beginning of autumn, Jean-Marc's daughter came
back from Paris to resume school. She was a senior in high
school and was planning to enter a university in New Delhi.
Obviously I couldn't go to his place anymore and he couldn't
come to our room, either. So the affair came to a sudden and
premature end. I would have handled this more gracefully if
Jean-Marc had made some effort to see me somewhere. But he
resumed his normal life and didn't even hide the joy of having
his little girl back. Every morning when Tala and I walked to
school, I saw him having a warm conversation with his
daughter in the car. He was taking her to school, too. I felt
possessive, mean, and jealous for the first time in my life and
began to spy on him. I walked to his house late at night, when
he came home from a party, to see if a woman was with him.
But it was only his daughter—a seventeen-year-old blond girl,
a female version of himself. But she was dull-looking, freck-
led, and charmless.

Once Jean-Marc saw me hiding behind the tamarind tree
in front of his house; he stopped and shook his head.

"Roya, I think you're acting foolish. This is an obsessive
behavior. You should meet a young man and begin a new relationship [as if it was that easy!]. You are young and beautiful [he lied to bribe me so that I'd leave him alone]. If there
was any way for us to see each other I'd do everything to make
it possible, but I can't risk my position at the embassy. And, of

course, my daughter. You understand? She is only sixteen [he made her younger to make the situation seem worse]. She found your little perfume bottle yesterday and interrogated me."

But I kept walking every night to his house and paced in front of the gate. I had gone out of my mind and thought that he was making love with his daughter upstairs. I remembered that once he showed me a very narrow red-and-white polka-dot bikini and asked me if I liked it. I thought he had bought the foolish thing for me, but he said it was for his daughter. One night he took me to his daughter's room to make love with me on her bed. Now I had no doubt that Jean-Marc was a sick pervert and I didn't love him anymore. But I walked every night to his house and hid behind the tree to watch his window. I'd fallen so low! I'd become a stalker.

This sad comedy ended when my handsome French diplomat, his daughter, and their dumb servant moved away (because of me?) and I never saw them again.

I CLOSED MYSELF off to men after that. It was our second year in India and Mali had sensed depression (or signs of madness?) from my letters and sent me money and transcripts and insisted that I enter a graduate school. The love-crazy couple finally got visas from the Swedish Embassy and left our room and our lives forever. The rent of the servant's room was heavy for us and Mali had to keep sending money every month.

Although I studied well (this was my only activity—work and leisure in one), I seriously contemplated suicide. The only obstacle was Tala. What would happen to her? Wouldn't they take her to an Indian orphanage? How could I send her back to Iran and freely destroy myself? I didn't sleep much, studied until midnight, then lay down on the bed with one arm over my eyes reminiscing about my prison time. I remembered the mad scenes of the Bathhouse. These were incidents that I hadn't been able to recall or write about. In particular, I remembered one girl who went out of her mind. She had my name, Roya, and her madness began when the guards cut her long, thick braids and shaved her head. First she stopped talking, then she behaved strangely, stayed in the shower even after water was shut down and rubbed her bald head compulsively, as if washing it. She had to be spoon-fed (I spoon-fed her for a while) and taken to the toilet. I heard Roya's voice only once and that was when the guards forced us to sit in cartons for a week to punish us. After a few days sitting in a box that contained her discharges, Roya shrieked and called the guards. She told them that the Great Leader's picture was carved on the surface of the moon and now she believed in the Faith and was ready to repent. The guards didn't believe her and sent her to the psychiatric wing—a wing of which she was the first resident. Other prisoners followed her afterwards.

Now I began to think about this girl obsessively and all the incidents related to her became vivid scenes in my mind. What if I was going mad like Roya? Then what would happen to my daughter? Where would they take her after taking me to the madhouse?

During this winter of madness, my old friend died in Kabul and was buried on the Hill of the Martyrs next to Pari. Comrade Mahmood sent me a few books and the Professor's unfinished manuscript. I looked in the small box and didn't find any letter. My old friend must have died suddenly and without a long illness.

Then two things happened that made the bad worse. The hospital in Tehran accused Mali of blasphemy and fired her. They told her that she was lucky that she wasn't thrown in jail. Now that my sister was jobless, she couldn't send us money. So I began walking in the streets, stepping in and out of schools, looking for a job. Mt. Carmel Catholic School gave me a few hours of teaching in the afternoons, but this wasn't enough and we had to take in roommates. After having had the servant's room to ourselves for a long time it wasn't easy to take even one person in.

So one day I went to Polika Bazaar, a crowded market of buyers and sellers, and sold my wedding rings. I had two rings. All these years I had worn my husband's rings on my middle finger. The gold rings fed us for a while and paid one month's rent, but then again we went back to the diet of bread, milk, and lentils and there was no rent money.

Desperate and unable to go on, I went to the Red Cross office and sought help. The officials were surprised that we were still in India. I should have found a sponsor and a country long ago, they said. I should have moved out of India. They arranged a small stipend and urged me to go to different embassies and find a home somewhere in the world. But who could leave the house in that heat to find a home in such a big world? Who could hang on the doors of crowded smelly buses all day like the rotten carcass of a dead sheep?

Tala had become a native and didn't know what heat was. With a group of laughing, chirping girls she walked to summer school and stayed there until afternoon and with the same gang she walked back and spent the rest of the afternoon and all evening in one of their houses or in the alley, playing, chatting, and studying. But I was suffocating, as if unhappiness had reduced my tolerance.

The water was rationed that summer and the air conditioner worked with water. At exactly two o'clock in the afternoon, when the heat reached its peak, the old machine began to growl and cough and this meant that there was no water circulating in it. I had to turn the machine off. I soaked a sheet in a bucket of water, which had been reserved for afternoon hours, and wrapped it around my naked body. I sat shrouded in the wet sheet in front of a fan and the sheet dried up in less than half an hour and again I dipped it and shrouded myself.

Who was punishing me? How had my life reached this point? What had I done to deserve such a life? Why did my country have mad leaders? Why had they taken my rights from me? Why couldn't I live in my own land? Had superpowers caused this dark destiny for our nation? If yes, then why? Who had given them the right to interfere in my country's affairs?

I was approaching thirty. My twenties were gone, wasted—in deserts, wars, shared rooms, storage rooms, without love and happiness, or with love and happiness lost.

It was around this time when Bijan's letter came. I'd seen this cousin when I was five or six but I did not remember him. He was Mali's age, had grown up with her, and she always talked about him affectionately. I always thought they had been emotionally close or even incestuously in love. After all these years Bijan's high school graduation picture was hanging on Mali's wall. He was my mother's sister's son—a first cousin. He had spent twenty-five years in America and was a bona fide American with an American wife. I had no doubt that Mali, out of desperation, had sought help.

Bijan sent a letter and even called Mr. Varma's house and talked to me. He advised me to go to the American Embassy and seek asylum. From the day that a kind American woman cried for us at the embassy and signed the necessary papers until the day that we left India another six months past.

Mr. Varma died in the last month of our stay. He had tuberculosis all that time and we realized now why he was so thin and yellow and why he coughed so badly early mornings, clearing his lungs. During the last weeks, almost every night we went to their bedroom to keep them company. For some odd reason, Mrs. Varma was also lying in bed next to her husband. Tala and I sat on either side of them, like a close family. Sandalwood burned next to the small statues of Vishnu and Siva and the servant boy brought food and fruits in trays and laid them on the bed. We ate, watched Indian movies on TV, and kept Mr. Varma company, until one morning Mrs. Varma knocked on the door and when I opened she said, "Varma left."

This incident marked the end of our Indian period. A week after Mr. Varma's death, we traveled to America with empty pockets and a ticket we bought with loaned money. I had just received my master's degree in comparative literature and Tala had finished the fourth grade. We had the whole summer in Houston to make her ready for school. Tala was excited and didn't cry when she left her friends, not knowing that later on in her windowless Houston room she would feel this loss and she would mourn the death of yet another period of her life. This was only a chapter from the long tale of her short life—a tale that had begun before she was born and would end sometime in an unknown future, hidden in a dense fog.

I CAME TO America with a child, one thousand dollars of debt, and an unfinished manuscript of a memoir in a language no one could read. Bijan lent me five hundred for the rent and his secretary, Mrs. Markar, a middle-aged Armenian widow, took us to a garage apartment she had found for us. After the night of our arrival, on May 7th, when Bijan and his wife took us to dinner at an Iranian restaurant, we didn't see our sponsor for several months.

Besides my cousin's wife and Mr. Thompson, who took our five hundred and gave us the key, Madison Kirby was the first American who talked to me. He was our neighbor across from the parking lot and I saw him for the first time at the bus stop. He seemed lonely and spent. He looked as thin as a twig, yellow in the face, watching that bloated gorilla on top of the tall tower dancing in the haze. He talked about books and music, his professor father, and his studies in philosophy and I found him interesting. I was lonely and hadn't talked to a friend for three years (since Jean-Marc) and was thirsty for friendship. I told him about my writing project and my desire to go back to school and get my doctoral degree.

What was wrong with becoming friends with Mr. Kirby?

I was not used to not trusting people. In the East if your neighbor offers you a loaf of bread, you don't think that he is a serial killer, scheming to cut your throat. You accept the kindness and return it if you can. If you can't, it's fine. The neighbor will understand. If your neighbor returns your bowl, in which you offered him some soup when he was ill, you invite him in. You offer him tea. You trust. So when I saw an ambulance bring Mr. Kirby home one day, I sent him a bowl of soup. I'd done this before for neighbors, relatives, cellmates, and friends. Mr. Kirby came back with a large magnolia in my bowl and I invited him in. I considered the flower a way to say thank you and I didn't interpret it in a different way. Maybe he somehow reminded me of my father, who had filled a saucer with tiny blossoms of star jasmine every morning.

Those days I had strong flashbacks of the people I'd lost. I would dream of my father every night and he would turn into the Professor. The two men would merge into one man and begin a long conversation with me in a language that was a mixture of all languages and incomprehensible at the end. This always happened in a room that looked out at snow-covered mountains.

Did Madison Kirby resemble my father? Not in appearance, but maybe in the way he talked—dropping a line of poetry here and there to explain something, using metaphors in his conversation, and a philosophical sadness, a despair that my father had. He bore no resemblance to the Professor. But it's possible that I trusted him because I secretly wished to find an intellectual friend like the Professor again.

Whatever my unconscious motives, I invited Madison Kirby for tea. Only when we took a walk and he showed me a pair of pearl earrings in a store window did I realize what his intentions were. I tried to pull back in a way that wouldn't hurt his feelings (because I knew he was ill), but he came to our apartment with the earrings and insisted. When I rejected him, he insulted me. When I came back late from work one night he blocked my way to harass me. He humiliated me by offering me money to live with him. He wanted to buy me. When I turned down his offer he hated me and planned to kill me.

I knew that Madison Kirby was ill; I didn't know he was mad. But how well I understood him. Hadn't I been there once?

One night he stopped me in the dark parking lot and urged me to go with him to his apartment—he wanted to tell me something. It took me a few seconds to decide and he thought that I was afraid of him. But I wasn't. He wasn't a monster; he was a lost man. I went up with him. We sat among boxes and odd objects covered with months of dust and he proposed to me. I was not shocked. I remembered myself hiding behind a tamarind tree in front of Jean-Marc's house in New Delhi, spying on him. I felt Madison Kirby's pain in my bones and left without a word. What could I say? Nothing. Didn't I know what he was going through? He was falling and I was a little twig he could grasp in midair. He was trying to hold on to something and survive.

Bobby Palomo was another American I met. He was like my brother at twenty and gave me the same kind of attention. Although Bobby was noisy and banged his bicycle against the walls and doors and didn't let me sleep at night, it didn't take me long to like him. All of a sudden, I was a child again, and Bobby was my brother Hamid and his room was next to mine. Bobby helped me, the way Hamid did. He found a job for me when I was desperate; he carried my heavy groceries upstairs;

he bought toys for Tala, and brought us good restaurant food almost every night. He was kind, young, and energetic, the way my brother was.

The day that Tony Santino fired me from my first restaurant job (because I didn't want the customers to flirt with me), I was so furious that I began to clean up the uncleanable yellow bathtub that had absorbed the filth of one hundred tenants before us. When I bent into the tub something snapped in my lower back and I couldn't move anymore. Tala called Bobby and he came to my rescue. From the similar incidents in the past I knew that I had to lie down on a hard flat surface with two pillows under my knees. Bobby cleaned up my doordesk and laid it on my bed. He arranged the pillows under my knees and covered me with a blanket. He was a dark angel hovering around my bed, nursing me. His black curly hair and dark olive-colored skin, which he said he had inherited from his Sicilian father, resembled my brother's. He biked to the pharmacy and bought me painkillers.

I remember that the next day was a solar eclipse and the world was dark. I had received two letters at once, from Mali and Simin. I missed them and felt homesick for all the three countries that I'd lost. Lying on the damned door, I held my tears back not to cry like a baby. The bedroom's two windows were blocked by plywood and I couldn't see the eclipse. For a reason that I never fathomed, Mr. Thompson had permanently covered the windows. Tala didn't care for me, didn't help, and didn't come to see what I needed. She was absorbed in a new world that she had discovered in the mesmerizing images of the American TV. She escaped from the reality of our miserable garage apartment into this colorful magic box.

Her numerous friends in Kabul and New Delhi had all become illusory images in the glaring box and she held long conversations with them in a hushed voice.

Bobby came to check on me and when he noticed that I had been crying, he helped me to get up and walk slowly to the kitchen. He sat me by the window, pulled the curtain up, and showed me the sky. The sun was a gray pill pasted to the dark sky and the world had no light. We sat together by the kitchen window, sipped hot tea, smoked, and watched the eclipse. Bobby was quiet and pensive that day and the sparkle had gone from his eyes. When I asked about his mother and half-sister in Chicago, he answered reluctantly. He didn't like his stepfather and didn't think he belonged to that family. I didn't ask about his father. I had a feeling that he was either dead or permanently absent from Bobby's life. But I remember that I asked about his plans for the future. I talked to him about college and the joy of studying and being with other young people. He shrugged and changed the subject. When I told him that a girlfriend would change his life, he smirked and told me that I sounded like his mother.

One afternoon, not long after the day of the eclipse, when I'd almost recovered and was working in the Sidewalk Café, Madison Kirby knocked on my door and insisted that we should talk. We sat at the bus stop, next to that miserable homeless woman (because I didn't want Madison inside my apartment anymore) and he warned me about my daughter. Tala had been to Bobby's place when I was not home. But I thought, so what? I couldn't imagine anything happening between the kids besides an innocent friendship. I didn't want to warn Tala or give her a lecture. This had been my mother's method and I resented it. I could clearly remember the day that my mother told me that a boy and a girl in a room alone were like fire and cotton. Fire would burn the cotton and consume it. I was thirteen then and had played with the neighbor boy, a boy with whom I'd grown up. The image of deadly fire created in me a mixture of fear and anticipation. Now I knew that I'd been destined to burn, and how dangerous and exciting that could be!

So, what could I do about my daughter? Would it be wrong to read her journals to see what she was doing? But how could I break into her most private world? Was it wrong even if it was for her safety? She was only twelve, after all. Sex was out of the question; it could hurt her for life. This way I debated and came to the decision to read her recent entries. I needed to know what they did in Bobby's apartment before I could talk about anything. She had her old notebook—a lined tablet we'd bought in Delhi for a few rupees. She had written her American entries with a green pen to separate them from her Indian stories that were in black. She was still a baby. More than anything else she had written about a treasure box in Bobby's apartment that contained fantastic objects like crystals, rocks, marbles, and such. She'd written that they looked into these transparent objects and saw different shapes. With a pair of binoculars they looked at far-away places and into peoples' windows and they laughed. I was convinced that I was right; they were playing.

Even later, after the shooting incident and several sessions of counseling, I could not believe that Bobby had possessed a gun. This revolver had been one of the items in the treasure box about which Tala had chosen not to write! Bobby had used my daughter to destroy himself. He had trained her to shoot and had set a specific date for this strange suicide.

I thought that Bobby was a happy young man who acted younger than his age, who was smart but immature. But I was wrong. I should have noticed that he tried to conceal a deep sadness under his cheerful appearance. I should have noticed a restlessness and an insomnia that was not normal for a boy his age. I should have paid more attention to his strange behavior—the way he carried his heavy bicycle up and down the steps every hour of the night to bike in the dark; the way he jogged and stayed in perpetual motion and then became stony and quiet and hid from us. How could I miss his long silences and his darkened eyes on the day of the eclipse? This was two weeks before the Fourth of July. He must have been contemplating suicide.

When I saw Bobby lying in his blood on the floor of his apartment and my daughter pointing the revolver at him, I heard the rattle of machine guns in my head as if Hamid had been killed one more time.

So it was July, our third month in America, and our life was a wreck. Tala had fevers most of the nights, talked to TV characters, and was sulky and demanding. Madison Kirby had escaped with Bobby's gun, and Bobby was sent to Chicago to his mother. To make everything worse, I had foolishly fallen in love with Tala's counselor, Ric Cardinal, but he had gone to El Salvador after bestowing on me a long Humphrey Bogart kiss in the airport. He had escaped from me too, from the fear of falling in love.

At times I felt that it was impossible and I couldn't go on. Long hours of the stupefying shirt-painting job, filling in the printed blanks (a skill an eight-year-old could master better than a thirty-year-old smoker with shaky hands); hours of waiting on tables at night; taking buses—numerous slow and smelly buses—in unbearable heat; coming home late at night drenched in sweat to Tala's demands and complaints, fever and tears; and hopelessly trying to write every night, a futile effort to re-create a past that had been hell, but now seemed better. I was going mad again, the way I had gone mad before. But no, this time was worse. Much worse.

I tried. I tried to remind myself of those endless nights when I was seventeen and I sat behind the bars of a cell in that old decaying prison, listening to the distant sound of children's laughter and wondering where it came from. I tried to remind myself of the days that I walked in a boy's disguise aimlessly in the ancient bazaars of Kabul to lose myself among the crowd of horses, carts, and people, wishing I would never return to the confined life of the refugee camp, where days and nights were stretched into a long, unreal monotony and there was no glimpse of hope that we would ever find a home again and begin to live a real life. I tried to remind myself of the servant's room, the groaning air conditioner, and that small storage room, my home for four years, and my yearning for a real home, a place I could call mine.

But was this garage apartment in the heart of Houston, Texas, my home?

I sat by the kitchen window, which faced the window of our new neighbor—an epileptic man by the name of Clifford who now occupied Madison Kirby's apartment. I smoked and thought hard and asked myself one major question: What were we doing in America? And where was the promising sound of the laughter in the distance? Where was that "home"

I was waiting for? My blistered feet resting in a tub of hot water burned and throbbed and the old shooting pain ran through the base of my spine. I'd been on my legs for twelve hours, painting shirts and then waiting tables. In the bedroom, Tala breathed heavily and moaned at times. In her dreams she traveled the length and width of four lands.

Now poor Clifford ran down the steps to wait for the ambulance before his seizure began. I had seen him before, standing in the shadows of the night, restlessly waiting for help. Soon a soundless ambulance stopped in the lot and Clifford disappeared into its dark belly. A minute later the alarming red light spun and the deafening siren filled the night. Then it was silence and I could hear a faucet dripping in Bobby's empty apartment. Tala sighed in her sleep, as if dreaming of the boy's curly hair.

I made a list of all that I had lost and I knew that this was not going to help. Mali would have advised me to make a list of all that was left for me. But had I ever been a positive person? I was a melancholy woman who always lingered in the realm of the dead and lost. And now that the dead and lost had outnumbered the people I knew, it would take me an awful long time to forget. I had to begin dreaming in English, I had to lose the images of the three countries I'd left behind, I had to forget the faces of the people whom I'd loved in order to heal and build a house for myself. Only when I found a home would I be able to make a list of things I still possessed.

I SAW RIC Cardinal for the first time, not in the office of the People's Aid Center, where Madison Kirby had sent me to seek help, but in Croissant Brioche, a small French café in the Village. This was my third day in America and I looked at everything and everyone with the eyes of a spectator. There were many things to observe and evaluate. The gorgeous, sun-tanned blond girls who walked practically naked in short shorts and narrow bras, the youths' freedom of movement, bouncing in their athletic shoes, the speed, the joy that rose from health and comfort and from the surface, not from deep within. The smiles, the wide, American smiles, showing well-brushed, well-treated teeth, and the cars, towers, and glass walls, imitation waterfalls, and replicas of other parts of the world, here and there imitations of Italy, France, India. A Mexican market without the aroma of tortillas, a Middle Eastern bazaar without the smell of wool, horse sweat, and saffron—all fake, all facade, all smiling America, noisy and fast, lacking silence, a magic globe containing the world, but illusory, deceiving.

I saw him, big and bearded, one eye covered with a black patch, sitting and bending over a small lined notebook, scribbling something fast and blowing cigarette smoke around his face, panting. He was an unsmiling American who didn't show his teeth. He looked like a pirate taking a written exam under immense pressure. To pass or to fail was a matter of honor or, worse, life and death. I saw him and my heart sank. This wasn't the way I had felt when I glanced at Jean-Marc for the first time. This was different. Love at first sight?

On my third day in America, one of the worst days of my life, I fell in love.

On this hot and humid day I applied for five jobs and experienced such shame and humiliation that flashbacks of my prison time played in my mind. I heard the jailer's voice shouting, "You ugly little brat!" I felt unattractive, short, mute, and incapable. I hated my accent and regretted that I'd listened to Mali and left my familiar environment in New Delhi.

I was fired from the first job after two hours because of not being able to lift heavy clay pots. This was a nursery and the big, booted, beer-bellied man expected me to carry the clay pots to people's cars. I had a bad back and couldn't lift anything heavier than a light chair. Sarcastically, the man called me "Princess" and asked me if I had done any work in my life before. When I said I had been a translator and a teacher, he fired me.

I walked out of the second job, because a greasy woman yelled at me when I burned the first bagel that I'd ever baked in my life. The third job, at a furniture store, was taken from me by an aggressive blond teenager, who spoke quickly in a sing-song voice, showing her tanned thighs to the manager, who had promised me the job. For the fourth one I was overqualified. This was at a day-care center and the woman looked at my application form and told me that she didn't need people with degrees. She showed me two girls who were squatting and washing children's urine and puke off the carpet and told me that there was no need for a college degree here.

So I had to grab the fifth one—T-shirt painting in a small warehouse. The owner, a young graduate of "commercial arts," on her way to becoming an entrepreneur, called this small, private business "Anita's Paw Company." There was no sixth job awaiting me and the frowning job developer at the Texas Employment Commission pressured me. If I didn't find something within a week, our seventy-five dollars in food stamps would be cut.

I worked at the Paw Company, or rather the sweatshop, all morning and Anita paid me two dollars per painted shirt. I was slow and painted one shirt and a half in an hour. The Vietnamese girls, who were fast and never took a break, painted four shirts an hour. They didn't know what fatigue was. I couldn't work like them. I needed a generous lunch break to be able to sit, eat, read a few pages of a book (how could I stop reading altogether?), and smoke and daydream before standing another four hours. I couldn't afford to buy the expensive sandwiches at the French café, so I snuck in my bundle of food and sat somewhere in a dim corner and ate quietly, away from the sharp eyes of the chubby French lady who managed the store.

Most days, I saw this one-eyed bearded man and I named him "the Pirate." He wrote in his lined journal fervently and did not once glance at me. I often imagined myself approaching him and opening a conversation. "If you're a writer, I'd like to tell you the story of my life. Listen!" And I'd tell my long story, like Sheherezade, night after night after night, and this way, I'd keep him with me. It may sound crazy, but I was fascinated with his hands. They were wide and big and strong with a tight grip on his felt pen. I imagined him holding my hand in his big hand and taking me home.

This was the period during which I met Madison Kirby a few times. I was often absorbed in my problems and preoccupied with Tala's mysterious fevers. Madison recommended the PAC and told me that he had sought help there a few years earlier and I should do the same. The counselor's name was Ric Cardinal, he said.

So one morning I was sitting next to the Cambodian refugees, troubled teenagers, senior citizens, and one or two street people, waiting. This was when I saw my pirate standing in a small office, talking on the phone. I was shocked. I'd thought that he was a Hemingway-type writer (although his small writing tablet was ridiculous) who spent his days writing, drinking at a bar, fishing on a lake, hunting on the weekends, and so on. But he was an ordinary man who had a busy job as a social worker in this agency. When the receptionist asked me who did I want to see, I told her that gentleman, and pointed at him with my finger. I told her that I'd forgotten his name.

She was probably used to foreigners forgetting American names, so she asked, "You mean Mr. Cardinal?"

"Is he Ric Cardinal?"

"Yes."

"Well, then that's him." I said, unable to conceal my excitement. "One of my friends sent me here—Madison Kirby."

"Oh. How is Madison?" the woman asked.

"He is fine. May I see Mr. Cardinal today?"

"Sure. Just wait till he's finished with this phone call."

And I sat right opposite the open door of his office and watched him pace the room, speaking with someone in a worried way, rubbing his forehead and pulling his beard.

That first day we met briefly and I noticed that he avoided my eyes. He made an appointment for the next week, when he'd be back from a short trip. When we shook hands he was grim and formal and didn't look at my face. I left PAC's building feeling uneasy and awkward. I thought that my accent was terrible and I'd made it worse by talking slowly and lingeringly. I laughed at my childish fantasies, too. I was thirty years old, a mature woman, but still had the mind of a seventeen-year-old high school girl. I felt that I had never grown up after I'd been released from prison and my suffering in the two preceding countries had taught me nothing.

I took Tala for two sessions and after each one, Ric talked to me for a few minutes. Now with his only uncovered eye he looked up into my eyes and made me nervous. I told him a few things about my past and he asked more questions. I was sure that he wanted the information to be able to help Tala.

This was when my new job at La Dolce Vita ended disastrously after the manager, Tony Santino, told me that I wasn't fit for waiting tables. Tony was a tall man eternally in a white suit, oil dripping from his slick black hair—a waiter who had climbed the ladder and was now the manager, as Bobby had informed me. No one knew who the owner of La Dolce Vita was. It was Tony who ran the place.

The first day, Bobby dressed me up in a tight black skirt and a white silk blouse (we did a little shopping at the thrift shop) and told me to take off my glasses, which I did and almost ran into the glass door. Tony liked me well enough and trained me and I began to work. The customers were middle-aged and old men who sat in booths with ladies, not always their wives, or girlfriends. They left me big tips and when they stood up to leave, they ran their hands over my breast or touched my butt. I stepped back and didn't let anyone touch me.

I could have made a living at La Dolce, quit the T-shirt job, and spent my mornings writing, if only I allowed the old men to molest me every night. There wasn't much to the work. If the tray was heavy, the busboy carried it for me. All Tony needed was a wide smile and a willingness to be touched. He blocked my way five times a night in the dim corridor, which led to the kitchen, and repeated that I was too stiff and needed to loosen up. Finally at the end of the seventh night, he called me to his office.

"You know, Roya, you look good, you look European, and you could make good money here. But honey, you're too serious. People come here to relax and have fun. You have to carry on a conversation with them and let them flirt with you. No one is asking for more. They have their own women with them. You see what I mean? Why don't you stop by here— let's say—in five or six months, by that time your hair will grow too."

I dropped into bed with a paralyzing back pain for two days and on the third day a girl who worked at La Dolce called and told me about a job in the theater district downtown. A minute later I was sitting on the bus.

The manager of the Sidewalk Café was a tall, red-haired woman in a plain but expensive khaki shirt and long skirt; her name was Joanna Bauer. When I told her about my background, she beamed, squeezed my shoulder in a friendly way, and said that she needed cultured people here. This was her own baby project, a café in front of the theater, and she wanted sophisticated youth to work for her. She was herself a curator of art and a freelance art critic. She had just come back from a trip to Europe and was now working for the city's Art Commission.

When I mentioned my new job and Joanna Bauer in Tala's session, Ric couldn't hide his surprise. He said that Joanna was his old friend and he'd like to see her. This is how Ric Cardinal came to the Sidewalk Café a few times and each time stayed longer. Of course, later he told me that the first time he hadn't gone to see Joanna Bauer, he had wanted to be with me all night.

That cloudy evening in June, Ric sat at a table in a corner with Tala, eating ice cream. I could hear him telling jokes and making my daughter laugh. I climbed up and down the steps with the heavy tray in my hand, working and glancing at both of them—my daughter was laughing for the first time in a long while. The same night a black homeless man walked into the café and insisted that he wanted to play trumpet. But he didn't have a trumpet in his hand. Joanna was terrified. She would lose her affluent, elite customers who sipped cool wine before the play began. They would get up and leave if the homeless man performed. But Ric asked her (in fact told her) to let the man play. As we were standing and listening to the tunes of the invisible trumpet (which sounded sad and real), Ric put his warm palm on my neck and my heart sank into my belly and my knees shook. Then it rained and we had to close the café in haste. It was a monsoon-type rain, the kind that had soaked me in India several times. Buckets of water poured down from the dark sky and no umbrella could protect us. Ric helped me with cleaning up and took us to his car and drove us home. I asked him in and he came up.

We were all drenched and had to dry off. But Ric was in a funny mood—he chased Tala and shook his muddy boot in front of her face; she screamed and ran around and our box of an apartment wobbled like a toy house. We dried off and I made us hot tea. It was still pouring outside and water ran down the windowpanes and it felt as though we were under the sea. In a minute Tala yawned and fell asleep on the floor; she was exhausted from the long day, the rain, and the last laughter. I thought Ric would leave then, but he sat on the couch and gazed at the blue screen of the TV—the weather channel. His big feet in thick, white stockings moved with a nervous tic under the coffee table and my heart beat in my throat as I sat next to him. He had landed in the middle of the couch and he was big and only a tiny space was left for me. Our bodies rubbed and I felt electrified and the base of my spine burned. It was strange, because I'd never felt such a strong physical attraction toward anyone. It was as if danger-ous currents buzzed and ran back and forth between us. He was slightly panting, the way he did when he wrote, and he shook his feet crazily under the table. Now he turned and looked at me.

"Feels lonely here at night, doesn't it?"

"For me?"

"For both of you."

"It doesn't feel lonelier than in India."

"And in Kabul?"

"No. We didn't feel lonely there. We had roommates. I've told you about them."

"Oh, yes. I'm sorry. One of them died."

"She was killed."

"You must miss them."

"Simin writes to me. She wants me to visit her. But how can I? It costs a lot to travel. Doesn't it?"

"For your budget, yes. A lot." He paused and said, "For my budget, too." He laughed.

"You never travel?"

"I did, recently. I flew to California to find my son. In fact, it was the same day that you came to my office for the first time. It was an emergency and a very low-budget trip." He paused as if recalling an image, then he said, "He was a mess. Sam, I mean. My son. I brought him back with me. But he left again. Just a couple of weeks ago."

"I'm sorry."

"It's okay. You know—I just want you to know—how can I put it? . . . It's not just you, we all have problems. We're all refugees in a way. Many of us, many Americans, live worse than refugees. This notion is wrong—this notion that we all prosper and we've all found that so-called American Dream. You see what I mean?"

I didn't quite see what he meant, but I wanted to hear his voice.

"Not everybody can follow Ben Franklin's advice, not everybody wants to open a business and become a millionaire. And those who don't, those who have different talents or abilities—for example, those who want to teach, to help people, to write, to paint, to do music and so on—are always poor. My son blames me for this. He can't understand."

He said all this with a voice that was full of tenderness. Then he became quiet and stared at the TV screen, pulling his beard absently.

He was so dear to me. Was this love?

Then he said, "When my son was younger, one day he accused me of not being a responsible father. Not protecting him. Why? Because I didn't bring in a big paycheck, I couldn't buy him a motorcycle or whatever. But I worked sixteen hours a day." Now he stood up and said, "I have a degree. Two. But I can't work in a corporation. I don't want to. And they don't want me, either. Why would they want me?" He paused and looked at me. "A shabby-looking old hippie? Huh?" Then he said, "But I'm very happy that you're planning to go back to school. They have a good English department at the university." He was embarrassed that he had talked about himself.

I walked him to the door and there he put the palm of his right hand on my neck, like earlier that afternoon. I closed my eyes and let him pull me gently toward himself. Now he kissed me slowly and delicately, as if my lips were flower petals and if he sucked hard, they'd wilt. The kiss took only a few seconds and he left.

He didn't contact me for a few days and I felt offended. Why would a man kiss a woman and not call her again? Then a strange coincidence happened. Cousin Bijan and his wife, who had seen us only once since we had come to Houston, stopped by one Sunday to check up on us. They had brought us their maid to clean our filthy apartment. After three months they had remembered that our place needed major cleaning, or maybe Mrs. Markar, Bijan's secretary, who'd brought us here, had reminded them that the place was a mess. The maid worked in the rat hole of the kitchen and Bijan and Sharon sat on the edge of the broken sofa asking questions about my life, pretending they were concerned, suggesting impossible ways to improve the existing situation.

Sharon, also an attorney, suggested that I should enroll in a computer class, because computer programming was very lucrative and I could find a good job like this (she snapped, meaning, "in a wink!"). Bijan nodded and suggested another option: accounting—a CPA degree. They completely ignored my specialty, my degrees in literature, and my wish to continue my education. They acted as if I had no identity and had to obtain one. But I was grateful about the maid. The filth was beyond my cleaning skills and physical strength. Germs had been accumulating since Mr. Thompson's first tenant in the garage apartment. At the end, my kind cousin and his wife invited Tala and me to a big Fourth of July party at their house. My uncle, Bijan's father, was arriving from Iran and I had to see him.

After they left I thought that this must have been the main reason they had invited me. The old man was coming. He didn't know English and the couple wanted me to keep him company. I was learning not to trust anyone and to seek hidden reasons for their kindness.

Knowing that we still didn't own a car, Bijan sent his secretary/chauffeur/errand lady, Mrs. Markar, to pick us up. Mrs. Markar was a tall, skeletal, middle-aged Armenian from Iran, who after thirty years still felt homesick for her old neighborhood in downtown Tehran. While driving, she asked me with her broken Farsi if the mullahs had closed the Armenian church on Hafiz Avenue, or if the apartment complex on Naderi Avenue, where she had lived for twenty years, still existed. I had forgotten the names of all the streets after eight years, but she still remembered.

IT WAS MID-AFTERNOON, the height of the heat, but in this exclusive neighborhood by the name of River Oaks, the narrow streets were shaded by tall oaks and a number of pines that normally grow in cold areas. Spacious mansions, miniature White Houses, sat back on emerald green lawns. European cars and oversized utility vehicles parked in driveways. Bijan had one of these White Houses with a shady, spacious backyard surrounded by tall palm trees, which cast generous shadows like umbrellas over patio tables. Fans created a heavenly artificial breeze and around a large oval pool, guests sat in bathing suits, or colorful shirts, sipping cold champagne and imported beer. The caterers fanned shish kebob, sirloin steak, and breast of chicken on gigantic grills. The aroma of charcoaled-brown meat and the smoke of kebob rose over the house and floated to faraway neighborhoods. Three waitresses in white shirts and black skirts offered cool champagne. Nondescript music, a new-age imitation of Indian tunes, poured from hidden speakers.

Tala, who was at first shy and didn't want to wear a swimsuit, changed her mind after she saw several boys and girls in the pool. Soon she was wading and screaming with other children. I sat at a table with Uncle Salim, like a respectable old lady, with all my clothes on. We carried on a polite conversation in Farsi. My uncle was a retired oil company employee who had just arrived from Iran. He spoke sluggishly with long pauses between his words. He was not used to humidity and suffered from jet lag. I asked about my sister, Mali. He said that he hadn't seen her recently (the price of the dollar was astronomical in Iran, people had two or three jobs and couldn't visit each other any more; he was doing some accounting in the evenings). But he knew that my sister was fine and after the government took her job from her, she was working for a publisher as a freelance editor of medical books. Nothing I didn't know. His wife (my mother's older sister) was a bitter, aging woman who cursed the government day and night and wrecked her own nerves. The children were all gone—one lived in Australia, one in America, and the third one in Japan.

"It's insane!" Uncle Salim raised his voice. "The goddamned mullahs threw a bomb in the middle of our country and scattered us around the earth."

As I was listening to him and nodding, I glanced at the gate and saw Ric coming in. I think I went pale, because my old companion noticed.

"What is it, dear? Who is it?"

I mumbled an "excuse me" and headed toward the door. Ric stood bewildered, looking for the hosts.

"I didn't know you and my cousin were friends!"

He tried to smile and pretend that he was not surprised, but I could see that he was.

"It's a small world," he said. "Sharon was PAC's attorney a few years ago; she is still a good friend of mine and calls me whenever she has a big party. She knows what a glutton I am. I love Persian kebob."

For the rest of the afternoon I planted Mrs. Markar next to my Uncle Salim, so that they could chat and reminisce and feel homesick, and took Ric to a bench at the end of the yard, behind a row of dogwoods. I was definitely smarter than I was a few years ago and didn't spend all of my time with old people.

At first we didn't talk much. Ric ate ravenously and I watched him, wondering if he was entirely human. With his big beard, one eye, and a supernatural appetite for food, he looked Olympian. Then after a cigarette, he spoke in his soothing voice and panted slightly, as if he had been running. He told me about his life with his dog, Willie, his only companion. I asked if he had heard from his son. He shook his head and became silent for a long moment, absently picking his teeth with a broken matchstick. Now he told me about his first and only marriage at age twenty and his divorce at twenty-four. His wife fled with another man, a mutual friend, and left the baby behind for him. He said he was so desperate that he went to the top of a highway bridge, and drank and wept until morning. Then in the morning he dragged himself home, washed his face, and fed the baby. He had to pull himself together and he did. He raised his son the best he could.

He talked and I felt that mysterious warm current passing through his skin and entering mine. I wanted to hear his voice forever.

When Tala appeared, wet and tired, we decided to leave. Ric took us home and somewhat guiltily I left my Uncle Salim behind.

IN THE PARKING lot of our garage apartments a different version of a Fourth of July party was going on. Mr. and Mrs. Thompson had planted little paper American flags all over the place and had decorated the entrances of the dark, dingy stairways with red and blue and white balloons. We had driven only a few streets from the land of haves to the land of have-nots. Old Mr. Thompson was at the barbecue grill chuckling, showing his large yellow dentures. Bobby was telling a joke, making him laugh. Mrs. Thompson with big rollers on her head handed out paper plates and cans of beer to her tenants. The old retired mailman, Mr. Whitefield, was out for the first time, spreading his hefty body on an old beach chair in the shade. His legs were fat and his feet in the plastic slippers were swollen as if he had gout. There were a few neighbors from the Thompsons' other apartments, most of them single men, drinking. Madison Kirby was shaky and pale like a ghost and I avoided him.

Now the fireworks began and everyone looked up to watch the fantastic shapes in the sky. In close-by neighborhoods firecrackers blasted and filled the air with the smell of dust and gunpowder. Suddenly we heard a bullet above our heads and glass shards fell down in the parking lot. In a split second I was back in the Bathhouse, covering my ears when the guards machine-gunned the inmates. Then I felt that Tala was not next to me and my heart sank. I ran upstairs, but no one was in our apartment. I rushed to Bobby's apartment and found Tala holding a gun (later I realized it was a revolver), aiming at Bobby and crying. Bobby was on the floor, a pool of blood next to his head. In a second everybody was up there, examining Bobby. They said only his left ear was hit. The bullet had taken the top part of his ear off. Everything was foggy and unreal after that. I remember that I sat on the floor, holding my daughter tightly in my arms; she still held the gun. Ric tried to take the gun, but couldn't; then Madison Kirby squatted in front of us and tried to take the gun. I heard Mrs. Thompson announcing, "No need for police—the kids were playing—just an accident—" Bobby was up on his feet, holding a towel on his ear, laughing. He said, "It's all my fault—I let her play with the gun." Ric said he'd take Bobby to the hospital and this was the end of the commotion. Now everyone left to eat the meat before it became cold and the party went on downstairs with the loud and excited comments of the neighbors about the kids playing with the gun.

Tala and I remained on the floor, both in tears. Madison Kirby knelt and looked at me for a long time. I remember that he said something about leaving forever. At that moment I didn't notice that he had put the gun in his pocket. No one did. He left with the gun and he left forever, leaving his boxes behind.

Only much later, more than a year after the incident, I realized that Madison had taken Bobby's gun with him to kill me.

There are all kinds of madness in this world and I've seen a few in prison and in exile. Madison Kirby's madness was the most natural—if a natural madness means anything. He was alone and he hadn't lived a life and now they were telling him that he would die soon. He didn't want to die. He wanted to have a chance to live. I had unexpectedly happened to him, and he had become obsessed with me. I was that little branch he wanted to grasp to keep him from falling. When he saw Ric with me he felt that he was falling. He took the gun to kill me before he hit bottom.

THAT NIGHT TALA demanded "our story" from the very beginning to the end—the shooting. I told her the whole tale, then asked her, Why? Why did she shoot Bobby? She burst into tears and confessed that she loved Bobby more than anyone else in the world (equal to me, she added after a pause!), and she had never wanted to hurt him. It was Bobby who had taught her the game. What game? Shooting him with an empty gun—except that this time it wasn't empty, she said. He had put a bullet in it and she couldn't understand why.

So Madison was right when he said that the kids were doing something up there. It wasn't sex they played at, as he had imagined, it was death. I gave Tala a sedative and put her to bed and sat behind the window, smoking and thinking. Thinking hard. What was happening to us? Had we traveled through the deserts and mountains, lived under fire, in the cold and hellish heat, in poverty and desperation, to end up here with our lives worth nothing? If my twelve-year-old had killed the neighbor boy, she would have been lost forever. And here—in America.

Ric came at ten o'clock and said that Bobby was okay and he'd stay only one night in the hospital. Ric had convinced him to take a break from his job and visit his family in Chicago. I asked him about the gun. How could a twenty-year-old possess a gun? He laughed and said that his thirteen-year-old students at the Juvenile Prison possessed guns. Bobby wanted to die, Ric said, the way his son wanted to die, the way most of the teenagers in the juvenile jail wanted to die. Then he sighed and said that it was amazing how these kids, who hadn't lived much, loved to die.

That night for the first time Ric talked about his side job, counseling at the Juvenile Prison. He told me that he was writing the minute details of his visits to the Juvenile in a journal, in the hope of making it into a book one day. He confessed that he worked with the boys thinking about his son, Sammy.

So what he wrote frantically in the French café was not *A*

Farewell to Arms, after all, it was a prison journal. But wasn't this more like him? I can't deny that I was surprised, but not a bit disappointed.

I was shaken that night. Weepy. I hadn't cried in prison when I was violated, had held back my tears when the jailers handed me my brother's bloody shirt, had no tears when my husband's corpse returned from the front, didn't shed tears for Pari and the Professor. But now I was weeping. It was as if those incidents were not real, but this one was. Prison and war were not the scenes of my real life—I'd stepped on a stage to act and I was to perform the role of a brave and strong woman and I'd done my best. But my real self in real life was a vulnerable girl-woman who had never grown up. When sometime later Maya of the PAC office told me that I was strong, I laughed at her judgment. She should have seen me the night of the shooting. I trembled like a five-year-old only because Ric was here to protect me and hold me in his arms. I was a schoolgirl again, I had a father, and I was free to feel hurt and cry.

Ric talked softly and tried to remind me of all the good things that were awaiting me. I was entering a doctoral program finally and PAC was paying my first semester's tuition. Soon I would find a good job. Tala would begin school and she would get help from PAC. Steven Will, his colleague at PAC, would do counseling with Tala. Steven was a clinical psychologist and an expert in teenage problems, he added. If Tala's moods did not improve, then Steven would arrange sessions with a psychiatrist who worked with them. He said all this and stood up to leave. Holding the doorknob in his hand, he added in the most casual tone that he was leaving the country in a few days.

I held my hand to the wall not to collapse, then took a deep breath. He explained that he was a member of a human rights committee and this was his third trip to El Salvador to investigate the army's crimes. Then, as if I cared who else was on his team, he explained that a nun, a professor of mathematics, and a journalist would go with him. The four of them were supposed to stay in an abandoned school in a village. Most of the men of the village had joined the revolutionaries and their women and children were living in fear. The army could massacre them any day.

Either I didn't matter to Ric Cardinal, or I mattered enormously; there was no third way. Either he was doing what he always did—living his active life—and I was just another client (but did he kiss all of his female clients on the mouth?), or he was afraid of falling in love with me and he had to leave to forget. In order not to lose myself again and act "obsessively" as I'd done once before, I stood cold and erect and looked at him quietly. I'm not sure what he saw in my eyes, but he cupped my face in his big hands and kissed me on the mouth again.

"This is not a very long trip," he whispered. "I'll be back."

I called Susan, PAC's receptionist, and she gave me the flight information. He was leaving on Tuesday at 7:45 A.M. All through Sunday and Monday I waited for him to call. I stayed up at night and thought hard, trying to figure him out. Why would a man like Ric, who had dedicated his life to people, want to play with me? Was he playing with me? He didn't call me and Monday night was ending. At 12:30, with a rage that I had only experienced when Jean-Marc had deserted me, I picked up the phone and for the first time called his house.

"I just called to see if you're going to say the last good-bye."

Pause. "I'm sorry. I was busy packing, buying certain things I need. Mosquito repellent, medicine, water, underwear—" He laughed.

"I know, I know. You don't have to explain."

"It's not that I didn't want to call." He said this in a serious tone and didn't continue. There was a long pause, then he said, "Don't miss Tala's sessions with Steven. He is good. He knows kids' language better than I do. And visit Maya. She'll help you find a job you deserve. I've talked to her and she has already started searching. You should be teaching, or—or translating somewhere, working at a newspaper or something—"

"Thanks for your concern."

A long pause.

"Well—" he said—meaning, he had to go.

"You have to sleep."

"I have to walk Willie. I'm going to miss him. He's going to be with the neighbor."

I was jealous of Willie the dog.

"Tala is going to miss you," I said after a pause.

"I'll miss her, too." Pause. "And you."

"Bye."

"Bye."

I couldn't sleep until morning. I was thinking that I could go to the airport and see him before he left. I could tell him that I was afraid that he would get killed and I'd come to see him before he died. I could make a complete fool of myself in front of that nun (a young woman? I was raised in a Catholic school and had seen a couple of them breaking their vows when they'd fallen in love). She could fall in love with Ric; she could seduce him in that deserted school like in a Hemingway novel.

Mad, like the time when I hid behind a tamarind tree to spy on Jean-Marc (now I was absolutely sure that I'd never been in love with that man), I got dressed at six in the morning, woke Tala, dressed her, and when she asked, "Where are we going?" I said, "We're taking a cab to the airport to see Ric leave."

"Is he coming back soon?"

"He will, he will," I told her. And to myself I said, "He has to."

It was not hard to find them. A seventy-five-year-old smiling nun, a tall, lanky, spectacled professor, a shabby-haired journalist with a camera on his shoulder, and the bearded, one-eyed Ric in his wrinkled khakis stood in a circle, talking. The nun first saw us approaching their group and smiled at us. Ric followed the Sister's gaze and went pale. He excused himself, walked away from the circle, and took us to a quiet corner. Before I could say anything he held both of my hands.

"I'm so happy that you came."

"Was I supposed to?" I was mad at him. "I used our week's grocery money to pay the cab." He was embarrassed. "I can understand why you have to take this trip, but I can't understand why you had to kiss me three times on the mouth. Is this the way in America?"

Panting slightly again and looking bewildered, he turned back and glanced at his friends, who were talking to each other but looking at us too, spying. Then without a word, he slid his right arm around my waist, pulled me toward him and kissed me in front of hundreds of eyes. Tala giggled and covered her face. The nun elbowed the professor and they both laughed. The shabby journalist smiled with fascination, perhaps wishing he could take a picture. The kiss was long, the longest I'd ever had and the most tender, as if he didn't want to take the whole juice out at once. It was a kiss anyone would remember for a lifetime.

MAYA WAS A bald woman with a big heart and smooth chocolate-colored skin that glowed in the light. She sat in her office in the PAC building, under crawling ivies and among her cactus collection and tried to solve problems. She listened to my story from the very beginning, when I was a comfortable child of a professor father, a gymnast, a straight-A student, heading toward medical school, up to age seventeen when I was orphaned, abducted, tortured, and raped in the Bathhouse, and the long years of exile that followed with my baby. And now, I was a shirt painter, a waitress, a mother of a troubled girl, an unpublished, unaccomplished memoirist, who knew four languages, using none, forgetting all, forgetting everything, even my roots.

Maya had solutions for everything. She didn't know what obstacle meant. For my chronic back pain, she fished in her purse and handed me two cards, a doctor's card and a white card saying, "HBA, unlimited number of classes." She told me that she was an amateur dancer and a member of the Houston Ballet Academy and this was her own membership card. I could use her card and take ballet classes for adults; they were good for my back. The doctor was a bone and joint specialist and the dancers frequently went to him. As for a job, she had already talked to the director of the ESL program at the community college and had made an appointment for me. I could teach a few classes for extra income. They didn't pay much. I had to keep my restaurant job, she said, until she found me something else. For Tala, she had an after-school activity in mind, a creative writing program for children, where she taught a few hours a week in a museum setting. For Tala's transportation, she had another idea. She would ask one of the mothers, a lady who lived not far from us, to pick her up. For my transportation she had a "revolutionary" solution: I had to buy a secondhand car, no matter what. In Houston, she said, one couldn't get from here to the next block without a car. When I said I didn't even have one hundred dollars, she shifted in her seat, rolled her eyes, and said, "What's the phone number of your cousin, sweetie? The man who sponsored you, I mean, who invited you to America. I'm planning to talk to him one of these days. A big talk!"

She fed me fajitas at Two Pesos, a semi–fast food Mexican restaurant in PAC's building, and talked about herself, her poetry, her dance, her activism, her women's organization, and her daughter. She used to have a husband, she said, long ago, but had divorced him. "He was no good," she said. "But I don't have anything against men. Some of them are as fine as we are," and she mentioned Ric and Steven as examples of the finest ones. She said that she had a woman companion and together they raised her daughter, who was a dance student at the High School of Visual and Performing Arts.

When she said that she was moved by my story and I was one of the strongest women she had ever known, I blushed and felt embarrassed. No one could understand that I had to survive; I had no other choice. And many times, my attitude in the face of hardship had been far from dignified. I saw obstacles where Maya saw open roads; I felt suicidal when Maya celebrated life. Maya danced and wrote, and helped people and raised a daughter, and felt happy. As a defeatist, I stopped my gymnastic exercises; I lost hope in my literary aspirations and left my project unfinished; I raised my daughter with fear and insecurity and brought her up as a needy, nagging girl who sought men's love and attention the way I did. Maya didn't need men; I did. I searched for love in each country I was thrown into and was in love now more than ever and longed for my lover to return. I was a hopeless romantic, a nineteenth-century blood-coughing sentimentalist, but Maya was a practical realist; she was the woman of the future. I had survived, because the other option was death and I was not free to die; Maya had lived her life fully, beyond mere survival, and I envied her.

After that visit, Maya became my first woman friend in America. I somehow knew that I'd never feel lost or desperate in this country as long as the bald, brown Maya Baldwin sat in the PAC's office among her ivies, trying to remove obstacles.

THE ESL CLASSES were held in a miniature school church, south of Houston, way out of the inner city. I taught two evenings a week for two hundred and fifty dollars a month. English as a Second Language. My students were Vietnamese, Cambodians, Ethiopians, and Salvadorans. I drove a gray, dented 1978 Chevy Impala, as large as a spaceship and as squeaky as an old wagon. I put two pillows under my butt to see the road. The car was of course purchased after Maya's phone conversation with Cousin Bijan. She never told me what she had told Bijan, but one Saturday Mrs. Markar, lanky and gray, who insisted on speaking her rusty Farsi, came and took me to a secondhand car dealer and bought me the space-ship. I sent a message for my cousin through Mrs. Markar that I considered this a loan and I would pay back his twelve hundred dollars. And I paid him sooner than I'd expected.

But the church-school, the Sacred Heart of Mary, was a dim, gloomy place that made me melancholic. I arrived early every Tuesday and Thursday and walked between the columns and under the arches. I listened to the echo of my own footsteps on the black tiles of the dark, cool corridors that the nuns had washed and scrubbed. I inhaled the smell of my childhood Catholic school and remembered all the kind and mean nuns who had loved me or punished me in that bigger version of this mini–school church. I remembered when I was only six, on one of the first days of the first grade, a Sister locked me up in a basement room in which tall statues of Jesus and Mary stood watching me with their wooden eyes. I was being punished for sliding down the shiny oak banister from the second floor to the first, laughing with fear and joy.

I went to the Sacred Heart of Mary a bit early to use the soothing silence, to meditate, to reminisce. The September breeze helped me think. Now my brain could breathe; the summer oblivion was removed. But was this oblivion because of summer or was America doing its work? I was losing my inner world. The last time I had written anything worthwhile had been in New Delhi. Where was I now? I asked myself and looked at the empty schoolyard. What was I doing here? Why did the sun set in haze? Why did the air give out a chemical odor? What happened to the mountains of my life? Where was that light, crisp air of Tehran that smelled of the sweet snow of Mount Alborz? Where were the chains of the brown mountains in Kabul, so close that I thought I could have reached and touched the small cave-like houses growing in their dark folds?

I paced and reminisced. Didn't the people of my past deserve remembering? Could they survive the passage of time and the rapid changes of my life (and myself) if I didn't resurrect them once in a while? No they wouldn't. I would forget them. I would forget Mr. Varma, even Simin and Pari. I would forget my old Professor too, the way I'd forgotten my parents, husband, and brother after they died.

Wasn't I finally acquiring an identity by forgetting who I'd been? This was my new self—a fast-paced, hard-working immigrant who came with a child and empty pocket and made it. I was a cliché now, a repetition of millions of other identities. That's the way it is in America.

What happened to my memoir?

IN A SMALL, damp classroom, with a window looking out at the brick church tower, I held the thick, callused hand of Melet and taught him the alphabet. He had been a peasant in Ethiopia. His family was starving; he had brought them to America. He said he couldn't even read and write in his own language, so we began from the beginning—A. My small hand wrapped around his big, rough hand and we wrote together—A. Then he wrote, A-A-A-A to the end of the line—day after day, week after week. And B and C came later, until we reached Z. He smiled, showing his snow-white, even teeth. Like a little boy he stuck the tip of his tongue out when he wrote. It was harder than breaking up the frozen soil. He perspired and sweat drops glittered between his kinky gray hair, balding in front. The day that Melet learned to write his first and last name, I dashed toward home in my dented spaceship, stopped at an expensive bakery, and bought a cake bigger than a birthday cake. Tala and I celebrated that night.

When I reported this to Maya, she shook her head, sighed, and said, "Girl, oh, girl, you are so sentimental!"

IN OCTOBER I had a job offer that sounded lucrative and permanent, but there was no way I could take it. And this was when the Sidewalk Café had closed (Joanna couldn't raise money for it) and the T-shirt painting would soon cease to exist. I would be desperate again. When I was hired, Anita didn't tell me that a few months before Christmas she would close her sweatshop and would open it again in the summer. We were twelve painters and we all knew that the day we'd painted the last Santa Claus and put the last red stripe on the candy cane, we would receive our last paycheck. We were all looking for something else. Meanwhile, Tala's school expenses were rising.

The lucrative job that I had to reject was offered to me, with bonus of a lunch invitation, on the phone. One night, around ten o'clock (as if knowing that I wouldn't be home earlier) a woman called. Her voice was cold and formal.

"Is this Roya Saraabi?"

"Yes."

"My name is Liz Watson. I'm Mr. Nelson's secretary. Mr. Nelson is the director of Public Affairs of ASINCF and he wishes to invite you to lunch."

"Invite me?"

"Yes, ma'am. Could you give me a couple of free lunch hours?"

"I'm sorry, but why? Why does Mr. Nelson wish to have lunch with me?"

"Oh, I should've explained more. I'm sorry. He has a job offer for you. You know Russian, don't you?"

"A little."

"And other languages?"

"Yes. But how does he know me? Through PAC?"

"Excuse me?" She didn't know what PAC was. "He knows that you're looking for a job."

"Oh, I see—" I hesitated. I had to think fast. But why would I pressure myself? I could think slower. Who was rushing me? "May I have your phone number, please? I don't have my calendar with me. I'll call you back." I took the phone number and put the receiver down.

I'd always considered myself a person without enough spontaneity, without necessary sharpness and shrewdness. This didn't have to do with my education, my languages, and all the other achievements I'd been proud of (or tried to be proud of); it had to do with my contemplative nature. I needed time to think about things. I couldn't respond quickly, without enough thinking. I would always fall in traps of fast-thinking people and they considered me slow, or maybe naive.

But now when I put the receiver down and stared at it, I thought that this didn't need much thought. This lunch smelled. But how slow they were. I had entered this county six months ago and now for the first time, they were calling me. When I was leaving India, it occurred to me that the CIA might contact me and ask me about Afghanistan. I even asked myself, what if they force me to collaborate with them, give them information? But then I laughed at my fantasies. What did I know about the government in Afghanistan? Nothing. One official (the gloomy Comrade Mahmood) was our contact and arranged our lives. True, we saw a few more of them, but I didn't know anyone well. My job at the radio station didn't have anything to do with politics. They gave me texts and I translated mechanically. The news came from the BBC, Reuters, and other foreign agencies. I learned a little Russian because of my own interest in languages. I was fascinated with nineteenth-century Russian literature (which was my mother's interest) and wanted to be able to read the original Tolstoy and Dostoyevsky. But we left Afghanistan before the Professor could teach me the language well.

What did Mr. Nelson want from me? What kind of a job was this? Did they want me to become a spy, to go to Afghanistan or Russia and bring them news? Imagining the dangerous scenes of James Bond movies, my heart began to thump louder.

The next morning, from Anita's office in the T-shirt warehouse, I called Liz Watson and with a fake, excited voice (I'd learned this way of talking from American girls, mostly from Anita, my boss) reported that coincidentally, I'd just found a perfect full-time teaching job and I didn't need a job anymore.

Before she could say anything, I sent my thanks to Mr. Nelson and hung up. Then I called the phone company, changed my phone number, and unlisted it. Anita, who was painting her nails, stared at me open-mouthed, the brush frozen in her hand.

STEVEN WILL, IRONED and starched from head to foot, was in his mid-thirties. He wore new-looking brown loafers and when he crossed one leg on the other his white socks showed; they were carefully folded on his ankles. He was younger than his colleagues, Maya and Ric, and looked very different. Maya wore loose-fitting, long skirts and flowery shirts and from her ears extra-large earrings hung that brushed her shoulders. Her shaven head, which she massaged with rosewater oil, was a sight. Ric was disheveled and his khaki shirt was never ironed and the pockets were badly wrinkled. His boots—which he wore summer and winter, day and night—were once brown, and now a dull, dusty yellow.

Steven Will looked at Maya and they communicated something with eye contact.

"You did the right thing. But if they really want you, they'll find you even if you change your phone number ten more times."

"I know," I said. "I've seen these things in the movies."

"But don't worry about it now. We'll see how serious they are. They're not stupid, you know. They know who you are."

"Which means they know I'm nothing."

"That's not true," Steven said. "You're everything. Especially to us. You're unique. Precious and unique. Maya and I want to ask you a favor."

We were sitting in the smelly Two Pesos again. Greasy smoke of burnt fajitas rose in the air and floated above our heads like a cloud. Tex-Mex music blasted out of the speakers on the four walls.

"What favor?"

"There is a Christmas fund-raising party," Maya said. "Every year we have a speaker. We invite rich and charitable people and some affluent senior citizens to listen to our speaker."

"And—?"

"Well, they donate money. Where do you think our funding comes from?" Steven asked.

"The more they like the speaker, the more they donate," Maya explained with a vicious smile.

"No!" I covered my face. I knew what they were planning for me.

"We can even invite Mr. Nelson to come and listen to your story," Steven said jokingly. "Then he'll be sure that you are not a communist agent. You are a young mother who took her baby and escaped for her life."

"Sweetie, you'll tell your own story, nothing more, nothing less. What are you afraid of?"

"I'm not a public speaker," I said. My face was burning.

"You're not doing this for nothing. We're aware that you have tuition to pay for your spring semester. PAC will give you another scholarship."

"I appreciate your help for the first semester."

"If it wasn't for our rich old ladies, we wouldn't be able to enroll you, honey," Maya said.

"But, please—I stutter. My voice won't come out. I have problems with speaking."

"Have you ever seen Woody Allen movies?" Steven asked. "You sound like him. A female Woody Allen." He got up and went to the greasy counter to pay.

"It's not even November, sweetie," Maya said and held my hand. "You have plenty of time to write something and practice one million times."

This meant that I had no choice. I had to do it. PAC was counting on me. They had helped me in so many ways. Now they wanted my help.

In America almost everything is a deal. Even when you're receiving the kindness of your best friends you should never forget that one day you'll have to pay this back.

The Christmas party presentation became my nightmare for the next two months and distracted me from the long and complicated Whitman paper in which I was trying to compare some of his lines with Rumi's. I had found amazing similarities between these two poets' thoughts and sensibilities and I was very pleased with my discoveries. But now I had to think about my damn life again and write it in English. To make everything worse, my back hurt more than ever and I felt wires buzzing and short-circuiting inside my spine.

WEDNESDAY EVENINGS WERE the evenings of my American Literature seminar. I took Tala with me. She sat on the tiled floor of the dark hallway of the English department and spread her homework around her. There was a snack room not far from the class, but she insisted on sitting behind the door of my class, as if guarding me. My classmates, who thought I was in my early twenties, were surprised to see my big girl. Since May, Tala had grown a few inches taller and her breasts were budding. Her childish behavior and her almost grown-up body gave her an awkward look.

Dr. Laura Mitchell was a restless woman and couldn't stay seated at the seminar table. While lecturing she had to walk around us and move her long, thin arms in every direction. Her lectures were ninety percent gossip about the writers she taught and ten percent substance. Now she circled around the table and waved her arms like an Arabian dancer.

"Willa Cather couldn't write when her upstairs neighbor made noise above her head, so you know what she did? She bought the neighbor's apartment and got rid of him. She lived across from Central Park. Those apartments were as expensive then as they are today."

I was there and I was not there. I was somewhere within myself. I remembered writing in Camp One, when explosions shook our project apartment. I remembered writing in a smelly storage room, the size of a coffin. I remembered writing when Bobby Palomo dragged his bicycle up and down the steps and banged against the walls. I remembered writing when Tala should have been asleep but called me from her bed one hundred times, demanding something. I remembered our story, our damned story that I had to repeat every night, like an ancient chant, to put her to sleep, and now I was forced to write the same cursed tale again and present it to rich old ladies to be able to go to school. How could I buy the upstairs apartment? Metaphorically, I mean. How could I buy my peace?

· · ·

IN LATE NOVEMBER, Ric sent two postcards to PAC's address; one was for his co-workers, the other was for us.

"I'm in San Jose de Las Flores now—a deserted village. There are only a few mothers and children left here who live with us in this school. We have some papers and colored pencils for the kids. They love to draw. They draw the bombs and the ruins of their houses. Their suns are round and yellow, shining in spite of all this bloodshed. I'll bring some of these drawings with me. I also have some slides to show. When I see little girls, I remember you, Tala. You have suffered and I know that.

"There is a small waterfall, my shower! I stand under it and rinse myself; then I sit on a rock and look at the green, deserted valley. This is when I think about you, Roya."

I ran home with the card and, before Tala noticed, took it to the bathroom and read it over and over again. I sat on the edge of the bathtub and reread the last paragraph, which was separate from the first and was only mine. I was careful to wipe my teardrops before they fell on the ink. I heard Maya's voice in my head: "Girl, oh, girl, you are so sentimental!"

SOMETIME IN DECEMBER, I saw Madison Kirby in rags across the street from PAC's office. He sat on a bench, gazing at the passersby. The air was cool and crisp. That short winter we had looked forward to was finally here and we could fill our lungs with more oxygen and less ozone. Maya and Steven had let me stay late in PAC's office and use the computer to prepare my term paper. Tala was with me, doing homework. When we finished, we turned the lights out and locked the door. Our car was in the grocery store's parking lot across the street. When we were crossing, I saw Madison on the bench. He had wrapped an old blanket around his shoulders. He saw us. There was no way to avoid him. With those cold eyes he looked at us and his thin lips stretched into a chilling, sarcastic smile.

"One of the PAC now, huh?"

"I use their computer."

"No computer yet? I thought you were a doctoral candidate now."

"Not a candidate. Taking courses."

He looked at Tala, who was trying to hide her chubby body behind me. "Tala—see? I remember your name. It means gold." He grinned. He had lost a couple of teeth. "Haven't tried to kill anyone else, yet?" He laughed. His face had red blisters and almost all of his hair was gone. A ghost, a horrible, laughing ghost.

I pulled Tala's hand and we walked away. After a few steps, Tala began to run toward the car, wiping her tears. I heard Madison's steps behind me. I smelled the odor of his unwashed body, the dust of graveyards, the corrupt, bittersweet smell of death. He whispered behind my head. He was so close that his breath brushed my neck.

"You ruined my life, Persian, and I'll ruin yours!"

How fortunate that Tala didn't hear him. She was already in the parking lot, leaning against the car, sobbing.

Steven Will had to talk for hours with Tala to help her through this new crisis—this wound that had been opened and scratched again. We couldn't work in PAC's office anymore, so I rented a small electric typewriter and worked at home.

I saw Madison Kirby one more time, in front of the Houston Ballet. My friend Marlina Haas and I had just finished a
class and were planning to have coffee across the street. It was
a few days before Christmas and the River Oaks Shopping
Center was busy with carefree, affluent people, who could afford the unbelievable prices of clothing and gift objects in the
exclusive stores. The open umbrellas of tall palms on either
side of the street glittered with Christmas lights and from
somewhere, maybe the open door of a café, Frank Sinatra's
jolly voice poured out: "I love those jingle bells bong—those
holiday jingle bells bong . . ."

Madison had worn the same colorless blanket like a pon-
cho and was following two young ballerinas, as if trying to
stop them and talk to them. The girls, who were advanced
ballet students I'd seen rehearsing in the *Nutcracker,* were no
more than sixteen or seventeen. They still had their pink
tights on, covered with little black skirts. Their flat chests and
narrow waists were sculpted in leotards and their cheeks
were still red from all the dancing. Madison was so immersed
in the girls that he didn't see us. Marlina was talking excitedly
about her theory of gravity. Although I'd told her many times
that we could speak German, she insisted on speaking English with her thick accent that always made me feel good
about my own.

"When you take one hour of ballet a day and you pull your
belly muscles in and every inch of your body up toward the
sky, then this becomes a second nature—are you with [wiz]
me? Or you're looking at other people?"

"I'm with you."

"It becomes your second nature and you always pull yourself up toward the sky. You defy gravity. Have you noticed how we walk after a dance class? Almost on our toes. Almost no weight! Who is this you're staring at, Roya? A homeless man? Oh, there are so many of them in Houston, so many."

I MET MARLINA Haas on the first day that I took the basic ballet class for adults with Maya's white card. I remember that I stood timidly in the dim part of the corridor watching the other adult students who had gathered behind the door of Studio 3, waiting for it to open. I was looking to see if anyone was as old and out of shape as I was. I was pleased to find a few much older people who were not quite fit. I felt relieved.

The soft voices and murmurs died in the corridor and music vibrated in the air. Everyone gathered at the open door and watched the pianist who, was playing for herself in the empty studio. This was not one of those short Schubert Études for a barre exercise; this was Tchaikovsky's melancholic piano concerto coming to life again in this dim December evening. Men and women in their tights and leotards, in T-shirts and tank tops, in their soft ballet slippers and leg warmers stood and listened. The red-haired Loraine, our ballet instructor, who'd just arrived to begin the class, stood and listened too. We all smiled and appreciated this spontaneous concert, this treat, which had become available to us.

"This is our new Russian pianist, Olga," Loraine whispered to the students.

The Russian woman was not here, in Studio 3 of the Houston Ballet; she was gone with her stormy tunes somewhere else, somewhere remote and cold, somewhere she had once belonged, but no more, somewhere from which only sounds had remained. These sounds were hidden in her narrow hands, dripping from the tips of her long fingers.

How well I knew what she felt and where she was.

We all applauded for her and entered. She blushed and in haste opened her exercise book. Men and women stood at the barre and began to stretch and bend, until Loraine clapped and began.

In front of me a skeleton of a woman stood, medium height, wearing an extra-large white T-shirt that extended down to her knees like a shapeless sleeping gown. She looked awkward and wooden, as if her joints were screwed together by an unskilled carpenter. She opened her arms like wings of a dead bird whose flesh had been eaten and spent. On her wide, rough hands paint drops had dried up. Her hair was dull, short, and thin and her scalp showed. While doing the demanding leg exercises, I could see three droplets of pearl earrings hanging from each earlobe and vibrating with each movement. I stared at the droplets all through the half an hour of the barre exercise and a vague dark feeling distracted me from the rhythm and the dance.

"Smile! Smile, for God's sake," Loraine screamed. "This is a dance class, not a funeral."

We all laughed and tried to keep smiling, but the exercises were hard on our not-too-young joints and muscles and the combinations needed brainwork. Who could smile?

In the short break after the first part of the class I followed the skeletal woman to the water fountain to be able to look at her earrings. She smiled and her creased face opened, showing large yellow teeth. In her smile there was something contrary to her old appearance, something young and girlish and a bit shy.

"I'm Marlina Haas. I think [sink] this is your second class; I saw you last week, but you left soon."

"Yes. I'm trying to begin again. I took ballet as a child, then switched to gymnastics in high school, then had a back injury and quit everything."

"Oh, you shouldn't have!" She covered her mouth as if in horror. "You shouldn't. I'm a doctor. Tell me about your back pain. Maybe I can help."

This way we became friends, but each time I wanted to ask about the earrings (she wore them all the time) I hesitated, then changed my mind.

It happened that I asked her about the earrings the same day that I saw Madison Kirby following the little ballerinas. We were sitting behind the window of the Epicure Café, sipping coffee and sharing one napoleon pastry so as not to gain weight (how could I tell her that she could gain some!) when I asked the question in a matter-of-fact way.

"Nice earrings—where did you buy them?"

She touched the last droplet, blushed, and in a girlish voice said, "They were given to me as a present, when I was hospitalized." Then she told me the whole story of her disease from beginning to end—her scientific research on viruses, her contamination with hepatitis C and forced resignation, her immersion in art, and so on. She talked about her few AIDS patients—some of whom had died, one who had disappeared. There were only three left.

"Was one of them Madison Kirby?" I asked.

She went pale and the cup in her hand shook. She put it down. "Yes. Do you know where he is?"

Something told me that I shouldn't ruin the image of Madison for her; something told me that I should withhold the truth.

"He was my neighbor, but for a very short time, then he moved out. I haven't heard from him. Probably you know him much better than I do."

"Oh, I know him. I know him." Her eyes were full of tears. "He gave me these earrings when I was unconscious. He put them next to my pillow with a beautiful note." She paused, looked through the window, and said, "Madison was a sensitive man. Very." She rubbed her eyes, pretending they were tired. "All I can say is that he was not made for this world. He suffered every minute of his life. It wasn't just his illness." She paused and looked out the window. "Do you see how they're digging up the street? Or sawing a tree somewhere else? The smoke in the air, the chaos in the city? Madison had magnifying glasses, he saw everything, felt everything. He suffered. But it was more than that. He didn't like himself."

I remained quiet.

BETWEEN DECEMBER 1990 and December 1991, when Marlina Haas died alone in her apartment, I spent quality time with her. We sat in cafés and talked and she gave me practical advice about my life, my health, and my daughter. I invited her to our small suspended cage and cooked Persian food for her. She invited Tala and me to her super-modern apartment on top of a skyscraper, showed us her paintings, and played the flute for us. Many times I wanted to quit the twice-a-week ballet exercises—because I didn't have time—but she didn't let me. Even when I wanted to leave the class after the barre session and skip the harder work at the center, she gave me a piercing look and ordered me to stay.

"It's good for you; don't leave. If you learn to stand on one foot and raise the other one, with all the muscles in your body under control and your breathing under control, then you'll take the same attitude to your life—the balance, the ability to endure, the control. You get me? Otherwise the earth will pull you in. You'll sink."

She was another Mali and reminded me of my sister all the time. It was as if I needed a Mali figure again in my life to tell me what was good for me and what was not. I liked her and respected her, but I feared her too, the way I always feared strong people.

Marlina mentioned Madison Kirby again only once and that was when she told me that her big painting, her "master-piece" (she said this sarcastically) was chosen for the AIDS ARTS Exhibition.

"Imagine! I wanted to destroy it and now they say they can sell it at auction for a million and raise money for AIDS patients. Can you believe this? If Madison hadn't given me a copy of that poem, 'The Ship of Death,' I could have never painted this picture. You have to see it when the exhibition opens. You'll find me on the deck of the ship; Madison is in the stormy sea." She paused, bent her head like a shy girl, and added, "I showed it to him when it was just finished and he didn't like it. This was the last time I saw him. It was a rainy day and I'd invited him to see the panel and have a sandwich with me. He saw it, we listened to *Tristan and Isolde,* then he vanished in the rain without eating. I didn't see him after that. He must have felt offended by my picture. I never forgave myself for using his image in my dark landscape."

I remained quiet.

AS THE FUND-RAISING event and my half-hour speech approached, I became horrified. The pressure was back-breaking (and my back pain told me so). I had to finish up the requirements of my seminar—an oral presentation, a long paper, and a bibliographical essay. I had to paint at least ten shirts a day to be able to pay the bills, and I had to drive to the end of Houston to teach the refugees for that meager salary. I didn't wait on tables now and I had more time on the weekends to study, but on the other hand, without a restaurant job, we were broke.

I wrote my income and expenses on pieces of paper to see how short we were and I'd leave these scraps everywhere—in my pockets and purses, between the pages of books, on the kitchen table, and in the car. I saw these figures every day and I was tormented. If we wanted to live in relative comfort, we needed five hundred dollars more a month. I had to cut unnecessary items from the grocery list—fruits, soda, wine, tampons, and many little items that could make life easier for me and more fun for Tala. After eight months in America we hadn't been able to go to a movie, or a place called Astroworld, where Tala's friends went every Friday night to ride the roller coasters. She could never join them and sulked all through the weekend.

But I could bear the pressure of poverty if this damn upcoming speech didn't torment me day and night. Even in my mother tongue I'd never been an eloquent speaker and had never volunteered to read anything aloud in classes. Whoever had killed my voice when I was a child killed it for good, and I never raised it again. But now I had to talk in front of one hundred affluent Houstonians and impress them so much that they'd open their purses and give money to PAC.

The fifteen-minute oral presentation on Henry James in the American Literature seminar was a disaster that killed all my hopes for the big event's speech. I had to speak about Henry James's life and work and I was prepared, even over-prepared. But every second of the talk, I was conscious of my accent and assumed that everyone was disgusted with the way I spoke. When my classmates nodded, I thought, oh, they're just being polite, but they're making fun of me, laughing at me. And to make it worse, I interpreted James's literary genius with anger and resentment. I lashed out at the bald, dead master because he had lived a comfortable life and used his talents to the full. I remember vaguely that I said something like, "If James had to work three odd jobs a day he'd never have been able to be inventive in fiction. The leisure his class status provided him made it possible for him to dedicate his whole life to literature." The graduate students nodded.

Tala mirrored my fears and anxieties. She was argumentative and demanding. I felt that she watched me whenever I was around and observed every single mood in me. She felt my worries and insecurities and I'm sure she read my deepest, most-buried secrets too, those I'd hidden somewhere even from myself, those that had to do with death or disappearance, the final solution.

When I felt ugly she felt the same way and she became ugly. She hunched and sat in front of the TV, like a shapeless sack of potatoes, like one of those plastic bin bags we had bought for ten dollars. She ate, overate. When I felt momentarily relaxed or a bit hopeful, she grew wings and ran around the house and shook the squeaky apartment with her heavy legs. She was there to watch me and police me and feel whatever I felt. She was a little me, made of me, but uglier and moodier, with that stocky body and those small eyes, which were not mine, but her father's. And the poor thing had to survive, had to endure our lousy life if she wanted to live in America.

Ric hadn't written anything after that postcard and I'd lost hope. Now I thought that even if he loved me, he didn't love me enough to not stay there for so long. I felt mad at myself for loving him more than he loved me. Maya, Steven, and even Susan, the receptionist, knew about my feelings and kept telling me that Ric was traveling and wasn't writing to anyone.

A few days before my speech, I entered a barbershop (not a beauty salon, but a men's barbershop, and a cheap one) and out of desperation cropped my hair again.

I avoided mirrors. I'd avoided them since I'd left the Bathhouse at age eighteen. We didn't have a large mirror in our garage apartment; we didn't have a dressing table, either. A broken, dull mirror was on the wall of the little bathroom; it was too high and neither Tala nor I could look into it. Tala had recently bought a round, two-sided mirror which sat on her desk with a plastic pink box full of fake, cheap accessories. She looked more and more into that mirror now and tried on different plastic earrings and squeezed her pimples in the magnifying side of it. In ballet class, while exercising, I stood far from the mirrored walls and looked at the head of the student in front of me. I didn't want to look at myself.

But now for the big event I had to dress up. Oh, how I missed poor Bobby, my friend and beauty consultant. I remembered how the day that I had interviewed for the job at La Dolce Vita, Bobby took me to this thrift shop, The Blue Bird Circle, and told me to pick a short black skirt and a white silk shirt. He advised me to wear black pantyhose and use a little makeup on my face. He said, "Don't wear these glasses even if you don't see anything." When I was ready, he said that I looked like a pretty woman, and not a high school girl on the way to the gas chamber. His jokes were harsh sometimes, but never hurt.

Now I had to resurrect Bobby's spirit and get ready for the big event. After trying on a half-dozen outfits and piling them on the floor, I ended up wearing the same black skirt and white silk blouse of my restaurant days. I had two reasons for my choice: one, Bobby had told me that I looked pretty in them, and I knew he didn't lie (he didn't? Bobby's whole life had been a lie!), and two, I'd worn this when Ric had first put his hand on my neck at the Sidewalk Café.

THE FUND-RAISING PARTY was in a big hotel and we were late. The parking lot was full. We had to park somewhere in the back and enter from a smaller door the servants used. We were lost in the hallways looking for the lobby and I was nervous and irritable, snapping at Tala, who whined that she was hungry. I thought that one hundred people were now waiting for me and I was rudely late. Fortunately, Steven Will found us and led us to the lobby. In his black suit he looked more starched than ever and I was dying to see if he was still wearing white cotton socks. Tala was happy to see her counselor and I was relieved that she'd leave me alone for a minute. But my heart pounded hard in my throat. What if my voice shook from the beginning to the end? What if no one understood a word? Now I remembered the worst instances of the past eight months, when I'd pronounced something wrong and someone had corrected me. Madison had embarrassed me a few times. So I leafed through my papers nervously to see if I had used any word that I couldn't pronounce. But all the lines were blurred now and I couldn't even read them.

"Hey, take it easy, relax," Steven said. "Look at our guests waiting for the food. You're going to talk after dinner, when they serve the dessert. Oh, by the way, Maya has invited your cousin and his wife, too. Sharon was our attorney once. Did you know that? This was before she chose the corporate world. I thought they should shake their pockets for us. And we invited someone else too—who was it?" And he pretended that he was thinking hard. "Oh, I remember—Mr. Nelson. We invited Mr. Nelson, too."

When he saw my wide eyes he laughed and said, "Just kidding. Now don't be so stiff. Go to that corner table and sit. Do you see Maya, fixing the mike? That table." And to Tala he said, "Do you want to come with me, Tala? I want you to see my baby."

There were twenty round tables—I counted them. People, mostly gray-haired women, sat and chatted and giggled and looked at the program. Maya wore the same type of outfit that she always wore, but in addition to all the layers of colorful blouses and skirts she had a few long chains hanging on her neck, as if this was still the seventies. Her fan-shaped turquoise earrings brushed her bare brown shoulders.

"Honey, you look gorgeous. Wow! Look at you!"

I'd been cold to Maya for the last couple of months. I thought that she and Steven had taken advantage of me and if Ric had been here he would have understood my fear of public speaking and my hesitance to pour out the accounts of my past miseries in a few minutes. Ric wouldn't have let this happen, no matter how much money it could've brought for PAC. So when Maya complimented my appearance I thought she was lying, and I felt worse.

The meal was three courses and served by white-tuxedoed waiters, but I couldn't eat. Tala, Maya, Steven, and his wife, June, who sat with a baby on her lap, ate all they could and I watched them. Steven's wife was a tall, big-boned woman; she was taller than her husband or anyone else around and I avoided standing next to her. She had a ravenous appetite and fed her newborn baby grown-up people's food. After eating and feeding the chubby baby, she kissed Steven on the mouth and packed to leave.

"I'm sorry I have to leave, Roya," she told me. "The baby will make noise when you're speaking. Good luck!"

When Steven announced that now Roya Saraabi, a political refugee from Iran, is going to tell you the story of her life, my heart began to bang inside my head. Somehow I managed to ascend the steps and stand behind the mike, which hit me at eye level, and Steven had to lower it.

"Ladies and gentlemen," I said. "I'll read my story from the text I've prepared, because I don't think I can speak without looking at the paper. I'm too nervous." People laughed, as if there was anything funny about being nervous. "This is my first public speech and it's in English too, a language I know, but I speak with a heavy accent."

No one laughed now, but some people murmured something. From the very beginning I had put myself down and called everybody's attention to my defects. I stared at the text and began to read and not even once did I raise my head to make eye contact with anyone, not even Steven and Maya, who would definitely smile back and encourage me to go on.

I read and read and reached the last paragraph where I said, "One day in New Delhi, when I was writing in a storage room the size of a coffin, a letter came from my cousin, who invited me to America—" I raised my head for the first time to see if Bijan and Sharon were there, but instead I saw Ric. He stood in the frame of the arched entrance, leaning against the wall, playing with his beard. He wore the same wrinkled khaki shirt and looked gray and dusty. I stammered for the first time and lost my line. It took only a second, but it seemed like eternity. I read the same thing over, by mistake, then rushed through the rest and ended in haste with "And now I'm here, in America."

When people applauded, I rushed down the steps and out to the lobby. Steven, who had planned a question-and-answer session, saw me leave and announced, "Well, I think we'll have an informal chat with Ms. Saraabi in the next room, where they're serving more wine. How about that? Now let's give this young and courageous lady another round of applause."

Knowing where I was heading, Ric stood in the narrow corridor, blocking the ladies' room. He looked tired and didn't have his eye patch on. His left eye was off center and there was a lot of white showing. Slowly I approached him and we stood looking at each other for a long moment. His blank eye didn't confuse me. I looked in the depth of his good eye, which was dark and inviting. Now he cupped his large hands around my face and looked at me carefully. He loved me, I told myself. This man, this tired, one-eyed, revolutionary pirate loved me.

In a minute all the ladies would rush to this hallway and this big man was holding my face like a rare object he had found in a desert. I pulled myself out of his grip.

"Were you here the whole time?"

"The whole time."

I covered my face. "Oh, no."

"Black tears are running down," he touched my cheek, "Go clean your face. I'll see you after I grab a bite."

HE HAD COME for thirteen days to spend the holidays with us. But he said he had to return. His mission was not over yet. That night, after the wine with the old ladies and responding to their questions, Tala and I sat in Ric's old Toyota and headed toward the garage apartment. He stayed that night and the rest of the twelve days and nights. We talked every night and slept late in the morning (the Paw Company had closed and I was out of a job). We sat every afternoon in his car and went to see his old dog, Willie. We fed him and walked him and once or twice hosed him down in Ric's little yard. Early evenings we cooked and ate and sat and talked for hours into the night, telling stories, in bits and pieces, about our past lives. Ric told a long story about his childhood in his grandfather's house in Cincinnati. Then he showed us his large opal ring, which had belonged to his grandpa and which his grandma had given to Ric before her death. When Tala went to bed he told me strange and morbid stories about his encounters with death. These tales seemed so unreal that I suggested he should write fiction instead of prison journals. He laughed and told me that it was I who should continue writing my memoir, but this time in English.

One night before Christmas, Ric suddenly realized that a tree was missing from our apartment. So we all headed out toward the store. On a bench in front of the grocery store in Montrose, a group of homeless people had gathered. Ric pointed out one of them and asked if I remembered him. Of course I did. This was the trumpet man, the black man who had performed in front of the theater last summer. Ric gently laid the palm of his hand on my neck to tell me that for him that night was a turning point. Now I glanced at the group of homeless again and cold sweat sat on my skin. Madison Kirby was on the bench wrapped in that threadbare blanket. His head was bare and patches of hair were missing. His face was ravaged beyond recognition and he wore that mad smile that chilled the blood. He was looking at us. But was he? It was hard to say. He might not have been looking at us, but through us, beyond us. He might not have been in this world at all. We entered the store and Ric never recognized him.

On January 5, 1991, I took Ric to Hobby Airport in my Chevy. In the crowded lobby, surrounded by the weary holiday travelers, reluctantly returning home, he kissed me in his old movies' style, then took his big black ring out and slipped it on my thumb. When he walked through a roped corridor, which took him away from me and led him into the mouth of the airplane, I watched his back and pressed the flat surface of the ring against my lips. Was I dreaming? Was I awake? Was it possible for a woman who had lost her early youth to be happy again like a child? Would this happiness last? And I looked at the square flat opal that had the shape of a gravestone. On this morbid stone, a white hummingbird was carved, wings open, struggling against gravity.

I returned home and wrote a note for Ric on the back of the picture that Tala had taken of us in front of our small Christmas tree. I mailed it to that deserted school in San Jose de Las Flores. He'd receive it within three or four days. I just wrote one line, nothing more, but he'd understand my meaning.

"And when you're gone to return to me some day, I'll let my hair grow long for you. Roya."

* * *

Fourth of July is his twenty-first birthday and no one knows. What would his dad do on this day? He would take him to Las Vegas. He is sure about that. He'd take him to his friend's casino, stuff his pocket with fresh bills, and say, "Put this in your pocket, kiddo, and spend it the way you like. You don't need to gamble. Go pick up a girl and have fun!" Then he would sit at the card table with a cigar burning idly in the corner of his mouth until it'd become a long column of ash. Bobby would put the money in his pocket and roam around, looking at glittering things, listening to small jingles and big avalanches of coins flowing out of the slot machines. The girls in slippery lamé gowns and glass jewelry flashing on their ivory skin would smile at him or even wink, but he wouldn't desire them.

What would his mom do? She would think about his malnourishment. She'd send him a package of food—a jar of olives, homemade polenta, a brick of Parmesan cheese, dried tomatoes—as if he were not capable of grocery shopping. She'd send a birthday card (always a pink angel, sending blessing) with a fifty-dollar bill in the fold, telling him how to spend it. "Treat yourself in a good restaurant, Bobby. Love, Mom." But this Fourth of July he

won't be here to get the smelly package and the card and the bill.
He'll be gone. Forever.

At dusk when people blast firecrackers all over town and thun-
der from the fireworks shake the city, his little friend will pull the
trigger and send him out of this life—without trouble, without
fuss. Poor little thing—his only friend, the only girl who loves
him. She will tremble and cry first, because the gun is not sup-
posed to have bullets. She will scream and call for her mommy.
But she'll eventually recover. She must. Didn't he recover when
his dad vanished? It was Saturday night and he was staying with
him, like all the weekends. They had eaten out and now they were
back; he was playing a video game—Super Mario Brothers—he
remembers now. He was falling in dark ditches and was lost in
long tunnels when he heard the front door slam. He ran to the
balcony and saw his dad's car speeding out of the dark alley.
Someone must be after him, he thought. He is running away be-
cause someone is chasing him—otherwise why is he leaving with-
out a good-bye? In his room he sat silently in front of the frozen
Mario in the dark, wet well. He waited. At midnight he picked up
the phone and called his mom.

He was only twelve when his father vanished, but he recovered.
Everyone will recover. His mother will recover from his absence
too. But, boy, oh, boy, how free he'd become, how weightless and
light. No matter how much he had run, no matter how many miles
he had biked, no matter how many meals he had skipped, this

heavy weight had pulled him down toward the earth like a gigantic magnet. He will be free now, a feather floating in the sky.

Let Tony Santino wait for him on the afternoon of the fifth, let the tables remain bare, let the salt shakers remain empty, let the customers sit and wait, and let Tony wear the white apron and wait on the tables himself. He'll be far away from this city, soaring in the sky, and everyone will forget him before long. And the little girl, to whom he taught shooting, will recover and forget him too. Soon, soon. She must.

✦ ✦ ✦

*He is in the fold of the mountain, looking down at the green val-
ley. A narrow stream runs through the silver rocks, climbs them,
reaches the top, and sprays down like a shower. Water pours onto
a basin of flat stone. He undresses, steps into the basin, and stands
under the small waterfall. The water is almost ice, breathtaking
and sharp. He gasps, but remains and rinses off the day's sweat. He
stays longer and looks at the green walls of the mountain and the
blue woods that stretch beyond the village—San Jose de Las
Flores—a ghost town, war-infested. He hears hundreds of birds
chirping crazily, drunk with life. He could stay here on this mountain forever. Couldn't he? He could become one of the villagers—
a peasant, a donkey man, a shepherd, a schoolteacher. He could
stay here among these rocks enveloped by the blue woods and shel-
tered by clean sky. This is a sky he had been deprived of all his life.*

*A girl with three sheep and her younger brother pass by the
basin and giggle at the sight of him. The sheep bells tinkle. He
could be a cyclops bathing in the mountain falls, a hairy god, a
creature of the myths—if the girl perceived him this way. But she
just covers her mouth and laughs and the little brother laughs too
and they pass.*

He puts on his clothes and sits on a rock. His wet shirt dries fast in the wind. He glances at the girl and the boy and the three sheep that are now small dots on the green pathway and then the tinkling fades away.

Could he stay here and be one of them? Haven't some people done this before? Vanishing? Acquiring a new identity? Beginning a new life? Haven't people disappeared before? What is there to lose, except those dazzling black eyes, waters of a dark fountain, eyes of a woman occupying his head so possessively day and night? What is there to lose, except a voice that like the soothing hum of this mountain breeze reverberates in his head, in sleep and wakefulness? Is there anything else to lose?

RIC

◆

Penitentiaries are quiet tonight. Children are fast
asleep. Or if one is awake, crying for his mother,
we do not know him, my love. We lie down
together in our suspended cage, straining to hear
that lonely child.

RICARDO CARDINAL

My First Encounter with Death

Let me begin from that yellow house on Vine Street in
Cincinnati, where I was born, became orphaned, saw death
for the first time, grew up to become a sad and restless man,
and left my old grandma behind.

I don't remember my early childhood much. My memories
begin from age six or seven, when I had a little collie by the
name of Willie, who walked me to school and waited for my
return at the corner of the street. And the zoo—there was a
zoo on Vine, not far from our house, and I heard the lions

roaring at night, dreaming of the jungle. And I remember that I cried soundlessly, under my blanket, thinking the lions were missing their dads, the way I did.

We lived in Grandpa Cardinal's house, on the third floor. My Uncle Albert and his wife Rosa lived on the second floor. They had a son, Tommy, who was twice my age, and a daughter, Lucy, who was twenty but acted nine. Grandpa and Grandma lived on the first floor. In the basement, Grandpa had his business. No one except Grandma and Uncle Albert were allowed to go there. Grandpa was an embalmer and he worked with my uncle from early morning until dark. There was no big sign on the door, just a small brass plaque saying, "Cardinal & Son: Embalming." The business was good and every Sunday at the dinner table Grandpa ate and ate, then leaned back, burped, and said thanks to the Almighty for providing him a good life. He had been a peasant in Naples before moving to America at age twenty-five. His hands were big and rough and he showed them to us like two priceless possessions whenever he was mad. For example, if Tommy didn't do his chores, or I didn't wash and polish his old Chevy as spotlessly as he wanted, Grandpa held his hands in front of his face and with his rough, husky voice said, "You see this? Eh? Can you see this? I tamed the hard earth with these hands and look at your hands! Look! Like a woman!"

Much later, when Tommy went into the junk car business and left the house and I was in the dormitory of Saint Anthony's Catholic School, coming home on Sundays, and Grandpa was long dead, Uncle Albert joined the business with an Irishman, and the brass plaque became bigger and changed to "Cardinal and Gilligan: Embalming and Mortuary." Now a long black limo parked in front of the house and caskets and baskets of flowers went in and out.

My father was not part of all this. He had rebelled against his father's business and taken off at age twenty-three (when I was born) and become an insurance salesman—the traveling kind—so that he wouldn't be home at all. But in a way he was connected to death, too. He sold life insurance—went door to door in his black suit and narrow black tie and smiled at people, sweet-talking about death to convince them to buy life insurance. He sent us money every month.

My mother was not an Italian from Cincinnati. She was half-Italian, half-Jew from New York City. She had spent one school year in Cincinnati at age sixteen, visiting her aunt. She had become my father's sweetheart and then had married him and stayed on the third floor of the yellow stone house the rest of her short life. After Father abandoned us when I was born and he went on the road, we saw him only three times a year—Christmas, Easter, and Fourth of July.

My mother died when I was seven and I moved down to Grandpa's first-floor apartment and Grandpa rented out the top floor to his cousin, Uncle Joe, the mechanic, and his wife Mary, who ironed people's clothes day and night for extra income. Father no longer came three times a year. I waited for him every Christmas—sometimes he came and sometimes he didn't. He married a blond woman in St. Louis and settled down there. I visited him only once, when I was in high school, and I didn't like the woman. She talked too much and too loudly and laughed like a drunk. Father had changed too—he was bald, spoke with a different accent, and drank cheep beer in front of the TV. I was almost convinced this was not my father. I never went back again.

But let me return to the yellow house and Grandpa's death. I had been living with my grandparents for a year now and I'd forgotten my mother altogether. She wasn't too hard to forget. She had never talked much, never hugged me tight, or tucked me into bed. Mother was a strange woman, cold and remote and absent from where she was, living in her head or somewhere else. I have never seen anyone as motionless and silent as my mother. She was like a wall, a plant, or an object that was just there, sitting by the window, looking at the empty street. She didn't cook, didn't clean, didn't prepare me for school, didn't take an interest in anything. She just sat doing nothing, stony and catatonic, her white hands resting on her lap. It was Grandma who slapped me, kissed me, spanked me, tucked me into bed, pinched me, told me stories, washed my dirty feet, cleaned my butt, forced me to pray, and prayed for me. So Mother died in bed one night and the loose wire that had connected her to life was cut. I had slept downstairs in Grandma's room and didn't even see how she died. Her physical presence in front of the window, that motionless mannequin I always saw while playing in the street, vanished and I never went upstairs again.

A year passed, I went to school and came back home, playing in the street with the kids. My cousin Tommy was thirteen or so and a real troublemaker. He smoked and ran with bad kids. He got whipped by his dad and our grandpa all the time. But I was little and didn't know what was going on, and I worshiped the bastard. Tommy, I mean. I followed him everywhere, begged for attention, and did his errands. I stole cigarettes for him and stuck nails in the tires of his enemies' bicycles. I carried his duffel bag to high school and passed his notes to his girlfriends, until the day that the police came to our door to arrest him for robbery and he ended up in juvenile detention. He was fourteen.

The same year, Willie was run over by a car and this was my fault—I whistled for him from down the hilly street and he ran toward me excitedly and a car hit him in front of my eyes. I was sick for a month. I had fever and chills and my teeth rattled as if I was at the North Pole. Tommy in jail, Willie dead, my dad absent for more than a year (he didn't even know his wife was dead!), and my mom gone, I felt orphaned and miserable. I slept in a narrow bed in the corner of my grandparents' bedroom listening to the sounds of the zoo, dreaming about freeing the lions.

Grandpa was rough and Uncle Albert was rougher; they couldn't show love and they stank of camphor. When they came home, I ran out or hid in the dark bedroom to not be with them. They both sat in front of the TV and watched Perry Mason and Johnny Carson and Grandma served them handmade angel hair pasta and Italian sausage. It was only for Sunday dinners that the whole family sat around the table.

One day when I was eight, I was playing with a silly plastic ball on the pavement, hitting it against the wall of the house, watching it bounce back to me, trying to catch it. Suddenly the ball hit the basement window and landed there. The window didn't break, but I was scared and didn't retrieve my ball for a few minutes. There was a strict rule not to approach the basement windows. But I wanted my ball back, so after I made sure that Grandpa hadn't heard or seen the ball and was not mad at me, I tiptoed to the window and squatted. It was late afternoon and the sun was just above the roofs across the street. Soon it would sink behind the walls and darkness would fall. It was autumn and the days were short and a cold breeze brought the smell of snow and the anxious anticipation of a long, cold winter.

I squatted, cupped my hands around my face, and pressed my forehead against the cold windowpane. The evening sun reflected in the pane and I couldn't see clearly. But then the sun sank and I saw as clearly as I could: Grandpa Cardinal standing in front of a table that reached up to his big belly. He was combing the long hair of someone lying on the table. This was a woman, young and beautiful, and very pale, almost blue. Grandpa kept combing and combing and I watched him, mesmerized. Why was it so mesmerizing, you may ask? Because I'd never seen the old man doing anything so tender, so loving to anyone. Once in a long while when he got a bit drunk with brandy, he pinched Grandma's butt. She would holler at him, and they would both laugh and tease each other in their crude peasant way. But combing a woman's hair, a woman who looked like a mermaid and was almost blue and had nothing on. I couldn't see her body well, but I imagined her naked with the bottom half of her body ending in a flat silvery tail. I just squatted and watched all through the sunset and Grandpa never noticed me. But just before I rose, I saw a tall shadow on the wall of the basement behind Grandpa's back, appearing out of nowhere. The shadow was imposing and seemed to be hanging over the old man's body, approaching him.

Grandpa combed the mermaid's hair, closed the lid of the

box, and I thought that he sighed, then the dark shadow covered him completely and I couldn't see him anymore.

That night in bed I strained to hear the lions and I thought that instead of roaring they gave out a sad and desperate moan. I dreamed again about setting them free from their iron cages.

I didn't think about Grandpa and the mermaid and the dark shadow until exactly a week later when, on a cold November night, Grandpa died while watching Johnny Carson. He drank his brandy, leaned his head against the back of his special velvet armchair, and died. They took him out in a black casket the next day. Uncle Albert blew his nose into a wide checkered handkerchief, Crazy Lucy wailed like an orphan, and instead of Grandma, who was unconscious, Aunt Rose made me ready for the funeral. When I stood in front of Grandpa's open grave, holding Aunt Rose's hand, for the first time I felt that I'd always loved the old man and I blamed myself for avoiding him. Then I remembered the dark shadow on the wall of the basement. I had no doubt that it had been Death that had taken my grandpa away.

Years passed and I didn't encounter Death. I didn't see Him even when there was a riot in our college in Tampa and my classmates were shot in front of my eyes, or when a cop's leather whip blinded my left eye. I didn't encounter Death when Uncle Albert sent a telegram that Grandma was in the hospital and wanted to see me. I didn't feel His presence when I sat next to Grandma's bed and she opened my palm and put Grandpa Cardinal's opal ring in my hand and said, "Keep it, Rici; this is your grandpa's ring!"

I didn't feel Death's presence; neither did I smell His camphor odor until I was twenty-four, young and reckless, on a revolutionary mission to Argentina. There I saw Him, in disguise, and man, oh man, what a disguise.

My Second Encounter with Death

Everyone said I was lucky to be beaten and blinded by the cops—I wouldn't go to the war. So I stayed in Tampa while most of my friends were shipped to Nam—some never to return. Uncle Albert said on the phone, "Sue the bastards for blinding you!" But how could I? And besides, deep inside I was happy. I was scared of the war.

So I stayed in college and continued my antiwar activism with a black patch over my left eye and a bushy black beard covering the rest of my face—Fidel Castro–style. I met Janet at a political rally when I was twenty and we married. Soon Sammy was born. We both worked odd jobs and didn't really have much to eat or a decent place to raise the baby. I'd dated Janet for only a month or so before she got pregnant and I didn't know her that well. She was twenty-one, older than I was, five feet two, with a curtain of blond bangs covering half of her enormous blue eyes. She talked in a dreamy way, carried a red velvet purse of pot and a flask of brandy, and chain-smoked even when she was pregnant. She kept sleeping with two or three other men even after we were married.

When I took her to Cincinnati with our one-month-old baby to spend the Christmas holidays with Uncle Albert and Aunt Rose, she passed out at the dinner table, face down in her plate. She was unconscious the whole night, and I had to tend the baby until morning with Aunt Rose's help. She slept the rest of the days and before we left, Uncle Albert put his heavy hand on my shoulder and said, "Take this girl to a doctor, kid. Something is wrong with her."

Nothing much was wrong with her, except that she was self-medicating with alcohol and marijuana. I was a kid myself and didn't know much, so I put up with her heavy pot-smoking, drinking, and passing out. I took care of the baby myself most of the time and joined the demonstrations and passed out leaflets and got arrested and got released and finally joined a serious left-wing organization. I read day and night to educate myself and become a revolutionary. I wanted to take care of the injustice and help the workers of the world. So I had to become a worker myself. I quit college, went to a welding school, and became a welder.

In the hot summer of 1971, the organization sent me to Houston. I had to help the comrades in their fight against the Ku Klux Klan. The bastards were burning bookstores. A job was ready for me in the heart of Houston's industrial area; I would become a welder for Westinghouse. So I took Janet and the baby, who was seven months old, and we drove from Florida to Texas. We lived in a friend's small room on top of a smelly Mexican grocery store until we could afford to get our own place. The comrade who took us in was John Eagleton, my connection in Houston. He had a sweet smile and soft, brown baby hair covering his forehead. He gave us his living room and I began to work.

Needless to say, soon Janet moved to John's room and I was left on the couch with Sammy and his supply of formula for the night. John and Janet took off a month later and abandoned the baby and me. In September 1971, my wife of a year and a half called from Denver to say that she and John Eagleton were planning to get married. She wanted a divorce. I was not yet twenty-one.

There is a bridge over the rushing river of traffic in Houston, not as magnificent as the Golden Gate or the Brooklyn Bridge, but quite interesting, especially in late summer nights. If you sit on this bridge after midnight, when the traffic is slow, on the horizon to the south you'll see the refineries coughing white vapor, and to the north the postcard view of the skyscrapers against a gray night. It seldom gets dark in this city—the haze, the acid clouds, the steam and smoke of the gulf and the many chemical plants surrounding the city defy the natural darkness of the night. We have no stars in the Houston night sky.

The first night after Janet left, I took a bottle of Bushmills to the top of this bridge and sat there on the cement, drinking. What was I doing here? What had I done? My twenty-first birthday was still two months away and I had a kid and no wife and I was in a city as strange as planet Mars. I drank and remembered my father, who was somewhere remote with a family I didn't know (I'd heard that he had a daughter now) and remembered Cincinnati, Vine Street, and the zoo with the lions still roaring in cages. I hadn't set them free and I hadn't set humans free, either. I'd just screwed up my own life—that's what I'd done. I drank, felt incompetent, a sorry loser, and passed out, facing the tall towers. Sometime around three or four in the morning, I woke in panic. Maybe it wasn't panic, but a realization mixed with fear—fear of "What if I'm not able to make it?" It was about the baby—a small, fragile human, more vulnerable than Willie the dog, more in danger than the lions in the zoo, and now left alone on the couch of John Eagleton's apartment on top of the Latina Grocery Store in a Hispanic ghetto. I threw the bottle away and ran home. The baby was lying awake in his crib, big blue eyes wide open, waiting for me.

I never drank heavily or slept on bridges after that night. I worked hard during the day and left the baby with a Mexican family in the neighborhood for thirty dollars a month and took him home in the evening and lay next to him with open eyes. I still strained to hear the lions moaning. I heard them and I heard all the creatures that were in cages and couldn't get out.

WHEN I WAS twenty-four and Sammy was in kindergarten, the organization gave me a mission; I had to travel to Argentina to find a missing comrade. This comrade who had gone earlier to join the Argentineans in their fight against the junta was missing now and I had to find out what had happened to him. I left Sammy with Dolores, his babysitter of three years, and left for Buenos Aires in an old suit, wearing dark sunglasses. I shaved my beard and didn't wear my black eye patch. My documents said that I was a shoe salesman.

In this old third-rate hotel room, someone—an Argentinean comrade (they hadn't told me the person's gender)—was supposed to knock on the door three times. I was supposed to say, "Who is it?" He or she would reply, "Jonathan's friend." I'd say, "Which Jonathan?" The person would say, "From the shoe factory." Then I'd say, "Come in."

So I lay in bed tired as hell and looked out the small, dusty window at a hazy view of red roofs, domes, and steeples. The view looked foreign, like those postcards of Europe Grandma Cardinal kept in her souvenir box and I looked at when I was bored. There was a brick tower, very close to my window, and a big brass bell hung there waiting. I felt lonely and homesick and didn't want to be in Buenos Aires. This was my first trip out of the U.S. and my first dangerous political mission. I lay down, looked at the evening sky, and thought about Sammy, who was fortunately not here with me and was sitting in his special tall chair in Dolores's steamy kitchen with four other kids, eating beans and tamales. Then I thought about Jonathan, a guy I didn't know, a guy like myself, who had come here to fight for justice and was now missing. What did it mean? Had they killed an American citizen? Kidnapped him? And how on earth could I be of any help? If I went on thinking this way, I'd lose my self-confidence, so I repeated the greeting sentences several times in my mind and fell asleep.

When I woke up it was 2 A.M. and the room was dark. A couple next door made love loudly and intensely and their bodies banged against the wall and the woman moaned and panted but didn't come. I thought about lovemaking, something I hadn't done for more than three years, in the peak of my youth. Then I remembered Janet and her tiny body in bed, her bangs covering half of her face like a golden curtain, whispering to me what to do and where to touch her. My heart sank and I felt sorry for myself.

Now for the first time, I realized how late it was and sat erect in bed feeling an intense sense of danger. Something was definitely wrong. My contact had to come before midnight and without a contact I didn't know what to do or how to start what I had to start. I didn't know the city and I knew only a few sentences of Spanish that had to do with a baby and food and a kitchen. They'd told me that the streets were full of armed soldiers who stopped people to check their IDs and I was traveling with false documents. The whole thing was ridiculous. I was supposed to be a shoe salesman and I didn't know anything about the trade. Shouldn't I have learned a thing or two about different kinds of leather and handmade shoes? Maybe my organization had thought that the Argentinean contact would teach me everything. But what if, for whatever reason, he failed to show up?

I sat for fifteen minutes, motionless, straining to hear something. The couple had calmed down and was probably smoking in bed or had fallen asleep. There was no sound except an angry ding ding—something hitting a metal post in a nerve-wracking rhythm. I slipped off the bed and opened the window. The air was warm and moist, but not heavy like in Houston. There was a pleasant thinness to it and an unreal scent rose up from the earth, as if a garden full of begonias was hidden somewhere in the dark. I found the source of the sound—it was a flag on top of the hotel door, hitting its post. But before I closed the window again, I noticed a tall shadow moving on the brick wall of the closed shops across the street. The shadow became taller in a split second and kept stretching. It took the shape of a woman with a narrow waist, then disappeared. In a sudden flashback I remembered Grandpa Cardinal in his basement combing a woman's long hair, a tall, dark shadow standing behind him on the wall. I closed the window, turned on the lamp, and lit a cigarette. I thought that I was anxious for no good reason and my mind was playing tricks on me. There was no shadow on the wall and if there was, so what? Then I decided that if no one came tonight, I'd go back to the airport in the morning and fly home. Thinking this, I felt relieved and prayed that no one would come.

But a few minutes later someone knocked softly on the door. Three times. I said, "Who is it?" A woman said, "Jonathan's friend—" So my contact was a woman. In haste I put on my eye patch while we exchanged the phrases to the end, then I let her in.

The first thing that I noticed was her height. She was tall and very slim. She wore a tight maroon dress and a wide, black leather belt pressed her waist so severely that I wondered how she could breathe. Her waist was very narrow and she made a point to show it by pulling that belt to the last hole. She had dark hair, but I'm not sure how long it was, because it was in a braided bun behind her neck. Her makeup was heavy and her lipstick was the color of old blood. For a comrade she was a bit too much, I thought. My fellow activist friends didn't wear dark red lipstick, and tight dresses were definitely out of the question. How could they move around?

She sat on the only chair by the table and I sat on the edge of the bed. In Spanish she said that her name was Marta. When she realized I couldn't speak more than a few sentences, she switched to English. Her English was good, which impressed me. After a few minutes of conversation about the political situation in her country and the army's increasing power and the missing people, she asked about my organization. She had a slow, relaxed way of speaking and tilted her

head to one side or the other and had a half smile that could
have been sarcastic and never left her face. I told her certain
things; I don't remember what—generalities, no details. I
didn't know any details myself. My organization was one of
the many small Marxist groups that had split and separated
from a bigger one because of one minor difference or another.
Even at that time I always felt that if our small organizations
remained whole and did not separate from the big party, what
a powerful force the leftist revolutionaries might become.
Anyway, Marta kept asking questions—now about our leaders—and frankly I didn't know any of them. I dealt with my
own contact in Houston, who was a bald, spectacled middle-
aged man working in a bookstore, and I knew a few other
comrades I worked with. She asked me about Jonathan, the
comrade I'd come to find. I'd never seen Jonathan, so I didn't
know much about him, except the fact that he had been a student at Kent and the organization had sent him and a few others earlier to help the Argentinean comrades. She didn't ask
anything more and instead took a flat bottle of Scotch out of
her purse and said that she was positive I didn't carry liquor
with me, so she had brought some with her. There were two
dusty glasses next to the sink. She rinsed them and filled them
with Scotch. For some reason, maybe jet lag, I was very tired
and on top of that a bit disoriented. To tell you the truth, I
hadn't thought that a woman might be my contact, and I felt
a bit self-conscious.

Marta's ass almost burst out of the seams of her tight skirt
and she gave it a slight side move when she stood in front of
the sink rinsing the glasses. I hadn't had much contact with
women for a long time and the only female I saw frequently

was Dolores, Sammy's babysitter, who was fat, had black blemishes on her face, and smelled of corn tortillas. I was speechless. Marta had bewitched me. The whole night, from the moment she arrived up to the moment that she kicked off her shoes, sat on my bed, and we began sharing warm Scotch, seemed like a chaotic dream to me.

Then something strange happened and all through these years I have been asking myself, what if it hadn't happened? How would the course of events have changed if that hadn't happened? As we were drinking and chatting, my neighbors began their lovemaking again. I remember that blood rushed into my face and I felt the crimson on my cheeks. The woman next door moaned, first in a low, murmuring way, then louder and they banged against the wall. Marta laughed. She tilted her head and kept laughing. We were talking about Cuba and Castro and she was nodding with interest, but now it was impossible to go on. We were both listening to this erotic show and we were aroused. There was no way out of it. I was almost panting with desire and she was obviously uncomfortable. I could see how her breasts heaved in her tight top. Now she slipped off the bed, put on her shoes and said she'd go down to tell the driver to pick us up later—in the morning. And she winked.

She went down and all the while I sat on the bed, hot and uncomfortable with that big erection in my pants. I was not sure what was happening and if this was right. But I told myself that it was okay, natural and okay. She was a comrade and was young and pretty, not like some of my female colleagues in Houston, who carried themselves like truck drivers. We were young, I thought, and there was nothing wrong with sex.

In order to justify what was about to happen, I even tried to recall the details of a story a friend had once told me. He said that when he was in Germany on a mission, a German girl, a comrade who had picked him up, seduced him and took him to bed. So it wasn't that all the female revolutionaries were as unattractive and puritanical as our girls in the Houston branch.

Marta came back and turned off the ceiling light. In the yellow, flickering light of the lamp she undressed and slipped under the blanket. I was hoping that the neighbors would keep going on, because I wasn't confident about myself. I could get cold like a piece of rock if they stopped and my cock would die. But, being in their second round, they kept banging against the wall and now the woman screamed with a mixture of pleasure and agony. Marta unpinned the bun behind her neck and a long waterfall of dark hair poured over my body. In a second, we were devouring each other.

I hadn't had more than one glass of Scotch, but I passed out after lovemaking and woke up in horror an hour later. I'd dreamed of my mother, my quiet, catatonic mother, who sat by the window like a blown-up doll. She'd whispered something in my dream and I held my breath in the dark and tried to remember. "Go away, Rici, Go! Go away before it's too late." But what did it mean? Why would it be too late? I closed my eyes and fell asleep again.

The next time I woke up, the room was filled with the blue light of dawn and Marta was handcuffing me. It's silly, because at first I laughed. I thought it was a sex game or something. I remember that I told her sleepily, "No, I don't like this kind of stuff—" But this wasn't a game, it was for real, because she shoved a big cloth, something like a linen handker-chief, into my mouth and then shut my lips with duct tape. My heart sank. She was not a comrade.

I lay in bed mute, my good eye looking at her with horror. She was in her black bra and slip, trying to dress me while she muttered something in Spanish. Her body gave out an un-pleasant odor that I hadn't noticed last night. Maybe it was her sweat, but it smelled of camphor. I knew the camphor smell. That was the odor my Grandpa carried with him upstairs every night. That was the smell of death. In the gray light of early morning, Marta's face was different too. She wasn't as attractive as she had looked last night. There were black shad-ows under her eyes and fine lines showed around her mouth. She was not that young.

What she muttered in Spanish under her breath sounded like complaining or even cursing. At one point when she but-toned up my shirt she stared at my blind eye and paused; she had that sarcastic smile. Where was my eye patch? I had slept with it, but now I wasn't wearing it and she was ridiculing my eye, which probably looked like the blurry white of a raw egg. Now she went to the bathroom, put on her maroon dress, se-cured her hair in a bun, and freshened up her makeup. She came back and sat on the chair, waiting. She didn't look at me anymore; no sideway smiles and tilting head, no muttering. She took a notebook out of her purse and began to write something (her daily journal?). After a while someone knocked; she opened the door and three men came in. They lifted me and put me on my feet. One of them pressed a gun against my back and ordered me to walk with him. They took me three stories down and out of the hotel to a black car. The concierge looked at me—mouth taped and everything—but pretended he was busy writing something. Marta sat in the front seat next to the driver and the two men sat on either side of me. I remember that I looked up to see the flag that was hitting the post last night. It was a purple flag with a black dragon on it, the sign of the hotel, and it was still hitting the post.

They drove me through narrow cobblestoned streets and I saw a few people lined up against a wall, armed soldiers checking their identifications. A tank passed with soldiers standing in it, guns in their hands, looking around. So was it this bad? What I saw was a city in the deadly silence before a war, or in the terror of the temporary cease-fire. Our car parked in front of a fruit market. The men pushed me out, pressed the gun's muzzle against my back, and led me into the market, then inside a store and through a back door to a basement. There were people around, but they all pretended they didn't see a person with a taped mouth. No one turned to look. A minute later I was sitting on an old wooden chair in a damp basement, facing a wet brick wall. They had tied me with a rope to the chair and my mouth was still full of that kerchief. I felt like vomiting and couldn't breathe well through my nose. There was a sharp, damp smell of wet cement or standing water that made my stomach cramp. I felt my insides coming up into my mouth. Through a long, narrow window at the top of the wall, I could see people's legs in the fruit market—old ladies, maids, children, and soldiers— many of them. Now an orange fell from the fruit stand, rolled toward the window, and hit the pane. This reminded me of Grandpa Cardinal's house—the day that my plastic ball rolled and hit the window of the embalming room, the day that I saw the shadow on the wall. Death was here again, for the second time, disguised as a tall woman in maroon.

I didn't see the three men anymore. It was Marta who came and left, came and left.

What did she want me to tell her? Or was this the case at all? They should have been smart enough to know that a guy like me didn't know much. I was a soldier of the revolution, selfless and ignorant. I didn't know. I shouldn't know. They didn't let me know. But she kept slapping me and asking about Jonathan, who, if still alive, was most probably in another basement being tortured.

This lasted until evening. The daylight faded outside the window and the people's legs vanished. She came at dusk for the last time, slapped me a few times, and threatened that she'd send me to the real prison, where they executed spies without a trial. I kept telling her that I was a U.S. citizen and I wanted to contact my embassy. I told her that they couldn't execute me; it was against the law. She laughed each time I repeated this and made fun of me. At one point when I said I was a U.S. citizen and I didn't know anything about anyone, she spat in my face. Her saliva landed in the middle of my forehead. I'd made love to this woman last night and now she humiliated me. Was this whole thing a nightmare? Was I still lying down on the bed of that hotel waiting for my contact to come?

When she took off my shoes and brought hammer and nails, I came back to reality. This wasn't a disturbing dream; it was happening. She knelt in front of me (she was still wearing that long-sleeved maroon dress and her body, after hours of hard work (!), gave out that deadly odor, sharper than in the morning). She knelt and nailed my feet to the floor.

As she put the nail in the hollow space between my big toe and the second one and hammered on it, she said that this was to teach me a lesson: not to come all the way to other people's countries to find anyone, or interfere with anything. She said that she was fucking tired and needed to go home and sleep and wanted to make sure I wouldn't move. She nailed my feet to the floor, shoved that same kerchief back into my mouth, and taped all around my face. She even taped around my eyes. It's funny to me now that when she was doing this I thought about the moment when she'd pull the tape off and how badly it would hurt. I didn't think about pulling out the nails, the burning pain, and whether the wounds would get infected—all I thought about was the damn duct tape; how it would hurt when she peeled it off.

She left me in the dark, tied to the wooden chair, feet nailed to the floor, face taped like the Invisible Man, in the basement of a dead fruit market. I hadn't eaten anything for a day and a half and hadn't used the restroom for twenty-four hours. Would I die here? What if I really wanted to throw up and when the vomit didn't find a way out it slipped back into my air pipe and killed me? Why didn't she put a guard here to watch me?

I spent the whole night half-crucified. My mind ceased working and my system told me not to vomit—breathe, only breathe! And I breathed until a man came at dawn and pulled out the nails with huge pliers—the kind carpenters use—and peeled off the tape too and I didn't feel much pain. Now he told me to follow him out. I looked at my feet—there was just one drop of blood on each foot and there wasn't much pain, but numbness. I looked around to find my shoes, but I didn't

see them anywhere. The man hollered at me to get up and follow him and I walked barefoot on the cold, damp cement out
of the basement, up the narrow stairway, and through the still
closed fruit market, and into a car. There was no need for a
gun at my back. He knew I couldn't run.

He dropped me off somewhere in a deserted street and
sped away. There was a bench there. I crawled toward it and
sat. It was still very early in the morning and the air was cool
and blue. I had on my undershirt and pants and nothing else.
I began to shiver. Now I realized that they had taken my
jacket and my pants' pockets were empty; my passport and
papers were gone. I sat in a daze and felt a sudden urge to uri-
nate. But before I could get up and go somewhere to pee, my
pants became warm and wet. I relaxed and relieved myself.
Where had all that water come from? I hadn't drunk anything since that damn warm Scotch. Now I smelled myself
and vomited. I had to do this when I was in that basement and
my mind and body had suppressed it from the fear of choking. Now I vomited my life out—yellow bile. When I was relieved a church bell rang. I counted—six. It was six in the
morning. Then another church bell rang and another, as if
one bell tolled and its sound reverberated. It was Sunday.
There was one bell very close, ringing with a deafening clang
clang. I looked up and saw a brick tower and recognized it. I'd
seen this tower from the hotel window. I looked around and
thought that this might be the alley behind the hotel and my
guess was right. When I looked back I saw the hotel's gray
building. Could I go in? Did I still have my room? I had already paid for a week and this was the second day, so I had the
room. I got up and, before the streets became busy with peo-

ple, dragged myself to the hotel and stepped inside. The concierge didn't seem to mind my wet pants, yellow bile all over my shirt, or my black and blue face (I saw the bruises later in the mirror), but he stared at my bloody feet. I went up and found the door open. Although I didn't feel thirsty, I drank a full glass of water and called the American Embassy.

THE EMBASSY OFFICIAL sat in the same chair that Marta had sat on the night before and I sat on the edge of the bed, my injured feet hanging to the floor. I'd told them on the phone that I didn't have shoes or a single penny to get myself to the embassy, someone had to come and see me, and they had sent this man. He was tall and broad-shouldered, in his thirties, wearing a navy blue suit, white shirt, and red silk tie. He shook his head and sighed.

"I'm sorry, Ricardo." He used my real name to tell me that he knew who I was. "But why do you guys put your nose in other countries' affairs?" He asked this and waited for me to answer.

"Don't you guys do the same?"

"What do you mean?"

"Doesn't the U.S. support the army and paramilitary in Argentina?"

"That's not true. That's Soviet propaganda."

"Okay, let's not argue, Mr. Summers. We won't get anywhere. We're both interfering. But the difference is that I'm for the people and you're for the murderers—the junta." He wanted to say something but I didn't let him. "People are being tortured and killed every day. I came here because I care, but how about you? They're a bunch of ants to you, aren't they? Now would you please put me on a plane and send me back? I know I need to be punished for using false documents, but not here. And I need a pair of shoes."

I'm not sure where this eloquence had come from, because I was starving to death and I was still disoriented. I couldn't quite believe that what had happened had really happened.

Summers, who was too young to be an experienced agent, babbled some clichés he had learned in training and tried to use a calm and convincing tone. I couldn't help but admire his looks, his voice, and his sincere effort to make the jargon convincing. He could have been on TV lecturing about the poisonous ideas of Marxism spread throughout the world by the Soviet propaganda machine and the American youth, who had fallen under the influence of the Left and idealized a totalitarian system and so on and so forth. When he actually began to lecture me, I cut him off and said, "Please! This is not fair. I haven't eaten and slept for a long time—"

He got up and told me that he had to talk with the ambassador. But before leaving, he fished into his pocket, took out my passport and wallet, and handed them to me. He looked at me for a long moment and smiled. His smile said something like, "See? I finally managed to give you a little shock, you smart-ass!"

I WAITED FOR ten days until the bureaucrats in the embassy sent me a pair of shoes. I felt fear and anxiety every night and dreaded the thought that Marta and her men would break in again. When I asked for a guard, the embassy assured me that

I didn't need one. But I couldn't trust them and didn't dare sleep. Besides, how could I sleep on that damned bed which still smelled of camphor? And I wrestled with my thoughts, my tormenting thoughts. Sitting by the window all day I gazed at that church tower and crucified myself one million more times for the stupid mistake I'd made. Shouldn't I have known better? When the woman began asking about the organization and Jonathan, shouldn't I have doubted? Comrades don't ask. They know they shouldn't ask. And then, sleeping with someone I didn't know? I lashed myself with self-criticism. I was weak, unprofessional, immature, and unfit for the revolution.

Finally on the eleventh day, Summers took me to the airport. He walked me onto the airplane, and sat me next to an American woman who breast-fed her baby all through the long flight. I smelled human milk, sweat, and vomit and heard gulping and burping noises, which were all good, warm, and healing. I was grateful to be sitting next to the mother and child. At Houston's Intercontinental Airport, two agents in civilian suits approached me and whispered to me that I was under arrest. They told me to follow them quietly.

From the jail I called my contact, Johnny, at the bookstore and he called a lawyer. Johnny told me that I'd be out after a few days and I was. At that time I wasn't sure how Johnny dealt with these matters and how he or the lawyer could free me so easily, but later, years later, when I realized who Johnny was, everything became clear to me.

So, I picked up my son from the house of poor, horrified Dolores, who didn't know what had happened to me and went to my ransacked house. When I was in jail, the FBI had tried to punish me by breaking into my apartment. Sammy and I had a small life then—a TV set, a stereo, an old car, a giant AT&T computer, and a very comfortable couch I'd bought from a thrift shop for next to nothing. The furniture and the computer were smashed to pieces and the car's insides were gone. But this wasn't a very effective way to teach me a lesson, because I cursed them and swore to expose their crimes in Chile, Argentina, Indonesia, and other countries of the world.

My Life with Blue Jenny

I lived another five years without a woman. Every once in a long while I had a girlfriend, but this wasn't anything serious or lasting. The incident in Argentina—Marta in her maroon dress, then naked in bed, and finally in the damp basement nailing me to the floor—had wounded me for life. When I made love, I closed my eyes and tried hard not to see Marta. But the more I suppressed the image the stronger it became, to the point that the girl who was with me transformed into Marta and I smelled camphor on her skin and couldn't go on. Something had gone wrong with me and I needed a shrink. That's how I met Steven Will.

Steven was a young clinical psychologist. I was older than him and didn't trust him at first. I wanted an old fatherly therapist—a Dr. Freud or something. I was suffering from re-curring nightmares, in which someone patted my shoulder and when I turned, there was a shadow. I said, "What do you want?" The shadow said, "I know where your grandpa is.

Follow me." That's it. And I always woke up not knowing if I followed the shadow or not. I wanted someone who could remove Marta and the shadow and all this mess from my head.

Steven was a friend of the organization and didn't charge for the sessions. I couldn't afford a Dr. Freud anyway, so I went to see him.

After a few visits with Steven, I remembered one day how Marta knelt in front of me and nailed me to the floor. Until that moment I'd forgotten this particular incident. The wounds had healed and they were no more than two white dots on the top of my feet. Now when I remembered the scene, cold sweat covered my body and I murmured the story with a voice that Steven could barely hear.

I had these sessions once a week and sometimes twice. I told him about this fantasy, or whatever you may call it, that I had about death. I told him that I saw the shadow twice in my life, both times on the wall before something horrible happened. And now these dreams. Was I crazy? Paranoid? Schizophrenic? Steven laughed and said that I was as sane as anyone—that I just had a rich imagination. Years later, this is what my wife, Roya, told me and she urged me to write these stories down.

Steven and I became good friends and planned to open a social work organization together. We needed an activist to help us and we found Maya Baldwin. We both knew this woman very well from her women's organization and poetry readings. She was well known in progressive circles. She agreed to work part-time for us. So we opened a nonprofit organization to help the most needy of the city—the homeless, the refugees, the runaway and drug-addicted teenagers, jobless single mothers, battered women—you name it. We didn't have any money. We counted on fund-raising and Maya was a genius at this. At first we got a loan and used a lot of Steven's monthly income. He worked full-time as a therapist and paid our rent and the loan payment. I put my whole life there—seven days a week—and before long, Maya agreed to work full time. We called our organization PAC—People's Aid Center—and formed a pack. We were loyal and dedicated, like dogs.

What made it possible for me to put all of my time into PAC was the decline of my political organization. A year after the Argentina incident, the Texas branch split because of some minor differences about Cuba and we became small. I mean, very small. Johnny led the split and there was me, a few comrades in Houston, and a few in Austin. We were so weak now that we couldn't do much. The big organization, which itself had separated from a bigger one in the sixties, also divided and now we had several small groups arguing with each other in our newspapers about this and that political issue. It was ridiculous. How could we even speak of a revolution before we could learn to live with each other? When I saw that I was wasting my time, I quit my job at Westinghouse and put my efforts into PAC. Sammy was nine now and I was dirt poor.

The other thing that I did, thanks to Steven's advice, was to enroll in college and finish up my degree. I'd already passed two years' worth of courses, but as a part-time night student it took me longer than I'd thought to get my bachelor's degree in social work. But I didn't stop at that; I got my master's too.

When Sammy was nine and I was taking night courses at

the University of Houston, one evening after a full day of work, I was sitting on the bench waiting for my class to begin when I saw this little girl. I followed her to the Fine Arts building as if hypnotized. I say she was little because of her size, not her age. She was barely five feet and had short orange hair that stood up on top of her head like a clown (she looked like the little woman in Fellini's *La Strada*). She wore a long gypsy skirt and big earrings and carried her carpet satchel on her shoulder and walked lazily to the art building. She was a painter. Every evening before I went to class I sat on a bench not far from the Fine Arts building to see her passing. I couldn't take my eyes off her when she walked. She was so different than Marta that I didn't fear her and there was something very innocent and, at the same time, brave about her. Who would make such a clownish appearance for herself? She looked like a child playing a game and knowing that the whole thing was just a game.

Steven encouraged me to ask her out. We dated; she liked me and I fell in love with her weird ways and we moved in together. Later, much later, I realized that in Jenny I'd picked someone who had resembled Janet—petite, childish, weird, demanding, and domineering.

The house we moved into was in fact Steven's present to us. He let us live there as long as we wanted. This was his dead parents' house and it was in a very old neighborhood of Houston, once populated with white people and now with poor Mexican immigrants who worked at the Ship Channel. The streets were dirty, ugly, and unsafe and the houses were shabby shacks. Steven's parents' house, which was a big old thing, once white, now yellowish, stood right in the middle of this narrow, muddy street like a sore in poor people's eyes. The living quarters were on the second floor and all the downstairs was a huge basement that could become anything. It could become a mechanics shop (which it became after we left); it could become a neighborhood community center for the kids (my idea) or an art studio (Jenny's idea). As you may guess, it became an art studio for Jenny. She spent her days and nights there with her buckets of paint and big canvases. Her artist friends came and went or spent the night in the studio and I didn't mind. They were all cool. But the coolest of all was my Jenny who came to bed with all these colorful spots on her skin and smelled of turpentine.

Jenny worked on a project that didn't need just brush and paint, but her whole body. She dipped herself in a bucket of paint and then rolled on this huge canvas that was spread on the floor. To me the whole thing was a game, but to her it was dead serious. Once when I underestimated her artistic efforts, she sulked and didn't talk to me for a month and slept in the basement. I apologized and she came back to me again. I remember that the first night, after the long sulking, when she came to bed her body was blue. She had washed herself but the paint hadn't gone and she glowed with a blue, translucent light. We had a tall window opening to the big yard and the moon was up above the old oaks and Jenny's naked body glowed like a little mermaid. I had a strange feeling. I remembered my grandpa combing the mermaid's hair, but I didn't tell Jenny what I was feeling or remembering.

Now that I think back on it, in the four years that I lived with Jenny, I never once talked about my past life. She was so fragile that she would break if she heard my morbid stories.

So my encounters with death remained in a file in my head and never came out. Jenny didn't talk about her life either. Whenever I asked anything about her family in Kansas, she shrugged and said, "They're a bunch of village idiots. And they're Republicans, too."

A little more than a year after we'd moved to this house and a few months after Sammy and I bought Willie the Second, the replica of my dead collie, Janet showed up. Janet, Sammy's mother, came to see her son after ten fucking years.

She seemed better than in 1970, but much older. Her hairstyle was the same—those thick yellow bangs covered half of her eyes. She said she had married a lawyer a year and a half ago and lived in North Carolina (I never asked what happened to our friend John Eagleton). She said she didn't work now but was planning to get her massage certificate and open her own business. She wanted to have Sammy with her for the summer or, if he liked it, longer. When we sat around the kitchen table to eat, Sammy stared at his mother with his mouth wide open. He didn't blink, just watched. He was deeply moved. Their resemblance was amazing. Now that they were both here you could see how the boy had taken almost every single feature from his mother and nothing from me. Large blue eyes, a bit tilted down as if they were always sad, hay-blond hair, straight nose, a bit big for their delicate faces, and Slavic cheekbones. To make a long story short, Sammy fell in love with his mother, who was a mirror image of him, and left with her for the summer. When he said that he was not coming back for the school year, I flew to Charlotte to check on things. What I saw was not bad at all—a decent house, Janet playing the housewife, Mr. Lawyer coming home tired, drinking a glass of whisky, Sammy having his own room and a little puppy, a bicycle, toys, and everything that a comfortable kid has. I even drove to the school and liked the neat, yuppie neighborhood.

Sammy didn't come back for three whole years and we visited a few more times. So I didn't see my son grow to become thirteen.

Jenny and I lived a happy life those three years because I'd learned to compromise and to take it easy. When I didn't like something, I didn't argue and when she was moody, I left her alone. I'd learned to put up with her friends too, who came and went as they pleased, as if our house was a public art studio. I never spied on them when they spent long hours down there painting, listening to the kind of music I didn't like, and dipping themselves in buckets of paint. But to tell you the truth, I never believed what they did was art or that Jenny was a genius. My very first notion stayed with me forever: she was a little girl (she was in fact older than me!) playing a game and she didn't want to grow up and end it. Sometimes I regretted that she was wasting her talent. I'd seen her earlier sketches and real paintings. She could draw and paint decently. But she kept experimenting in crazy ways.

I thought I was happy with Jenny, but what does happiness really mean? At that time it meant not worrying about bills, going home at night dead tired, finding Jenny in the shower, humming and washing the blue paint off her tiny body. Happiness meant massaging her with violet oil and kissing that little scorpion that was tattooed on the small of her back. I knew that these weren't enough, because of the fact that we never talked, never connected. We were together and we were not together. Our inner worlds, so to speak, were poles apart. And this became worse when Sammy came back.

As I said, I went to Charlotte a few times to see Sammy and each time I felt relieved that my son had a good life, maybe even better than the life he could have with me and my bohemian Jenny. The lawyer was a level-headed man and treated Sammy a bit coldly, but politely. And Janet (who never opened a massage business) spent a lot of time with her son. I even noticed that she meddled too much in Sammy's little life, but I didn't find it harmful.

But I should've known better. Janet was crazy and probably had periods of sanity and insanity. It happened that she divorced the lawyer, shipped Sammy back, and moved somewhere in California. I'm not sure about the details, but it seems that she did to the lawyer what she'd done to me. She left him for another guy. She gave up that comfortable life and abandoned her son, too.

At age thirteen, Sammy came back to us, angry, betrayed, and confused. I'm not sure how things would have been different if Jenny and I had had a deeper relationship. Would we still have split? Weren't four years enough for a couple to build up a foundation? Sammy became an issue now. First of all, he wasn't a kid anymore. He had the shadow of a mustache above his lips; his voice broke now and then, and he showed anger and aggression. He was resentful and unfriendly. I took him to counseling, but things got worse. He argued with Jenny and she cried and complained every night. Sammy this and Sammy that was the nightly report.

Life became hell. Did she expect me to throw out my son? I cursed myself one million times for letting Sam go with his mother when he was ten. Had he stayed, things would have been different. But how could I have prevented this? It was Sammy's right to be with his mother and the woman seemed to be fine and her family life was in order. Didn't I go up there and see it with my own eyes?

Three major incidents happened during the summer and fall of 1983, which led to our separation. I'm not sure which one was the most important, but I'll list them anyway.

Jenny was working on a secret project, a special painting for me—and this was the first time that I was being honored in this way. She painted all day and hung a black cloth over the canvas when she didn't work. No one was supposed to see the panel. Apparently, one afternoon when Jenny had gone somewhere, out of curiosity, Sammy unveiled the panel and forgot to cover it. To make it worse, Jenny caught him when he was leaving the basement. When I got home, there was a commotion in the kitchen. From the yard, where I pulled in the car, I could hear them. Jenny was shouting hysterically and sobbing, Sammy was hollering. I tried to make them quiet down, but Sammy ran out of the house and banged the iron gate. Willie followed him. The boy and the dog didn't come back until dark and I had to drive around the neighborhood to look for them. Jenny went to the basement and tore the canvas with a razor. She destroyed my painting and I never saw what it was. Then a long period of coldness began. She slept in the basement and didn't come up to eat with us. Sammy was sulky and sad, too. We ate separately and went to our rooms.

Summer was ending and I had to enroll Sam in a junior high school in our district and the schools were bad. The kids were gang members or gang apprentices and carried guns to school. When I went to enroll him, the sight of the Coke machines being chained and padlocked and the armed security guards walking in the yard as if this were a penitentiary broke my heart. I didn't want my son to spend his long days in this prison. We had to move out of this neighborhood and live somewhere with a normal school, in which kids felt happy and bought Coke from unchained machines and didn't see the police all the time.

It was August and if we wanted to make such a change, we had to do it fast. The schools would start in a couple of weeks. I sat Jenny, who was still sulky, at the kitchen table and told her about the problem.

"We have to move out of here, Jenny. This neighborhood is dangerous for Sammy. I saw the school the other day. They'll eat him up. They'll shoot him. He's different. You know what I mean? There aren't many blue-eyed kids around here. I didn't see even one."

"Then how about my work?" She was pale and her orange hair was dirty and ropy and stood on end.

"You can work in our new place."

"Will we have a big basement like in here?"

"I don't think so. We have to rent an apartment. We can't afford a house with a basement. And we have to pay, you know? No more free house."

"How can we pay?"

"We'll manage. Don't worry about that."

"Where would I work?"

"We'll get a two-bedroom apartment."

"You mean all my stuff in a bedroom? Are you out of your

mind? My projects, my huge panels, my barrels of paint—where the hell would I take them?"

"Any of your friends have a place? You were generous with your studio for years. It's their turn now."

"No one has such a space." And she burst into tears like a four-year-old.

To tell you the truth I understood her predicament and felt sorry for her. Why was life changing? Damn! I kept cursing. Why did we have to move? But my anger was irrational. It was like saying, damn, why did Sammy grow up? Children will grow up and life will change.

Sammy had to go to school, so I rented an apartment not far from PAC's office and enrolled him in a decent public school, racially mixed, with good teachers and unchained Coke machines. I gave the apartment's address to the school, but we didn't move in. Every day I dropped Sammy at school and after school he walked to PAC and stayed with me until my work finished. Although I had to pay rent for a place we didn't live in, we could probably have gone on like this for a while, if the other incident hadn't happened.

One October afternoon I went home unexpectedly, because I had forgotten a client's papers on the kitchen table. I pulled into the yard and saw another car, an old orange VW bug parked behind Jenny's little Toyota. I'd seen this car before and I knew it belonged to one of her artist friends, but I didn't know which one, so I wasn't surprised. Before picking up the papers, I went down to see Jenny and say "hi." We'd become a bit closer after I'd rented the apartment and agreed not to move into it. And summer was over and Sammy wasn't around much. There hadn't been a crisis recently and Jenny was back into my bed. So I went down to surprise her and steal a kiss. There was the familiar scene—two or three canvases spread on the floor, barrels and buckets of paint, panels on the easels, and numerous done and half-done paintings leaning against the walls. But Jenny wasn't there. We had a little laundry room at the back of the basement where the washing machine was, and where the dog slept when he was cold. I knew that Jenny never did the laundry (I did the laundry every Sunday), but I thought she might be mixing paint or something in the laundry room.

To make a long story short, Jenny and a guy were making love on a white canvas next to the washing machine. Her body was blue and she was twisting and wriggling like a fish out of water in the arms of this tall, naked man who had jet black hair and a sharp goatee and I couldn't remember if I'd ever seen him before. With each move or turn Jenny made, a blue impression marked the canvas. She was doing her ultimate experiment. But I didn't care about that; what amazed me was Jenny's scorpion. When she rode on the man and waved and wriggled her body, the little insect on the small of her back crawled, as if alive.

I didn't want them to see me, so I turned to go out, but Willie, who had followed me to the laundry room, barked. Jenny slipped off the man's body, turned, and saw me. I left in haste and didn't even go upstairs to get the papers. I couldn't go back to the office. I couldn't go anywhere. I drove aimlessly for a while and found myself on Allen Parkway. I saw some benches facing green grass and the quiet bayou. I parked the car and sat on that bench for hours, staring at the thin silver water gleaming down there, until it got dark. I was in pain, but I had to get up and go on—Sammy needed me. The boy was alone and injured and I was the only one he had. So I went to the office and told the worried Maya—who had stayed late with Sammy—that my car had broken down on the freeway and I had to walk a long way and so on.

Sammy and I packed that weekend and moved to the empty apartment. We left Jenny behind. I told Steven that it was up to him to let Jenny stay in his house or tell her to move out. Steven wasn't happy about the whole thing. He didn't want to act like a lousy landlord, so he let her stay and she lived in that house and painted in that basement for another six months. I never went to see her, but Steven said that she felt very lonely in the big empty house and finally moved out. Where to? He didn't know.

Isn't this strange? We didn't even talk after I saw her with the man. She never attempted to explain anything and I never asked for an explanation. I just moved out and she accepted it passively. Did she ever love me? Had she been unfaithful to me all through our relationship? Or was this the first time? Nothing was explained. Our souls were closed to each other from the beginning and remained closed to the end.

All those years with Jenny the shadow of death remained trapped in my memory and the marks of death, the two identical spots on my feet, remained unnoticed. Jenny never saw the white marks on top of each foot and no other woman discovered them until Roya saw them and insisted on knowing what they were.

Jenny's story ended in the autumn of 1983, but she stayed with me for a long time. In the very depth of my dreams, and even in wakefulness, when I drove at night and forgot where

I was, I whispered her name in the dark, "Jenny, little blue Jenny—"

My Life with Sammy

Among many rights that are taken away from parents, the right of feeling wretched is the most important one. If you're a parent (much worse, if single) you don't have the freedom to feel depressed; you have to pull yourself together every morning, wear that wide smile, switch your motor on, and get going. All through Sammy's junior high and half of high school (that's all he did) I felt lonely, wretched, and depressed and I wasn't free to feel what I needed to feel. I turned my engine on every morning, pretended to be cheerful, made breakfast, took him to school, and made an effort to have a conversation with him. I took him out, sat through action movies, ate burgers and fries, played baseball and basketball with him, and so on. I lived the life of a poor, lonely single father with a teenage son, a life you can imagine for yourself.

But those were the good days. Sammy's anger and aggression changed to a dark depression when he approached fifteen. He began to skip school and use drugs; he distanced himself from me and became hostile. I'll just sketch one day of our lousy life and you can imagine the rest.

I was at work early one morning, trying to help this Cambodian family, who were six people living in one room. The husband and wife and the baby slept on the bed and the old mother, who was the size of a child, slept on the same bed, horizontally, at their feet. Two older kids slept on the floor.

The roof leaked and there was a bucket and the drip, drip of water all night was like Chinese torture. I was trying to make phone calls to get a subsidized apartment for them when the other phone rang and a recorded robotic voice told me that my son, Samuel Cardinal, was not at school today and I needed to talk to the principal as soon as possible. I gave the Cambodians' case to Maya, who gave me, in return, one of her famous dirty looks—because she was working on something else— and rushed to Sam's school.

The principal, a middle-aged, middle-class, white woman, whose kids had most probably gone to private schools and were now out-of-state at good universities, told me that if my son kept skipping classes, he'd be dropped. There were "alternative schools" for troubled kids, she said, there was a list of them with the secretary. I didn't feel like arguing with the lady about their whole lousy school system, crowded classes, and lack of individual attention and their unqualified, indifferent substitute teachers who appeared frequently in classes instead of the real certified teachers who were overworked and underpaid and took off whenever they could to deal with their stress. I left, swallowing my anger, and the secretary handed me a list of alternative schools.

That night I didn't say anything to Sammy. First I needed to find out where he spent his time all day. The next morning I dropped him in front of the school but didn't leave. I pulled behind a tree and watched him. He met some boys and instead of entering the school they turned into a back alley. It was raining lightly and the sky was getting darker by the minute. Like a detective, I followed them at a distance. They walked a few blocks until they reached a vacant apartment that was about to be demolished. They sat on the steps, under the eaves, and began to smoke. The way they held the small cigarette and took deep drags and passed it around, I knew they were smoking a roach. It was only seven-thirty in the morning and Sam was using marijuana. What the hell did he do the rest of the day? What else did he use?

I couldn't talk to him that night because he locked his door and turned off his lights and sat in darkness. I went out to the balcony and from the narrow crack of the shade looked into his room. He sat on the edge of his bed looking at the opposite wall. There was a picture of a unicorn taped to the wall. Sam had lit a small candle under the picture, as if this were a shrine. He stared at the unicorn and the white animal glowed in the candlelight.

I told myself that this was no good. This wasn't a fucking teenage crisis, it was insanity and I needed help. I talked to Steven and he sent Sammy to a teenage group that his colleague ran in a local church. This was something like a kiddy AA meeting and the boys and girls were all messed-up with serious drug problems or alcoholism. I wasn't quite sure if this would help Sammy, but Steven said that Sammy had to see the kids who were in worse situations than he was and hear their stories and see what would become of him if he continued using drugs.

I never forget the first time that I took Sammy there. It was a cold winter afternoon and the kids were standing in the courtyard of the church smoking. They were all pale-looking and emaciated; some had purple hair, earrings, and nose rings, or wore dark shades that covered their sunken eyes. Girls were not dressed properly for that chilly weather, their arms and chests and even bellies were out of their short blouses to show off their tattoos and the rings on their belly buttons.

Sammy and I went upstairs and sat in a large waiting room until the counselor called us in. Sammy didn't sit next to me. He sat on the other side of the room, as if he wasn't with me, and pulled his baseball cap over his eyes and stayed motionless. There were two large windows opposite each other and I was facing the one that looked out to the church's backyard, where a kindergarten was. In my sitting position, all I could see was the top of the monkey bars. It was dusk and the sky beyond the playground was deep blue with the last streaks of orange. The waiting room was becoming dim now and someone had to turn the lights on, but no one did. So we sat in darkness and I kept looking at the monkey bars outside. Now a little boy appeared on top of the bar and hung like a chimpanzee and swayed, then he dropped himself and I didn't see him. A minute later he appeared again and sat there and looked around with a sad wonder, as if he didn't expect the darkness to fall. I'm not sure if it was the lack of light or our life's gloom that gave me that strange feeling, a feeling that is hard for me to describe. That boy playing alone in the empty playground was me, my childhood. My father had gone again and I was alone, playing by myself. And then he was Sammy too, when he was little and I took him to playgrounds and sat and watched him. Now Sammy and I were both sitting in this dark waiting room unable to talk to each other, our future foggy and blurred.

I felt all this until the purple sky became pitch black and I couldn't see the kid anymore and a little later the counselor opened the door and called us in.

I'm not sure if that group therapy or kiddy AA, or whatever it was, helped my son. For Steven's sake, Sammy went a few months and then he stopped and I couldn't force him. Then he quit school and said he wanted to work. I thought work was good for him and said okay, he could help me with the expenses, too. He worked in a fast food place all day, but didn't help me with the expenses. He bought himself this and that, which I thought was okay. And, of course, he smoked the rest of his money away in narrow alleys.

Only once was I able to take him to a psychiatrist for a test. Of course he was diagnosed with depression and the doctor prescribed an antidepressant, but said as a teenager Sammy was more than likely to come out of it. Monitoring his medication became another problem. He took it for some time, then resisted taking it, and there was no way to force him. He was sixteen now, as tall as me with a voice deeper than mine.

Sammy resented me, as if I was responsible for his unhappiness. He never talked to me and our occasional movies and hamburger dinners were now a childhood memory in the remote past. He was sulky and used his room like a tenant and longed to move out but didn't have money to do so. He mostly ignored me but he quarreled with me one night and said what he had wanted to say for a long time. He poured everything out.

It all started when I knocked on his door to call him for dinner. He almost never ate at home. He bought his own dinner or ate at the fast food place. But it was Sunday and it happened that he was home and I thought it would be nice to cook something for him. So I made some pasta and meatballs and set the table. He could at least sit and eat, I thought. I wouldn't force him to talk. So I knocked on his door, but his heavy metal music was so loud that he didn't hear me knocking. I opened the door and stepped in. He was lying on his bed with his eyes closed soaring into that psycho land where the music had taken him. He sensed me and opened his eyes. I was wearing my apron and holding the spatula in my hand and smiling like a happy, fat chef. I invited him to the table with a hand motion. He turned off his music and said:

"Can't you knock before you come in? Don't you think it's rude to walk into someone's room?"

"I knocked, but your music was too loud. Come and eat now. I've cooked for you."

"I'm not eating," he said. "And please leave my room."

"Sammy—"

"I said, leave my room. Out!"

"Why are you so unhappy, Sammy?" Now my smile had vanished, I was using my counselor voice and I couldn't help it.

"Why am I unhappy? Do you need to ask?"

"Didn't you want to work and have your own money, be more independent?"

"I had to have a job. Don't you understand? How could you support me with your lousy job?"

"Oh, oh . . . you better watch the way you talk, Sam. I don't consider my job lousy."

"How much do you make, huh? Twelve hundred a month? And you expect me not to work?"

"Money has never been an issue for me, Sam. I work for people."

"But you have a son, man. Sometimes I think that you never give a damn about me. Why did you bring me into this fucking world if you wanted to sacrifice your life for people? So, how about me? You keep saying finish high school and go to college. Let me ask you something, Dad. Have you saved for my college? Where is my college money?"

"We're not affluent, Sammy. Affluent people save for college. Poor people use student loans or work hard and pay for college."

"Do you think I can save anything working in that smelly fast food place? Do you know what kind of a job I have? I scrub grease all day. That's my life." He paused a few seconds, then added, "Thanks to my dad."

"You never talked to me about your job. We could find something else—and it's not too late now. I'll look around and find you something better, Sammy."

"Thank you, but I won't be here for long."

"What do you mean?"

"I'm leaving."

"Where do you want to go?"

"To my mom."

Three weeks after this conversation, Sammy packed and left to find his mother. Janet had sent four postcards in the past three years, each from a different small town in Northern California. The last one was for Sammy's sixteenth birthday and had an address on it. Sam went straight to that address.

I'm sure that I couldn't have stopped my son from leaving me, but to tell you the truth, I didn't make much of an effort, either. I was exhausted and I needed a break. Not a break to have my own life, but a break to be left alone and feel miserable. Does it sound cruel? Inhuman? A parent cannot feel exhausted, you say? A parent cannot want to be left alone?

But the irony was that Sammy left the poor parent for the semi-homeless one. His mother was a drifter in fact and lived in different towns, changing boyfriends and temporary jobs. I was sure that Sammy would come back very soon, but I was wrong. He stayed for more than two years and came to visit me only once—in December 1989. But this was a short stay. He left me again to go back to his mother. In the summer of 1990 Janet called me and said that Sammy was lost. I flew to Mt. Shasta to find him. He was in a cheap motel, confused and suicidal. I brought him to Houston, but he flew back again.

My son was a crazy bird banging himself against the walls, looking for his mother's nest.

My Life with Willie the Dog

But let me not jump ahead. When Sammy left in the spring of 1987, a couple of months after his sixteenth birthday, I began to work at the Juvenile Detention Facility as a counselor. Steven thought I was trying to substitute the troubled jailbirds for Sammy and he might have been right, but the truth of the matter is, in Sammy's absence I found myself left with a lot of extra time. I didn't have a life, so I gave my time to these so-called bad kids.

The Juvenile Detention Facility is right at the edge of River Oaks, one of the fanciest neighborhoods in Houston, famous for its glamorous mansions and quiet, shady streets. JDF has a red tower that, if you stand—let's say, on the roof of one of these rich people's houses—you'll see its top. On each of the six floors of this tower (counting the basement), boys and girls of nine to sixteen are locked up in dark cells. They get out a few times a day to sit at greasy white tables that are bolted to the floor and play dominos with the moody guards or eat smelly food. They wear orange uniforms and plastic slippers. Those on minimum-security floors are allowed to have combs and little pencils, the size of a pinky finger, and a little plastic jar of Vaseline to grease their hair or hands and everything else around them (and that's why the tables and chairs are always greasy). The sixth floor is the psychiatric wing; here the kids have shackles on.

I worked as a counselor for JDF from 1987 to 1992, when I had to quit because of another demanding teenage crisis at home. Tala was acting crazy now and all this was too much for me; I had to quit going to the damn prison. I had finally burned out.

During the five years that I worked for the facility, I had all kinds of kids from lily white to blue black, all shades of human brown, and from age nine, when they still have tiny, kiddy voices, to age sixteen, when they're almost grown-ups. I worked on different floors and even one whole year in the psychiatric wing. One semester I worked in the girls' unit and the girls were wilder and rougher than the boys. I couldn't go on. Most of the five years I chose to work in the basement, where the younger children were locked up.

You do understand what a basement means to me, don't you? And I worked in the basement of a prison for five years—true, only ten hours a week—but still in a basement, where you can only see the tires of cars and people's legs walking freely in the street, a patch of yellow grass, a thin portion of life. Steven believed that I was reliving my former three basement experiences—I was, on purpose, choosing to spend ten hours a week in a dark underground jail when I had a choice to work on the sunny floors, because the basement experiences had not been resolved for me. What Steven had meant was that my problem with death had not been resolved.

And weren't these children living in the shadows of death?

THREE HEAVY IRON doors had to buzz open and click shut before I could mount a graded, carpeted corridor that led to another thick iron door. When I pushed the red button and the security guard saw me on his screen, he buzzed the door open and I entered the third floor. Everyone entered the third floor first—this was the check-in station. From here, one could climb the steps to the upper floors or descend to the lower ones. On this floor kids were in handcuffs and shackles, chained together at their ankles, waiting to be sent to their units. They were either sitting on the floor against the walls, or walking baby steps in groups to the corridors. This is an indoor jail. There is no courtyard. This is a vertical prison—a tower.

So I see all this every time I enter the third floor and each time I have the same feeling that I had the very first day—something throbs like a time bomb in my throat and I hear the lions roaring in the distance, in a corner zoo, far away, awaiting me, patiently awaiting me, but in vain. I see the shackled kids, who look at me, some in anger, some in hope (maybe because they think that I've come to free them) and I pass another buzzing door and run down two stories to get to my dark basement. Here, the door buzzes and I feel the cold breeze of purgatory on my skin. The tall, fat guard (most of them are tall and fat to intimidate the kids) leads me to a narrow corridor and there are cells on both sides. Behind each dirty, greasy, scratchy square window of a cell, a small head appears—one smiles, one shows a *V*, one mouths, "Take me out!" One cries, one bangs his head against the window.

I have good and bad days with the boys. One day I touch a boy's shoulder and ask him how he is and he yells at me, "Don't touch me anymore! Okay?" Another day I help a black boy by the name of Little D to finish his art (he can't draw the handle of a dagger) and when I'm leaving he says, "I love you!" The boys laugh at him. I say, "I love you, too," in return, and the boys slap their thighs and laugh more.

Love is a laughable matter in the facility.

There are days that the floor supervisor comes and interrupts whatever we're doing. He puts the boys in their cells and shuts down the unit.

"Short of staff," he says. "We have to close the unit, Mr. Cardinal. See you next time."

Boys sit in segregated groups. At one greasy table the black kids sit, at another the Latinos, at a third table the whites. Occasionally, there is a fourth table for the Asians. The guards don't let me mix them.

"They fight and beat each other up," they say. "Let them be."

There are days that we have a mean guard who just picks on a boy and constantly harasses him. This happens when the guard is Hispanic and picks on a black boy, or he is black and picks on a Hispanic or a white boy. Most of the white guards pick on the colored kids. The harassment starts like this: every few minutes the guard says something to the boy, "Don't make noise! What is in your sleeve? What are you whispering?" And finally when the boy gets angry and reacts, the guard takes him to his cell and locks him up. "No lunch and no shower today!" I can't interfere with the guards' decision. They rule the facility. The warden, a big, mannish woman, seldom, if ever, comes inside the units to check.

There are nice guards, too—some too nice. I've seen them rubbing the boys' necks, massaging their shoulders, gazing at them as if they're pretty girls, and giving them chocolate bars to take to their cells.

My counseling is not the conventional type. I don't advise them to do things they can't possibly do. I don't say, "Don't get into trouble!" I know that trouble is at every corner. Their family is trouble. The neighborhood is trouble. Trouble is who they are and where they've been born. It's like sending someone into quicksand and telling him, "Don't mess up your shoes! Keep your pants clean! Don't sink!"

Among many social workers and counselors I've met at the Juvenile, only one or two have deeply grasped the situation. The problem has deep roots. Most of the kids are not to blame. Give them parents, a decent neighborhood, good teachers, love, and security and see what will happen. What we do here is hopeless, but I keep going. I can make a little difference today, can't I? I ask myself. If not for everyone, maybe for Little D.

I read to them and let them write their stories. We draw, watch movies, and discuss. I talk to them one by one, too. But

I mostly listen. They have stories to tell that put best-selling thrillers to shame. This kid tells me how he and his brother planned to kill their crackhead mother. They did it one night with a gun they'd bought from the pawnshop. The brother shot the woman in her bed. They emptied the trunk and put her corpse in it and fled to Galveston. Soon after, they were caught. Now the brother, eighteen, is in the adult jail and this kid, fifteen, is in the juvenile. He told the whole tale in a cold, detached tone. He said their mother had become a piece of trash. She had to go.

I shift my chair from one table to another and listen to their stories. I sit with the Latinos, the blacks, and the whites. They're all pleased. A fourteen-year-old shows me the picture of his baby boy. He is already a father and his girlfriend is here too, on the second floor. They'll go out soon. They were caught shoplifting. I don't ask what they were trying to steal. Diapers? Milk?

One day, when we have a nice guard (a young man who is new in this job and hasn't become cruel yet), the black boys ask permission to rap and the man says okay and then the kids rap together. In a minute I find myself excited, snapping and jerking and singing with them like a fat bear. I'm a big man, with a sizable belly. Since my half-ass crucifixion I walk a bit awkwardly, like a flat-footed person. You can imagine how I look when I snap, bang my hands on the table, and dance with the kids. The white and Latino kids, who are at first reluctant, join in and rap with us. So we rap and rap and rap until the floor supervisor comes, throws me out, and shuts down the unit.

This is a happy story. The saddest is when I enter the unit one day and everybody sits gloomily, doing nothing. The guard whispers into my ear that Jose, the jaundice-faced boy who rarely talked and yelled at me when I touched his shoulder, hanged himself from the shower last night. He says this is the second such incident in five years. That day, I cannot do much. I pass papers around and we all sit in silence and draw. The kids draw big black crosses, gang symbols, daggers, and guns. I doodle and think about Sammy.

In JDF, kids come and go. Some come and go for the second and third times, some for so many times that they grow up in the Juvenile and are moved to the adult prison, where they meet the real criminals. They learn serious crimes in adult jails and whether they stay or go free, their lives are ruined. Little D, who is released one day, gets arrested the next month and is back in the basement with a big smile. He has sold dope again to support his addicted mother. How could he not sell?

I overhear a social worker telling a kid who is being released, "Now, be a good boy, okay? I don't want to see you here again!" Why bullshit the boy? I never say this. I just shake the kid's hand and say, "Good luck, man! Take care of yourself; it's a jungle out there!" Then I go home and lie in bed next to the warm body of my dog (and later my wife) and strain to listen to the faintest sounds coming from the basement of that tower. If I strain hard, I hear Little D crying for his mother and for himself.

AFTER SAMMY LEFT, two more things happened that made my life gloomier than it was. Let me begin with my father's death.

You may ask where my father had been all these years? I

haven't mentioned him after that brief visit to St. Louis when I was fourteen. Apparently, he lived with his second family for a good ten years and when his daughter was eight or nine he divorced the loudmouth lady and went to Florida. I'm not sure what exactly he did there, but whatever he did, his last years were in a mobile home with a woman much younger than himself. She owned that metal box. He was a heavy drinker now and he and this woman shared my father's small retirement money, drinking it all away. He was sixty-something years old when he had his first stroke and he didn't have any close relatives left, except for old Aunt Mary (cousin Joe's wife) and Crazy Lucy, his niece, who still lived in Cincinnati with Aunt Mary, helping her with the ironing business. Uncle Albert was dead and Aunt Rose was in a hospital with Alzheimer's disease. His St. Louis wife and daughter didn't want to hear about him.

I went to see my father after his first stroke in 1985. I hadn't seen him since I was fourteen and I'd never felt that I had a father. Lying in his hospital bed, pale, bald, and bloated, he was a stranger to me and I'm sure that he felt the same way about me. I could tell this from the way he looked at me and smiled faintly and maybe shyly. But when I said, "Bye," and rose to leave he called me and said, "Rici—" (this is the name that only my close family used). I returned to his bed and said, "Yes?" He looked at me then shut his eyes. I felt very sad and left. What did he want to tell me? And why didn't he?

Now in 1988, the second stroke happened and it was massive. When his girlfriend called me (I never got her name right: Marie or Maureen?), I flew there immediately. I knew the old man didn't have anyone. He was dying alone with this

Marie or Maureen, who was just a drinking friend, at his bed-side. I got there soon enough to see him in the hospital bed. He was unconscious and a tube connected his nostrils to three bot-tles on the floor. My father's blood ran through the tubes and filled them. All the blood vessels in his head had blasted, I guess. In the corner of the room, Lucy stood and stared, try-ing to remember me. Aunt Mary sat on a chair and mumbled a prayer. Crazy Lucy was fifty-something now, but she acted like an underdeveloped twelve-year-old with greasy gray hair sticking to her little head. She had definitely grown up, but at a very slow pace. I asked her about Tommy, her brother, my favorite cousin. In a flat tone she said, "Tommy lost his busi-ness." Aunt Mary said, "Tommy Cardinal is back in jail for the third time. Embezzlement. I don't think he's gonna come out this time."

My father's girlfriend wasn't more than forty-something years old, but she looked wasted and spent. Her skin was yel-low and dry and white bags hung under her eyes. She sobbed by the bed, as if she was losing a lifelong husband. Now the door opened and a young woman in a business suit entered and went straight to my father's bed. She bent over him and looked at his bloated, gray face. I knew who she was, but I didn't say anything. She didn't acknowledge anyone, either. She ignored everybody as if she were a superior being. I went to find the doctor. He was a young Indian man and told me that my father was still breathing, but it was just a matter of hours. He'd die soon. I left the congregation of crazy women and went to find a hotel. I was just there to take care of the arrangements; I didn't need to be in the hospital. Let his dear daughter stay at his bedside.

I got a motel room at the beach, the only inexpensive place I could find. It was the beginning of summer, June 2, to be precise, and happy vacationers were everywhere. From my motel balcony I watched the kids playing in the sand, making a castle, and I tried to remember if my father had ever taken me to a beach. He hadn't. His longer visits were on Christmas and Easter and these were not beach times. In the summer he stopped by for a short visit and took me to that corner zoo and to the billiard place a few blocks down the street and then to the drugstore, where we sat and sipped cream soda.

I watched the kids building a sand castle and reminisced. I tried to remember my childhood. I took the files out of my brain and opened them and closed them and put them back. The images were all gloomy. The happiness of dad coming home was always ruined by the sadness of his leaving. When he left with that black briefcase in his hand, I didn't stand at the door next to my mother and Grandma to wave at him. I ran upstairs and hid under my blanket for hours.

That night I called the hospital every two hours and asked about my father. He was slowly dying, as if all of his blood had to drip into those stupid bottles. And I was in a motel room in Miami Beach, chain-smoking and resisting the urge to buy a drink, because one would lead to more and I had to be sober for my father's death.

So this way I waited for him to die.

At one point, I felt so lonely that I wished Sammy were with me—the sour, resentful Sammy, my flesh and blood, my son. I just wanted him to be here, as sour as he could be, and let me feel that I had someone, too. Then I thought to call

Steven, wake him in Houston, and tell him where exactly I was and what I felt. But before I made a fool of myself I dismissed this and sat on the balcony, looking at the white tides, waiting for the phone to ring.

To make a long story short, I waited for my father to die that night and he died around five in the morning. In the blue-gray dawn the cab took me through the deserted streets and I saw the silent ocean and the quiet sand and didn't feel anything much, except gloom. I'd waited for him to die and he was dead now, and I'd make the necessary arrangements and leave. One or two more days here, then I'd be gone. Let old Aunt Mary and Crazy Lucy take his casket to Cincinnati and bury him and send me the bill. My job would be over.

And my job was soon over. I sat in the airplane and flew back. But as I was looking at a magazine and listening to the radio with the headphones, a soft waltz began to play. I listened. It was very familiar. I'd heard this before, but long ago. Then I looked at the window and saw the thick, puffy clouds under the plane, like patches of iceberg, and suddenly this image appeared in my head. It was Christmas and in our living room the tree was decorated and all the presents sat neatly under it. My father wore a dark suit and his hair was combed back with oil and water like a handsome movie star's. My mother wore a long, white chiffon dress and smelled of lilacs; they were going out to dance and before leaving they waltzed around the room. My father was happy and my mother was not a stone statue; she laughed and whirled around the room. I sat next to the presents and watched them and I was not sad that they were leaving me at home. I wanted them to go out and be happy. They kissed me and told me to go down to

Grandma and they left. But I remember that I stayed for a while until the big record on the gramophone made scratching sounds. The waltz was over and I felt lonely.

For a while, longer than a month, that waltz played in my head. I even tried to find the piece. I went to all the music stores in Houston and stupidly hummed the tune for the sales clerks; they couldn't find it. Then I became so busy with work that the waltz died in my head.

THE OTHER THING that happened was Johnny's death. Johnny was my organization contact, remember? My comrade and mentor, the man who saved me from jail when I came back from Argentina. It was sometime in the winter of 1989 and by then my small amount of political activism had been reduced to zero. Johnny had left Houston in 1984 and the Houston branch had become orphaned and paralyzed. We were all doing something else. I was busy with PAC, which was growing out of proportion, and other comrades had gone back to school, or had just remembered they needed to have a family and live normal lives.

One December day, I was sitting in Dot, this smelly coffee shop near downtown. My client, Madison Kirby, liked to visit me there. After a long absence I had an appointment with him. He had problems again; he was delusional and paranoid and had lost his job. Now he wanted to see me and I was wondering how I could help him. Would he be able to handle another job?

Madison was a peculiar guy—smart and well read, but confused and antisocial. He was angry with people and it was no easy matter to find him a job. Waiting for him anxiously, I sipped my coffee and glanced at the headlines. At the bottom of page one, something caught my attention: "FBI Agent Shot in Cairo." And then there was Johnny's picture and underneath it a name: Malcolm Barry.

I read the article to make sure this was Johnny, and then left a note for Madison that I had a family emergency and had to leave. I rushed out of the coffee shop before he arrived and saw me upset. I didn't want my clients to see me distressed. At that moment I was devastated and didn't know what to do. This incident was not like my father's death. This was the death of my past life, my youth, my political ideas—my identity so to speak. I couldn't drive, so I left the car in the parking lot and began to walk the length of Richmond—a street that connects downtown to the end of Houston, where wild grass grows. I began to walk in a straight line along the endless identical shopping centers toward eternity. I panted and walked.

When something like this happens it's hard to say what kind of emotions we have. At first, I only walked without feeling anything. I was numb. It was later, way into the night, two or three in the morning, when I was tossing in bed that the realization came to me. All those years—from 1971, when I was twenty-one and came to Houston to work with the organization, up to 1984, when I fulfilled my last assignment—an agent, an informer, had been leading and advising me. My strings had been in his hands and I'd been working against the revolution instead of for it.

So what was the difference between Crazy Lucy and me? In our grandparents' kitchen Lucy sat and peeled potatoes for years, then picked up her red ball of yarn and began to knit a sweater for herself. But this thing, this sweater, never took shape, never became anything, because Lucy confused the stitch count or skipped or something and Grandma told her to tear everything apart and begin again. Every few weeks, when the thing became long enough to look like a red piece of something hanging from her needles she tore it apart and began from scratch. Now my young years, my energy, every single bit of work I'd done for the revolution, every danger I'd experienced, and every sacrifice I'd made (or that I'd thought I'd made) for the revolution was directed by this agent, who pretended to be a comrade and acted like one. Everything had been meaningless, a theater of the absurd, and I was only a puppet and someone pulled my strings from above. My whole life was Lucy's unfinished, crooked sweater, a wrong product, torn to nothing. I had done nothing to make the world a better place, nothing was done and every-thing had been meaningless.

But at that time these emotions were not so clear. I mourned Johnny more than I had mourned my father. When you love a man, work for him, trust him, and eat and drink with him, it's not easy to curse his soul when he dies. Even if he turns out to be devil. You can't help missing him, mourn-ing him. I thought then, and I still think, that Johnny's grand acting as a revolutionary leader had been blurred with real life. He had become one with his role, like a Method actor who at times cannot separate himself from the role he plays.

I took a week off from work and walked the length of var-ious streets in the rain and wind, thinking about Johnny and recalling different incidents. Not even once did I sense that he was fake. Not even once did I feel that he was insincere. When our old comrade Joe Schaeffler had a heart attack in the middle of an antiwar demonstration in Herman Park and fell on the grass and died, Johnny sobbed over his body. How could this have been role-playing? When he, Johnny, was beaten by the KKK in 1978 in Conroe and the rednecks smashed his camera, I dragged him out of the crowd and tried to convince him that we had to save our lives, but he cursed the Klan and ran back to beat them up. And there were more incidents, none indicating betrayal, all proving that Johnny, the informer, had become one of us. But had he?

If he hadn't and if he had been a superb Method actor who could slip into the skin of a revolutionary for fifteen years and slip out of it, then couldn't we assume that there were other superb actors in other branches of other cities, all around the country, all around the world, who sabotaged the revolutionary movement? If the answer is yes, then no wonder our organization split one hundred times and became nothing and finally dissipated like Lucy's sweater.

But did I really believe that everything had been absurd? Was I now a faithless nihilist? I didn't think so. It was too late for me to lose faith. Call me an idealist or an idiot, whichever you want, but I remained a soldier of the revolution, an advocate of the people's rights, because I thought there wasn't anything nobler than seeking justice in this lousy world. Was there? Was there any cause more human than fighting for a better life on earth?

Even in 1991, when the Soviet Union fell apart and we heard and read that the commies were shooting themselves in the temple, I remained faithful to my cause. Lenin's revolution had gone astray after his death and I'd known this since I was young. This was a sad historical fact and all that was happening now was the crumbling down of a house that should have fallen long before. Ironically, the Soviet empire had maintained a balance in our world and if this balance was disturbed, wolves would rule. But could I stop struggling because the wolves would soon fatten up? Was it right to leave the deprived people alone, now that they were more helpless? Or must I stay with them to the end, work for them, and give them awareness?

My years with Johnny were lost, true, but I had made a difference here and there and I would go on doing my work. So I made a slogan for myself: Make a little difference every day in people's lives. The day that the army of the deprived organizes itself and finds its leaders, as it has always done, be a soldier under its flag. Now call me an idiot if you wish, call me Don Quixote the Second. But being an idealist is better than being a nagging, whining, passive consumerist. Isn't it?

So in this way I maintained my equilibrium, or thought that I did, and I kept working. But I can't deny that one big part of me was massively injured, and that was my soul—that vague, elusive thing inside a person that has to do with love of life, happiness, and sense of our survival. I stopped taking care of myself and my life with Willie the dog became a hell of a doggy life. I went home in the evenings after my prison job and Willie and I ate on the dusty porch that looked out on the abandoned railroad track until it got dark. We had a shot of whisky, which gradually we cheated about and made two and then three and more, and we fell asleep right there, on the broken wicker chair that had once belonged to the landlord.

We dragged ourselves to the bedroom at midnight or, to be precise, Willie woke me up and reminded me that it was more decent to sleep in bed. We shared the bed, Willie and I. He warmed me and at times licked me, and gave me more love and affection than any human being had ever given me, since the time I'd been born. So this was my life with Willie and I wasn't aware that I was going downhill with the drinking and my gloom and lack of a normal relationship with a woman, until I met my third "J"—in my worst possible condition.

THEY WERE ALL "J"s, you know, Janet, Jenny, and now Joanna. But my third, I have to confess, was the sanest of the three and the most gorgeous. She was a tall, natural redhead, half-Jewish, half-Irish. A professional woman, smart and sophisticated and a true nagging, whining, passive consumer, and of course, a bit of a snob. I liked her and I despised her equally. I despised her when she talked in that arrogant tone, shaking her delicate white finger in the air, which showed a carefully manicured fingernail, the way she used graduate school words like *rapture* and *closure* and *fissure* and so on in every sentence to show off her sophistication, the way she tried to prove that she knew it all. And then I liked her long white legs, her red curls rubbing her shoulders, her cute little freckles, and her voice, her soft, girlish voice when she didn't argue "issues," the voice that said something contrary to all that arrogance. I met her first during the week-long meetings at the Texas Committee of Nonprofit Organizations that Maya had sent me to instead of herself, to raise money for PAC.

At the end of the first meeting Joanna Bauer invited me for coffee. I was reluctant, because I didn't like the way she carried her beautiful self. Too much confidence, you know? Too much for me, at least, who didn't have much left. But I followed her passively, like a dog, to the Black Labrador, the restaurant next to the Montrose branch of the public library, where our meeting was. I followed her only because I didn't have enough energy to say no, I don't want to have coffee with you; you're too much for me. But we ended up sitting longer and having an early dinner and I liked the bar and the restaurant's fireplace with real wood burning in it. So we kept going there after each meeting and ate heavy English pies and drank together. We chatted like high school kids and I laughed— God knows, after seven or eight years. Joanna was a charmer and had a superb sense of humor.

I'm still not sure what she liked about me. My unwashed, wrinkled shirt? My shabby beard? My long hair, now in a braid behind my neck? My black, mysterious eye patch? Or my lingering way of talking, my slow-moving jaws, indicative of long-neglected depression? But she said later that she fell for me! And I told her that she probably "felt" for me. She insisted that she fell for me and wanted to be with me forever. This scared the hell out of me, but I kept seeing her.

Then I began to clean up my house, which was like cleaning a hobo jungle. I disinfected it patch by patch, humming something while washing and scrubbing and spraying Pine-Sol on everything. And this humming! I couldn't remember the last time I had hummed anything. I stood in front of the mirror and studied my face; I tried to see what Joanna saw. I'd never removed the black eye patch in front of her. I could

never forget that devil's reaction after seeing my eye in the
morning. I'm talking about Argentina. Marta. Anyway, I
shaved the shaveable parts of my face and shampooed my
beard and combed my long hair and braided it carefully. I
even foolishly told myself—as if I were a sixteen-year-old—
that if Joanna wanted, I'd cut my Samson hair short finally
and would become civilized, but she liked it long. She un-
braided it in bed and praised its thickness and softness and
braided it back. She covered me with kisses from head to foot
and stupidly insisted that I was not overweight, but my bones
were large. She said she wanted me the way I was and the way
I looked and not a bit different.

We made love in her apartment, of course, a luxury two-
bedroom, with a large deck overlooking the woods and the
bayou on Memorial Drive. She'd seen my place only once and
had wrinkled her little nose, so I went to her place, first once
a week, then more, until I became addicted to her comfortable
leather furniture, her silk sheets, her red curls brushing my
chest, and the tips of her long, crimson nails scratching my
dead scalp in a soothing massage. She treated me like a child
sometimes, undressed me and washed me with rose water
from head to foot. She massaged every inch of my body, but
she never saw the white nail marks on my feet. I told myself
childishly, superstitiously, that the day Joanna notices my crucifixion marks she'll be mine forever. She never did.

This amorous affair lasted a good six months, from September to December of 1989, when Sammy called me one midnight
from the Greyhound station. This was a night that I was home,
otherwise Sammy would have had to walk all night and get
home in the morning. He didn't have a penny on him.

I drove to Greyhound with Willie panting in the back seat. I took the dog with me because I was afraid of what I was about to see. And I was right; Sammy was a mess. His face was covered with a bushy beard and his hair was dirty, straggly, and disheveled. The smell of outdoors on his filthy clothes turned my stomach, but the worst of all was his way of talking, which was incoherent and confused. He mumbled things that I could not get; he said things that didn't make sense.

"Hey Sam, good to see you back, son!" I turned on the engine—my cheerful, carefree, fatherly voice. But inside I felt desperate.

"I've been here before—" he said in a flat tone.

"You mean Houston?"

"No, here. I mean here."

"Willie is in the car. Look at him, he is excited to see you." He looked toward the car and saw Willie, but didn't react.

"Where's your stuff?"

"I don't have anything."

"Nothing?"

"I left everything at Mom's house."

"How's Mom?"

"She's found a new friend—I mean a man—we couldn't get along."

"Oh, I see."

"She's quit smoking, you know?"

"Your mother?"

"Right. Now she makes herbal medicine. She went to a class for it. She sells herbs."

"Good. Now let's go home. You must be tired. We can pick up some burgers on the way—"

"Wait a minute!" He strained to listen. He listened for a long minute, then chuckled to himself. Now he shook his head in regret.

"You okay, Sam?"

"Yeah—yeah—it was Taza."

It took me a while to take him home. He was a mess. He was ill in a bad way, as if a bomb had blasted in his brain and everything was in ruin—chaos. I had to do something fast, before it was too late.

The next morning I called Steven and told him about Sammy's return and his condition and I took the day off. Steven called a doctor friend of his, a famous psychiatrist, and asked for an urgent appointment. I convinced Sammy to wash and come with me to the doctor and I was surprised that he didn't resist the way he used to when he was younger. He was passive and stony and chuckled to himself and shook his head all the time.

In a dim room, where we could barely see each other, the doctor talked to Sam for half an hour and then talked to both of us. Then he asked Sam to leave the room and told me that most probably my son was schizophrenic. I told him about Sam's previous depression, the picture of the unicorn, and all those years. He said that those were symptoms, but now the illness was at its peak. Soon after the test tomorrow, he'd prescribe medication.

I became involved with Sammy and cancelled my dates with Joanna. At first I didn't know that this was the end of our relationship; I thought that it was temporary. I thought that after I got Sammy on medication, life would find its routines and I'd find time for Joanna again (I knew that it wouldn't be like before). But to my regret, Joanna didn't understand. She acted like a child, felt jealous of my son, and accelerated the breakup. She was offended that I had to spend all my nights at home with Sam. She told me that I didn't even have a tiny space for her in my life, which I said was not true, but I knew that I was lying. When my son's mental health was collapsing in front of my eyes, I didn't have any space left for Joanna. How could I leave Sammy alone all night, talking to the imaginary friend in his head, and enjoy Joanna's caresses? Joanna had been my earthly heaven, my pleasure and delight. The gates of that heaven had been closed on me that night in the Greyhound station when Sammy brought with him the odor of death.

My son had lived the life of a homeless man in Mt. Shasta and thanks to his crazy mother I wasn't informed of his symptoms. Only two weeks before his departure, he had forced himself to work a few hours a night to be able to make enough money to buy a ticket and come to me. He had been disappointed with his mother and distanced from her and didn't want to ask for money. He told me a few things about his homeless days and dishwashing nights when I took him to Corpus Christi for a short vacation.

It was a month after his arrival, sometime in January, and the medication was beginning to work. I rented a beach house by the water and took him and Willie in the car. During this short trip, Sam talked to me more than ever before or ever after. I realized that my son had lived a life, seen things, matured, but ironically had lost his mind. In Corpus Christi I realized that there was no hope for me to have a healthy, jolly boy who'd go to college, get a job, and then make a family.

Sammy was ill and lost, and either I had to care for him the rest of his life, or I'd lose him forever.

On our second day at the beach, late at night, when we were watching TV, Sam left with Willie for a walk, but fifteen minutes later Willie came back alone. I waited for him for an hour, but he didn't show up. I began to worry. Our rented house was at the end of the row and the beach was empty. It wasn't vacation season. There were no lights outside and the beach was dark and I didn't have a flashlight with me. With my plastic slippers I walked toward the ocean to find Sam and I found him a few yards away, standing motionless, facing the water. It was so dark that all I could see was the waves' white foam, gleaming here and there. All I could hear was a rhythmic hum. I stood next to Sam and didn't talk. Then we both began to stroll along the beach. He didn't say that he didn't want me there, so I took it as approval and kept walking with him. Could I begin to talk? Could I break the silence and ask him to say something? What was there to talk about? Sammy was now much older, a nineteen-year-old, and I didn't want to ask anything that wasn't my business. There was this wide distance between us, a dark ocean. When was the last time we had said anything meaningful to each other? When he was twelve or thirteen? When we ate hamburgers and fries after an action movie? Now Sammy's inner world was a massive darkness like this night, and I couldn't enter.

"Remember Johnny?" I don't know why among all the things in the world I brought this one up. Maybe it was dark and I didn't need to wear a happy mask and I said just what was most important to me.

"Yeah, sure. Uncle Johnny."

I almost said, he was an informer, an agent. But I didn't. My silence became long.

"What about Uncle Johnny?"

"He died."

He didn't say anything and we heard the tides slapping each other, then sliding away. "He did?" Sammy asked.

"Yes. He is dead. Someone shot him in Cairo. Your Uncle Johnny—"

"The pyramids in Egypt are made by aliens. Did you know?" He paused, then said, "This screwed you up, didn't it? Johnny's death."

"Oh yeah, it did."

"He babysat me many times."

"Many times," I echoed.

We kept walking in the dark and now turned away from the water and climbed a hilly, cobblestoned street with houses on either side. The houses were all dark, which meant they were summer rentals that were vacant now. We walked for a long time in the ghost town and the plastic slippers I had on began to hurt my feet and I took them off and walked barefoot on the stones. Now we reminisced in fragments—the years with Johnny, the big house and Jenny's basement, her paintings, Sam's schools and people and places that had faded and gone. Now we realized that we were lost and we didn't know how to go back home. We laughed at our stupidity and walked downhill, not knowing that we had turned somewhere to the right or the left and we were in a different street which looked like the first one. Now all we said was, "Was this tree here when we went up the street?" or "Did we pass a church?"

Suddenly Sammy said, "It's cool, let's get lost."

"Okay," I said and laughed. "Willie will wait for us. Dogs don't get worried the way humans do, or do they?"

"There was this crippled man," Sam said and at first I thought he was responding to what I'd asked, but he was telling me a story. "This crippled man was a beggar who begged in the streets all day and slept in the kitchen of the restaurant where I worked. His name was Taza. I don't know what kind of a name this is and I never had a chance to ask him. He was mixed race; he had a strange body and features. Sometimes he looked like an Indian, sometimes he was a black man, but he was a white man for real and he told everyone he was Caucasian. He was very small. Five feet one and he was thin and wobbly. When he lay down in the kitchen next to me, he looked like a twelve-year-old, hairless and brown like a troll. That's when I thought he was an Indian. Native Americans don't have much hair on their chest, you know?"

"You slept in the kitchen?"

"Yeah, the last two weeks I worked for this seafood restaurant and they let me sleep in the kitchen."

"You didn't want to stay at your mom's?"

"I left my mom's place five months before the kitchen job."

"So where were you staying?"

"In the parks, streets, under the bridge." He laughed.

There was silence. I had asked too much. I might have ruined everything. The story he was about to tell. We were walking downhill forever, toward the ocean that glowed silvery, like a mirage in the dark.

"Do you want to hear Taza's story or not?"

"Oh, yeah. The little Indian."

"I said he wasn't Indian, he just looked like one—sometimes."

"Tell me."

"He was crippled, you know? In a bad way. Like he couldn't walk very well. You know why? They had thrown him down a building in San Francisco once."

"Why?"

"He hadn't paid the dealers. He didn't have money."

"Drug dealers, you mean?"

"Yeah. He was a crackhead, you know? And he didn't have money to pay for his crack and the dealers threw him down."

"Then he moved to Mt. Shasta?"

"Yeah, he was in Mt. Shasta, begging. He opened his purse one night and he had all this money. I mean a lot."

"But could he make a life for himself with that money?"

"Nope!"

"He couldn't."

"He spent most of it on drugs. Whatever he could find."

"Did he use them in that kitchen?"

"Sometimes."

There was silence again and we walked but we didn't get one inch closer to the ocean.

"One night when I was washing the dishes and the pile kept growing and it was taking forever and more dishes were piling up next to me, I just walked out."

"You did? I thought you left when you made enough money."

"Nope. I hadn't made enough money. I needed more. I needed some money for food and my cigarettes, but I didn't even get my last paycheck and I walked out and went to Grey-hound and bought a ticket with whatever I had and left."

"I guess you were sick of that job."

"I didn't say 'bye to Taza."

"Or to your mother."

"Not to her either."

"Anything happen between you two?"

"Who?"

"Your mom."

"No. She just invited that man. We were living together before that and we didn't have a bad life. We both worked; she cleaned the rooms in a hotel and I worked for a mechanic shop. Every night we smoked together and chilled out, watched TV, and made herbal medicine. Everything was cool. Then this man came to our place and settled there. You know what I mean?"

"Yeah. You didn't have a girlfriend? I mean—a date or something?"

"How could I, huh? You think it's easy? Girls need money. You got to spend on them. Girls need a car. You got to pick them up."

"True."

"I wonder why we don't get to the damn beach."

"We walked a long way up."

The rest of the way we were silent. He was irritable and wanted to get home. Talking about his mother had made him angry, so I didn't say a word and we got to the ocean and found our way back. Only when we reached the steps, Sammy stopped to say something.

"I wonder what Taza is doing now."

"In that kitchen—" I added.

"No. He won't be there."

"Why? Didn't you say he sleeps there?"

"He slept there only because I let him in every night."

"I see."

"Yeah. I'm sure after I left, the owner kicked him out. I made him homeless, Dad."

"You didn't make anyone homeless, Sammy. Taza was a messed-up addict. You didn't do this to him."

"I took his kitchen from him and winter up there is cold, very cold."

SAMMY STAYED WITH me and I monitored his medication. He took three different jobs, one after the other, and quit or was fired. His co-workers harassed him and took his money; the managers abused him. Finally I took him to PAC's office and gave him some database job to keep him busy, but he couldn't sit still, worked for a few minutes, and rushed out to the streets and walked around for hours. One day in early March, he said he had a bad cold and couldn't go to work with me. I told him to stay home and rest; I'd cook some soup for him in the evening. When I went home after work with a bag of meat and carrots, he had gone. There was a note on the kitchen table. On the back of the now cracked and yellowish unicorn postcard (he had kept the card in his pocket all these years) he wrote:

"Dad, winter is coming and I need to go and find my friend Taza in Mt. Shasta. If I don't go, he won't survive. I'll miss you . . . and don't forget that I've always loved you (in my own weird way). Your son, S.C."

I kissed the card, put it in my chest pocket, and sat there, gazing at the hairy ends of the carrots. The sobs came like forceful waves and I let them come for half an hour. Then I blew my nose and picked up the phone. I called Janet and told her that Sam was on his way to Mt. Shasta and had stopped his medication and will definitely feel confused. Then without giving it much thought, I packed my stuff to go on my first trip to El Salvador. In those days human rights delegations traveled to San Salvador to observe the war. Our government was helping the El Salvador military and the "death squads" and different human rights delegations went there to take pictures, interview people, and prepare reports. They brought this material back and showed it to the congressmen and senators. Their slogan was: "The U.S. funding of the Salvadoran military has to stop." I knew that one such delegation was leaving soon—one of my journalist friends had asked me to join them but because of Sam, I had excused myself. Now I picked up the phone, called Jeff Brandon, and told him that I'd go with them.

You may tell me that I could have gone to Mt. Shasta, instead, to find Sammy. But would he have come back with me? He was not a child anymore and I could not chain him and put him in the car, unless I'd decided to commit him. But how could I? How much can a parent do, singlehandedly, for a mentally ill nineteen-year-old? Is a parent capable of doing everything?

I stayed for a month in San Jose de Las Flores, a ghost village destroyed by the military. I interviewed women and old men who had survived. With my teammates, a nun, a math professor, and Jeff Brandon, we stayed in an empty orphanage and slept on kiddy beds. There was a mountain right in front of our eyes and every day we climbed it by foot or on donkeys, taking slides and pictures of the burnt village. When I came back to Houston, there was a message from Janet that Sammy was fine and living with her again. He was taking "herbal medicine," she said; his system had to be "cleansed" of all the medication he had taken. I was relieved that Sammy was okay and figured that Janet's boyfriend had left and they were living together again, mother and son, in their strange codependent way. And I was not going to be worried about the next boyfriend and whatever would happen then. I'd think about it when it happened. But I also knew that when Janet said, "He's fine," it didn't mean that he was really fine, because the woman had never been fine herself. But I didn't think about this for too long, either. My life was very busy with PAC and I traveled frequently to El Salvador, and when in Houston, I showed the films and slides of the Salvadoran war in different public and private places. I made appointments with many authorities and gave public talks. This was my cause now, and I'd just begun to feel a bit better about myself.

I DIDN'T SEE Joanna again until the summer of 1990, when Roya mentioned her name as her supervisor in the Theater District. I went there one evening, more to be with Roya, but I can't deny that I was curious to see how Joanna was doing. I was surprised to see my redhead goddess so cheerful and fine. Her job as the coordinator of the "Downtown Project" was demanding and she seemed to be very excited about it. After our sad break, her affluent mother had treated her to a trip to

Europe and that tour had freshened her and taken care of the pain I'd caused her.

Ironically, that summer evening in the midst of jazz, soft breeze, the click of wine glasses, and the European ambience, which Joanna had created in the dead Houston downtown, I felt attracted to the small Persian woman, more than I wanted to admit. So I sat with her twelve-year-old daughter, Tala, and followed every single one of her delicate gestures when she ran up and down the steps of the Alley Theater, bent and unbent in her short black skirt, and waited on tables. I could tell that she had done many arabesques on the narrow surface of the balance beam in her past life and had flipped and somersaulted and pirouetted in competitions. But the most irresistible was not her small, muscled body, but her enormous black eyes, which met my one eye many times and made me feel hooked or nailed to where I was. I felt trapped when she looked at me and had a near suffocating sensation. I didn't want this to happen to me; this was like sliding down a long and slippery thing that would lead me to nothing or to everything. My heart raced. I was aroused, and I felt fearful like an adolescent. I think Joanna caught our glances and sensed my anxiety and, as happy as she was for me, a shadow ran over her face. Instantly, she pulled herself back from me.

So this way a period of hide-and-seek began that surprised and pained me at the same time. I was confused about my feelings and wasn't aware that I might be offending and hurting Roya by my sudden disappearances. More than once I kissed her and then took off, deciding to avoid her. Once—the night before I flew to El Salvador for the second time—she called me and in a sulky voice reminded me that I hadn't said good-bye. I thought that would be the end of it. I was a rough and rude man who had kissed a young woman passionately and then flown away without saying a word. But the next morning she showed up at the airport and when I saw her approaching, I began to slide down that slippery surface again. Forgetful of the time and place and the people around and her daughter, who stood there staring at us, I pressed her to my heart and took her breath out of her half-open mouth.

To forget her all together, I stayed longer in San Jose de Las Flores—from the end of July to the end of December—but every single night when I lay down in that orphanage, I saw her large, wet eyes and her small, muscled body pressed against mine in the airport. I'd never felt such a combination of sexual attraction and emotional closeness toward anyone. Lying in the dark in a dead child's bed, I tried to review the story of her life, the way she had told it to me in my office, and how I had listened with the cold detachment of a counselor. In my mind I imagined her in the prison, under the rough hands of the torturer, or sitting alone in her cell, counting the bullets that pierced her brother's chest. The strangest of all, something that had never happened to me and will never happen again, was the feeling that what she had gone through was one and the same as my own experience. When I saw her in her cell, I saw myself in the next cell, nailed to the cement floor, someone slapping my face. It might simply have been the intensity of emotion, the power of desire, and my immense solitude that made me feel one with her. Sister Ann-Mary, Dr. John Harris, and Jeff Brandon had all gone back to Houston in mid-December and I was still here in that deserted school-orphanage, resistant about returning for the Christmas break, trying to forget her, but daydreaming about her obsessively. What a name, I thought to myself, and repeated it in the dark: Roya, meaning "sweet dream," "Saraabi"—"belonging to a mirage." A sweet dream that belongs to a mirage! Was this where I'd ended up after a long and eventful life?

Steven and Maya's postcards came frequently and in the last one Steven mentioned Roya's upcoming presentation at the Christmas fund-raising party. "She is very nervous about it and makes us nervous, too," he wrote. "She has lived such an unbelievable life and still doesn't have self-confidence!" he added. "I feel so bad, Ric," Maya had written. "Roya doesn't come to see me anymore. I have burdened her with this damn fund-raising speech."

I read these lines over and over again and imagined Roya's predicament. Dealing with Tala's ongoing problems, her heavy doctoral courses at graduate school, her struggle with odd jobs and bills, and now this imposed presentation in a language she didn't feel confident about. I felt guilty for sitting on top of a hill looking at a green valley, listening to the murmurs of a spring while she went through hell in Houston. What kind of an asshole was I? So I packed to go and help her. That's what I told myself. But as the plane was landing in the foggy gloom of Houston night, all of a sudden I realized that there was nothing, absolutely nothing, awaiting me in this city except Roya. Nothing could make me happy except the hope of being with her. My friends' report about her had only been an excuse, something that I needed as a push to be able to end my conflict. Flying to Houston to be with her meant something more than just being helpful. But what did it mean? I was afraid to name it.

I pulled off my eye patch and put it in my pocket. Let her see my ugly eye, I told myself. Let's see how she will react. Then I stood leaning against the door, next to a young waiter, who was listening carefully to Roya's words with the tray frozen in his hands, devouring her. She read from her notes with a voice that was deep and distanced, as if rising from the top of a cold, remote mountain. She was detached from the story of her own life, reading a report, not exactly in a story-telling tone, but in the voice of someone who had been there, witnessed, but this wasn't her life she narrated. This alien-ation effect was one hundred times more powerful than an emotional speech, than looking into the eyes of the audience. I glanced at the old ladies, our guests, sitting motionless, mes-merized. I glanced at Steven and Maya and read their minds: "Yes! You made it! We got the money! We got all we want for the next year!" Almost at the end of her text, she raised her eyes and saw me; now she stuttered and lost her line. My heart raced. I mattered to her. As she found her line and read the rest, I traveled with the speed of light down that slippery slide to somewhere dark and warm and infinite. "Oh, man, oh, man, you're in love, you son of a bitch—" I told myself and rushed to the corridor to block her way and kiss her life out in front of the old ladies' eyes.

I stayed for thirteen days in her apartment and we cele-brated our first Christmas and New Year together. The very first time we made love (which wasn't the first night or even the first week), the dim light of a winter moon reflected on her skin and her body glowed like gold. She was timid and re-luctant and kept whispering that she hadn't done this for a long time and it might hurt. So I was very gentle with her, as if I had a sixteen-year-old virgin in my arms. After making a slow and quiet love with much suppressed passion, I ran my hand over her spine and traced the ligaments that were pulled when they had hanged her upside down in the prison cell. Then she sat in that semi-darkness next to me and ran her hand over my body until she reached my foot. There she stopped and played with the rough spot on my skin and examined it. She had seen it. She had noticed it even before we'd made love. After she reached for the other foot and found an identical mark, she sighed, lay down, and whispered into my ear, "Who has done this to you? Tell me."

I had to go back to El Salvador, though—my work was not completed. When we were about to part in the airport, I took Grandpa Cardinal's black opal ring off my finger and slid it on her thumb. "Keep this for me," I said, "until I come back."

I was stuck in San Salvador for almost a week, because there was a real war in the city and no airplane flew to San Jose de Las Flores. From my hotel room I heard the bullets and machine guns and the wailing of women over their men's bodies. When a bullet pierced the window of my room and hit the bathroom door, I sat on the bed and prayed to Death not to take me now and He had mercy on me. When I finally got to San Jose at the end of the week, Sister Ann-Mary greeted me at the door of the orphanage and handed me an envelope. There was a picture of us, Roya and me, smiling into Tala's plastic camera. On the back of the card she wrote a poem for me about letting her hair grow. I remember that every particle of my body danced with joy and the only human being in the vicinity of a mile was the old, shrunken Sister Ann-Mary.

So I hugged her and squeezed her skeletal body and said silly things that made her laugh. She laughed hard and loud and showed her long, yellow teeth and I hugged her again and told her that I was going to get married soon.

And this was January 1991.

My Third Encounter with Death

I've told this story so many times that I'm truly tired of it. But I guess I have to tell it one more time, in writing. Roya wants me to do this. She thinks I can write and so I should. It's me that Death visits and no one else; that's what I want to say.

Three times in my life, the Prince came to visit me and each time He taught me a lesson. The first time, I was a child. He cast his tall shadow on the wall to scare me and took my grandpa with him. The second time, I was young and reckless; I thought I could challenge the damn, crooked world and set it right. He appeared in disguise and nailed me to the floor to prove my weakness. The third time, He came to take me, but for some reason changed His mind and took someone else's life in front of my eyes. And when did this happen? The day that I was about to move my family to our first house.

This was December 1991. On November 1, Roya and I said our "yeses" and signed the paper in a lawyer's office and were officially husband and wife. We were packing to move to our new place. Tala was happy; but I guess her happiness was more due to Bobby's presence than anything else. Bobby had returned from Chicago and Tala was a child-woman who couldn't hide her love for the handsome boy.

282 • FARNOOSH MOSHIRI

But how can I tell this story without first talking about Madison Kirby?

On July 4, 1990, Madison took Bobby's gun and fled. He waited for the right moment to kill me or, to be precise, he waited five months. During this time he followed Roya and me, like a shadow, everywhere. He was scheming, trying to catch us together. Not that he wanted to kill us both. No, he wanted to kill me in front of her eyes, to torment her the rest of her life.

Madison didn't talk to me after he saw Roya and me together. So I had no idea that she was the same woman that he had told me about. How could I have known? I didn't know where Madison lived and Roya didn't mention his name when she came to my office. (Later, she told me that she had told Susan, our receptionist, that Madison had sent her.) Moreover, Roya had a daughter. In Madison's story of a Persian neighbor, there was no mention of a child. I remember very well that Madison described the woman as "not opinionated," while I had found Roya a woman with strong opinions. Anyway, this was a big misunderstanding on Madison's part, thinking that I had grabbed his girl and betrayed him. I wasn't a young man who fooled around anymore, and besides, I was preoccupied with my son's problems and my personal life was a big mess at that time. I didn't fall in love with Roya at first sight. It took me longer, much longer, to know that I had any feelings for her. I was overweight, chain-smoked, felt that I'd failed my son, and my political ideas had gone down the stinking drain of history. I had a gorgeous woman friend whom I didn't want to see anymore and preferred to share my bed with Willie the dog. Love and lust were the last things on my mind. All I wanted at that point of my life was to see Sammy well and settled. But this wasn't in the agenda—it was wishful thinking. Since age sixteen, Sammy had been slipping out of my hands and at nineteen he was gone.

Roya came to my office sometime in June or July of 1990. She sat on the other side of my desk and with her big dazzling eyes framed in thick eyelashes looked into my eyes. She wore no makeup but drew black pencil lines around her eyes to accentuate them. I thought she had cropped her hair on purpose to draw attention to her eyes. No, I didn't fall in love with her that day. I avoided her eyes to not fall into something bottomless and dark. I thought about her voice, though, after she left. It was a voice I hadn't heard anywhere. You know that I'm sensitive toward women's voices. I get irritated when they're loud. High-pitched voices, cheerleader-type voices annoy me. I like soft-spoken women and that day, after Roya left, her voice reverberated in my head and crept into my brain cells. It became part of my unconscious, as if it had been there forever, as if it was the voice of someone I'd known from the remote past. And her accent was of course different—foreign. She was definitely interesting, very sexy in a unique way—in a way that many men do not appreciate. But, as I said before, I avoided women. I wasn't in the mood, so to speak.

And her story—though it was sad—didn't shock me or make me cry. I'd had Iranian clients with such stories, and before them I'd had many Vietnamese and Cambodians, Chileans and Salvadorans with horror stories. Part of my job was listening to the refugees' tales. I knew what they had gone through—families lost, executed, houses bombed, burned, prison, torture. I'd heard stories about swimming across rivers, crossing minefields and mountains. Being alive was a miracle for these people, but this new life was not an easy one, either. America was no Utopia. Some of them could not speak English, could not say who they really were, who they had been. Some survived all that misery, made it to America, and got lost here.

I guess what I'm trying to say is this: I didn't betray my old client and friend; Madison had gone out of his mind. The disease had eaten up his brain. If on the Fourth of July—when he saw me with Roya for the first time—he had pulled me aside and told me in plain and simple English, "Hey Ric, this woman is the same person I told you about—" then I would have left and never seen Roya again (although I knew she was not interested in anyone but me). But still, I would have acted like a gentleman; I'd have withdrawn.

But he didn't say anything. He drew the conclusion that he wanted to draw, took the gun, and left to join the homeless. Roya and I gradually became closer and finally less than a year later we were a family and decided to remain one. We found and leased a little bungalow on Heights Boulevard with a backyard for Willie. Tala's moods improved and she looked forward to being in the new house, where she could have her own room.

Now let me tell you about Bobby Palomo. He came back from Chicago in October, one month before our wedding. He felt embarrassed about what he'd done, but Roya and Tala were so happy to see him that soon he felt like part of the family and spent most of his time with us. When we married in the shabby office of my friend, an old civil rights attorney,

Bobby was among our close friends—Roya's German friend, Marlina Haas, and, of course, Steven and Maya.

Was Bobby a happy person now? It's hard to say. He was relieved to be back and to be accepted into the family, but I don't think he was deeply happy. He had been badly scarred as a child. He needed therapy, time, and a lot of attention. One day, when we had all gone to a picnic in Memorial Park, he told me about his father's disappearance in the most matter-of-fact way. "You know, Ric? My dad left me one night when I was a kid, and never came back." I asked him if he wanted to talk to me some more, in my office. He didn't say yes, but after a week, he showed up and asked me to listen to his story.

We talked once a week and I was glad to help him. I liked this boy. He had qualities that I'd seldom found in young men (including my own son). He was kind, caring, and sensitive—more sensitive than many girls I'd known as a counselor. The shooting incident had shamed him and he wanted to talk about it. But the root of all his problems and his huge identity crisis lay elsewhere. He was eleven or twelve when his father left. His parents were separated. He stayed with his dad every weekend. One Saturday night his dad took him out to dinner. Back home afterwards, Bobby was playing a video game in his room and his dad was on the phone with someone. Bobby heard his father slam down the phone and bang the door. Then he heard the car speeding away. He thought his father would come back. But he didn't. His dad left without saying anything to him, without a good-bye. Bobby sat alone, for a long time. Scared. Way after midnight, he picked up the phone and called his mother.

In one of our visits he told me that while staying at his mom's in Chicago the previous summer, he discovered the reason for his emotional problems. Bobby was close to home, but still not hitting. I have eight tapes of our conversations; this is part of the last one.

"TELL ME."

"I was born and raised in Chicago, you know? But my dad moved us to Houston when I was in fifth grade. He wanted to open a restaurant with his friends, but before they opened it, he took off and didn't tell anyone where he went. At that time, we had everything—two houses, three cars, and God knows how many bank accounts. But I guess he was in debt and my mom and I didn't know anything. Maybe this was why my mom lived separately. He'd become rough with her. So I lived with my mom and visited my dad on the weekends. I looked forward to the weekends, because my dad took me to fun places and bought me toys and clothing.

"After he left that night, life became very hard for my mom. She had to move out of that house and rent a stinky garage apartment from Mr. Thompson. She had never worked before. Now she had to wait on tables in a cafeteria and I was in school and couldn't help much. The creditors took everything we had. All that remained was a bunch of junk. Useless objects in a red tin box."

"What happened that your mother left Houston?"

"She was lucky, I guess. She was saved. This guy, an old high school sweetheart or something, saw her in that cafeteria where she was working and they started to see each other. He proposed to her—like in the movies, you know? So she left. I don't blame her."

"You didn't want to go with her?"

"She asked me to go with her. But I didn't feel that she really wanted me. It didn't look good—to get married and having a big son. I had started to shave my face. I was taller than her."

"Did you go to visit your mother?"

"Only once. She had a little girl. Funny. I have a kid sister. She could be my own daughter. The whole thing was weird. It was not the life I knew. I came back and waited on tables and never graduated from high school. These people at La Dolce Vita knew my dad and gave me a job. Maybe they felt sorry for me."

"Did you feel lonely?"

"There were so many things wrong with my life that being lonely was the last on the list. Ric, why did I want Tala to kill me?"

"You were suicidal."

"I didn't know."

"Some people don't know."

"And how could I do this to Tala?"

"You were afraid to do it yourself."

"Do you know I've never had a girlfriend? The boys at the restaurant made fun of me. They thought I was gay."

"And this made you angry?"

"This made me think about it. What if I was? Who knew? But this wasn't the whole thing. I had my dad's stuff in my room. I don't know why my mom left this stuff for me. It was a mistake. His silk ties and suits were hanging in my closet and these little knickknacks he'd given me when I was a kid—all in this red tin box. I wanted to get rid of them. I wanted to give them to Tala. And the ties—I was trying to give them away to people. I gave one to Madison once."

"Why did you want to get rid of your father's things?"

"I didn't want to remember him. I'd remembered him enough."

"And now—how do you feel now, after visiting your mom? Did you have a good talk with her?"

"I'm not sure. I wanted to tell her what happened here. I mean the shooting. But I didn't say anything. She was so happy—you know what I mean? I didn't want to ruin it."

"Did she say anything to you?"

"She cried and said that she was proud of me for making a living for myself. Then she told me to go to college. She said she'd help me with tuition."

"Do you want to do this?"

"I guess."

"What are you interested in?"

"I'm not sure. Anything that doesn't have to do with restaurants. You know? That's a lousy business."

"After a year or two in college, you'll find out what you're interested in."

"You know, Ric? I never had a chance to grow up. I was playing a video game when my dad left. I guess I've stayed in one of those dark tunnels that Luigi and Mario were trapped in. I stopped growing up. When I was playing guns with Tala, I was really playing. It was a game for me, but at the same time a depressed man inside of me was scheming at something else. This surprises me."

"It's good that you're thinking back, trying to figure things out."

"Ric, you guys mean a lot to me. You're my family."

THIS WAS IN October 1991. Bobby applied for college and everything was set for the spring semester. He even reserved a dormitory room on the campus. Between October and December when we were planning to move, he spent most of his time with us. He gave us a hand with everything. I had to clean up my messy house and return it. Bobby helped me. We had to paint the bungalow we'd leased (the landlord wouldn't do it); he helped us. When Bobby was around, Tala was talkative and cheerful. With Tala, Bobby was a kid again. They told jokes, chased each other, and laughed at everything and everyone. I enjoyed looking at them. They were my adopted kids.

On the twenty-third of December, all the boxes were packed and scattered around Roya's garage apartment; Bobby and Tala were taping them. Around five, Roya said that she had to go for an hour or so to this exhibition at the Menil Collection—a small museum not far away. Her friend had died a few weeks earlier and now her painting was in this AIDS show. She said she had to see Marlina's painting for the last time, before they auctioned it. It was important to her. She wanted to go alone, but I told her I'd go with her. I thought she might become upset, cry or something, and I wanted to be with her. It's funny, I was superstitious that day. I didn't want anything to go wrong when we were moving to our first house. And Roya had been a bit moody for a couple of weeks—not only had her friend Marlina died, but her dead friends' corpses had been violated in Afghanistan. She had heard that the Islamic regime in Kabul had bulldozed the graveyard, taken the bones of the dead out, and powdered them with quicklime. Remembering her friend Pari and that old professor, she cried in bed every night and I held her tight until she could sleep. And the moving troubled her. Now she doubted everything. She woke me in the middle of the night, frightened.

"Ric, tell me you're one hundred percent sure that we'll remain married forever."

"Baby, I have no doubt about it. No doubt."

"I don't mean that you would leave me. What if I would go crazy and leave you?"

"You'll never leave me, baby, never. I've no doubt about it."

"I like the way you say, 'I have no doubt about it.' Say it again."

"I have no doubt about it." I repeated again and again, sleepily.

So I didn't want her to go to this AIDS show alone. I let the kids keep taping the boxes and told her that we'd go together and on the way back, we'd get some pizza. We had called the movers for the early morning because I didn't like the idea of moving in the dark. Willie was already in his new doghouse in the yard of the bungalow in the Heights, waiting for us.

I SAW HIM sitting on a bench in front of the museum, but Roya didn't see him. There was a small crowd behind the door, waiting to get in. The bench was blocked by people and Roya, being tiny, couldn't see anything. I saw him but, of course, didn't recognize him. It was as if you see someone

you'd known once, in a different life, and you don't even remember where and when. I glanced at his thin, yellow face
and realized that I'd known this person before. He had on a
dirty knit hat and the light in his gray eyes was dying. His suit,
or what was once a suit and now a wrinkled, beaten rag, hung
on him and was torn here and there. He had something like a
blanket covering his legs. They opened the glass door and the
people in front of us entered. When Roya went inside, he
pulled my sleeve and separated me from her. He kept pulling
my sleeve. Roya was already in. I stepped out of the line to see
what this man was saying.

"Don't recognize me, huh?"

I looked at him.

"It's not such an awful long time, Saint Cardinal."

When he said "Saint Cardinal" my heart sank. This was
Madison Kirby.

"It rings a bell, huh?"

"Madison!"

"The mad, mad Madison—" he said in a wheezy voice and
laughed a loud, phlegmy laugh. People turned to look at us.
He had no teeth, except one or two in front. "Just stopped you
to say something. What you're gonna see inside has something
to do with me. Hear me? Look at the huge panel carefully—
I'm in there."

Then he let go of my sleeve and I didn't know what to say
and what to do, so I just went inside. I wanted to find Roya. I
had an uneasy feeling, the feeling that something was going to
go wrong.

Roya was standing in front of her friend's panel, gazing. I
stood next to her and held her arm. She was quiet, thinking.

I'm not an art person. Art is my weakness (or maybe I resist it because of Jenny and our pathetic relationship). Anyway, for whatever reason, when it comes to visual arts, I'm blind. What other people find interesting and admire in a modern painting remains blank to me. I have no eye for colors and combinations and sometimes I think maybe having only one eye has something to do with it. Anyway, I stood there, holding my wife's arm, watching what she was gazing at. To me, this was something a child could do—dark gray water, a ship, badly drawn, and disproportionate figures, as if the painter didn't know how to draw a human body. Some of these little people were drowning in the black water, some were in the sky, sitting on a piece of cloud. This tall, skeletal woman with a black hood stood, or rather hovered, above the ship's deck, like death personified. The title of the painting was *The Ship of Death,* signed, "Marlina Haas, 1990."

I couldn't figure why Madison had said I'd find him in this panel. Where? In the murky water? Or on the fluffy cloud?

I wanted to get out of this place. It was getting dark outside and I wanted to take Roya away from this gloom. But she was inside the panel, with her dead German friend.

Finally we left and although I took Roya from a different door, I saw Madison again. He didn't approach anymore. He was pulling someone's sleeve, saying, "Look at *The Ship of Death*. You'll find me there." I pulled Roya toward our car and in the last minute before I opened the door, Madison raised his hand and waved. He had been watching us.

We bought some pizza and went home. The kids had taped all the boxes and with black markers had written numbers on them.

"How am I supposed to know what is in box five?" I was teasing them.

"We have a list here," Tala said. "Five means clothing."

"What if you lose the list?" I kept joking to draw Roya into conversation. She hadn't spoken one word since we'd left the museum. Had she seen Madison? Or was she on the deck of that damned ship?

"I packed Mr. Thompson's lamp by mistake, then I had to open the box and take it out." Bobby said.

"That lamp is a priceless antique. I'm glad you didn't steal it from the old man. We'd be in trouble," I said.

"By the way, Mrs. Thompson sent us some sandwiches," Tala said.

"So let's eat. Who prefers Mrs. Thompson's peanut butter sandwich to seven-topping special pizza with thick crust?" I managed to make Roya smile.

There was no place to sit. So we sat on the boxes and attacked the pizza. We kept the peanut butter sandwiches for breakfast.

"This place looks so gloomy." This was the first thing Roya had said since we'd come home.

"Why gloomy, dear?" I asked.

"I was just remembering the day that Tala and I moved in. It was May. Hot. The first thing I noticed was this huge gorilla on top of the tower. It reminded me of the King Kong movie."

"I saw you with that lady, your cousin's secretary," Bobby said. "I said Oh, God have mercy on me—an old lady and her daughters are gonna be my neighbors. I thought you and Tala were sisters."

"I saw you taking your bike downstairs that first night and I told my mom, 'Our neighbor is crazy, he's biking at night!' "

The three of them laughed, but there was a shadow on their faces. They were reminiscing about darker days.

"One day they brought Madison Kirby home in an ambulance, remember?" Bobby asked Roya.

Roya nodded.

"That apartment is doomed," Tala said. "After you left?" she told Bobby, "This guy—? Mom, what was his name?"

"Clifford."

"Oh, yeah, he moved in and he was epileptic. Once in a while he called 911 and rushed down and stood in the parking lot waiting for the ambulance."

"No kidding!" Bobby said.

"And you know what?" Tala was excited; she talked fast as if someone was chasing her. She had recently acquired this teenage girls' accent—putting a question mark at the end of each sentence. I looked at her and couldn't believe how she had grown tall in the past year. She looked like a sixteen-year-old and wore a bra. She was only an oversized child of thirteen and I had to raise her.

"What happened to him?" Bobby asked, concerned.

"One day he called 911 and rushed down, but the ambulance was late. He fell and had a seizure. My mom and I ran down to help him."

"You never told me this." I held Roya's cold hand and squeezed it. "Why?"

"You were in El Salvador, remember?" she looked up at me and smiled. She was still sitting on a box. Her hair was long now, sweeping the tip of her shoulders. When she turned her head to me, her hair gave out a faint scent of rose water and each time this happened I felt an uneasy feeling in my pants. My wife's scented hair gave me an erection.

"We rushed down," she said, "but I couldn't do much. I looked for something to put between his teeth like I'd seen on TV. Couldn't find anything. Tala took her slipper out and we put it in his mouth. We were afraid he'd bite his tongue. Then, Tala and I sat next to him until the ambulance came. Tala was, of course, crying."

"Mom, the man was jerking and shaking like a giant fish, with my plastic slipper in his mouth. I'd never seen such a sight."

"Where is he now?" Bobby asked gloomily.

"He moved out a few weeks ago. An old couple, his parents I guess, came and packed his things. I don't know why they'd let him live alone in the first place," Roya said.

"The doomed apartment is empty now," Tala said.

There was silence for a few seconds; each of us had flown somewhere. I was wondering why on earth we were talking about the epileptic guy now. This wasn't a good subject for conversation.

"Okay, back to work!" Bobby said and went to the kitchen. "Roya, do you need this big jar of beans on top of the refrigerator?" I heard him saying this from the kitchen, not knowing that this was the last thing I'd ever hear from Bobby Palomo.

Before Roya could respond, a bullet hit the window, glass blasted, and shards spread around.

"Lie down!" I shouted, knowing that someone was shooting at us. "Lie down!" I screamed and dropped myself on my wife, who was standing right in the frame of the window. Another bullet hit the window, and then another and another. I lost count. Tala screamed and from where I was—on top of Roya, pressing her hard against the floor so that she wouldn't bounce up—I saw Bobby come out of the kitchen to approach Tala. I was thinking maybe he'd left the kitchen (which was a safer place) and walked through the shower of bullets because he assumed that Tala was injured, or he thought that the shooting had ended. I yelled at him: "Go back to the kitchen!" But he was already moving toward Tala and the next bullet went through the top part of the windowpane and hit him. The bullet hit the boy right in the middle of his forehead, between his eyebrows. There was one last bullet that hit the glass jar of beans in his hands. And we had a firework of red beans and glass and blood and Tala's hysterical screams and animal sounds, crying and hollering and dropping herself on Bobby's body and shaking him, shaking him hard and calling his name. She was saying words that I couldn't understand, words in her mother tongue—powerful and horrible and ancient-sounding—as if this little girl's mouth was freeing all the pain and agony of humankind from the beginning of man's sad history until this very moment: December 23, 1991, Houston, Texas, America, 7:05 in the evening.

SO THE DARK shadow of death visited us and has vanished for, who knows, thirty or forty years, when we'll all be old and have to go. But the Prince did what He could to show me there isn't much that I, or anyone, can do when it's time to leave. The kid wanted to die in the summer of 1990, planned for it, trained his little friend to pull the trigger, but it didn't work. He stayed alive and lived a little longer, tried to find himself and set some goals for his future. Now he wanted to figure out his problems and sought help from me, but his life was cut short by a madman, who had meant to kill me but had made a mistake. Bobby was the son I wanted to have and the brother Roya had lost. He was little Tala's first friend in America and the first man she had loved.

I tell Roya Death came to visit me and no one else. She says this is all fiction and I have a good gift for it. She says I'm mythologizing death, whatever—personifying it, the way Marlina did in *The Ship of Death*—and she uses a few big words that she has learned in her Ph.D. seminars which she is using for her dissertation. She says it was Madison Kirby, not Mr. Death, who visited us. Madison, she says, wanted to kill her, because she had rejected him. I tell her Madison wanted to kill me, not her. It was I who betrayed him (he thought, in his sick mind). And Madison was not Madison anymore, was he? He was Death himself. How could that figure in front of the museum have been the Madison Kirby I'd known for years? The washed and starched man who quoted Shakespeare and babbled German philosophy? I tell Roya, "Don't be so literal-minded, use your imagination. You've gone far into the shadows of death, more than once in your life. Do you see what I'm saying?" She smiles and shakes her head. "Do you want to finish that memoir of yours?" She nods. "Then use your imagination. Who is interested in what really happened?"

♦ ♦ ♦

Evening slowly changes colors. An opaque haze veils the row of distant oaks. The Transco Tower waves like a pillar of quicksilver behind the smoke, as if painted by the deliberate hasty strokes of an impressionist. A restaurant in the shape of a boat—a semi–fast food place by the name of Captain Benny's—harbors at the rushing sea of Highway 610. He climbs the roof of the boat from a ladder and spreads his threadbare blanket on the dust. He lies on his side, fetus-like, the palm of his right hand under his cheek, the left hand pressing the hot gun in his trouser pocket. He has chills; his teeth clatter. The December air is cool and penetrates through every pore of his clothes. He pulls the collar of his old jacket up to cover his neck. Now a gust of wind blows the smoke of burnt meat onto his face. He remembers he hasn't eaten anything for a long time. He shivers.

From where he is lying, enveloped in smoke, he looks at the silver tower behind the net of haze. The gorilla is gone. He thinks that they have taken the air out of the beast and his reign is over. Now they are blowing up another helium animal. He smiles when light in certain rooms of the tower form a Christmas tree. Then all of a sudden he murmurs, "Oh, Lord, oh, Lord, I killed someone. I

just killed someone. Grant me my death now before they come."
He prays and pleads for a sudden death, but death does not come.
He hears sirens, alarming sounds, and murmurs around the food
boat. But they pass by him and silence falls. The tower sways and
blends with the evening light, then sinks into dusk. He remains
curled—a baby in a cradle on top of a fake boat. Something ticks
in his chest pocket with the rhythm of his heart. He knows that he
is still alive and bursts into sobs.

"Father, help me. Father, help!"

◆ ◆ ◆

On her fourteenth birthday she tattoos a revolver on her belly. When she gains weight, which most of the time she does, the gun stretches and becomes larger, almost the size of a real gun. She stands in front of the mirror, naked, and observes. She smiles with satisfaction.

When she is fifteen, she close-crops her hair and colors it purple. She pierces each ear five times, each nostril twice, two piercings on each corner of the lower lip. She plants one gold bead on the tip of her tongue, pierces her belly button too, although she is too big to be able to wear a short blouse and show off the gold ring. Her name is Tala Saraabi, but she insists on being called T.S. "Call me T.S.," she says to Mr. Hamilton, her teacher at Dawn.

Dawn is a small school in a building that used to be a house. The narrow courtyard faces a quiet boulevard on which the students of St. Thomas University occasionally walk. Dawn doesn't have a cafeteria, a gym, or a lab. There is a netless basketball hoop, but no one ever plays. There are only a few teachers at Dawn. Dr. Catherine Middleton, a psychiatrist, is the principal and two psychiatric nurses and three volunteers work with her. Occasionally, Dr. Middleton hires an art teacher or a creative writing instructor for extracurricular activities.

The junior class is small—six boys and girls sit around an old wooden table; Mr. Hamilton sits with them. If the kids leave the table and sit on the couch in the rest area and do nothing, it's okay. If they play with the computers, leaf through National Geographic, *or draw something at the art table, it's okay. There is no pressure, no restriction. This is a special school—its name is Dawn, indicating hope. Dr. Middleton and her staff and the children's parents—who pay a good sum of money for the tuition—hope that this small, friendly environment will help. It helps sometimes and it doesn't help many times.*

Today a young woman, a graduate student in creative writing, a would-be novelist, begins a writing assignment for Mr. Hamilton's class. "I remember—" she writes on the board. "What do you remember?" she asks. "Begin with this phrase and go on. When you're through with one memory, start a new paragraph and remember something else."

The class begins, except for Sarah, a pale small girl with long, brown hair. Sarah stares at the paper, motionless. When Mr. Hamilton whispers something in her ear she begins. But it takes her the whole class time to write a line.

T.S. curls her thick arms around the paper and makes a wall to protect her words. She writes fast, hoping this wall will keep the memories from flying away. She remembers a dark night, three women and a child walking in a desert. Turbaned men with guns rode on horses. The men hadn't told them that the dark earth on which they stepped was a minefield. The women and the child were escaping. Her mother whispered into her ear, "We have to be silent—" and sealed her lips with a kiss.

T.S. remembers living in a vacant school, where on her body sores as large and watery as the wounds of lepers grew. She remembers the smell of dust and excrement rising from a ditch; sun pouring fire on the earth at noon. The constant buzz of flies still reverberates in her head. This town was ruined by the war and it was called Nimrooz—Midday.

Now she remembers a city in the shape of a bowl, surrounded by a dark range of mountains. She was trapped in the bottom of this bowl and missiles and bombs fell on houses and people. She ran to the window and screamed, "Fireworks!" and laughed crazily. The lights were out. At night, the lights were always out.

She remembers an open grave—a woman who used to tell her stories lay in the cold, dark earth. It was raining, but they stayed motionless at the graveside and looked. She remembers that she counted the shovels of dirt covering her aunt. Now she has forgotten how many there were or what her aunt's name was.

She writes about a small, hot room with people crowding it, crawling in it. She had a corner for herself where she slept on a mattress against the wall. She hated this room and longed for school, which was in the open under tall almond trees. When the teacher in her rainbow-colored sari recited a poem she raised her head and looked at the sky and the tangled branches of the trees among which monkeys sat. If the monkeys were in a playful mood they dropped nuts on children's heads and disturbed the class. The teacher waved a long broom to chase them away, but they laughed, made happy noises, and showed their big yellow teeth. They invited the children to play. But this life ended too and she had to move on.

In this new place, she learned the shooting game. She was almost twelve and had a grown-up friend—a twenty-year-old young man. She calls him B.P. now, as if his name is a secret she cannot reveal. B.P. had a red tin box full of magical objects—a set of binoculars that brought the remotest people close to them, five large marbles filled with ocean water, crystals that created seven different rainbows on the wall, and a gun. They lay on their bellies on the cool, wooden floor and opened the box. They looked into the binoculars and brought the old head of Mr. Whitefield, the retired postman, close to them. He typed another letter to a sweepstakes company to win something—a plastic cup, a pen. He plucked a nose hair, looked at it, dropped it, and typed again. T.S. and B.P. laughed and now held a blue marble in front of the light and looked inside. Little papery particles, tiny fish-shaped things, floated in the water. B.P. said that this was ocean water and these blue things were alive. Oh, how badly T.S. wanted the marbles, but B.P. said, not now. One day these will all be hers, he said. After she learned her shooting lessons.

So he taught her to hold the revolver. He taught her to shoot.

The gun was always empty and when she pulled the trigger she heard a dry click. B.P. kept promising her the marbles and, later, the whole red tin box, containing all the magical objects, even the binoculars. They played with the empty gun many times until on a Fourth of July when there were loud explosions outside, he took her to his apartment to play the real game. She didn't understand what he meant by "real," but she was excited. They played and when she shot the first bullet, the revolver clicked. When she shot the second time, it clicked again, the third time the same. Now B.P. said, Aim at me! She aimed at him and shot—a dry click. B.P. said, Here! Aim at my head. She shot and a real bullet hit him. B.P. fell and a stream of blood ran under his head. But he didn't die that day. After months of practicing, T.S. had missed the target.

Four boys and girls are done with their stories or have left them unfinished. They are in the rest area, at the computers, at the art table, or just sitting and doing nothing. Mr. Hamilton moves to the rest area to watch them. A few days ago, Joey attacked Travis with a sharp pencil. Sarah and T.S. have remained at the table. Sarah writes one word and stops for ten minutes, then another word. She is not done with the first line, yet.

The writing teacher, this young woman with a long black skirt and honey-colored hair down to her waist, paces up and down, and sometimes glances over T.S.'s protecting arms. But T.S. doesn't want to stop. Her hand hurts from gripping the pen tightly; there is more to remember.

She remembers the evening of moving. There were boxes all around; they would soon be in a new house. Her mother and stepfather and B.P. and T.S. were having pizza. Yes, B.P. was back from his exile and was now part of the family and the shooting incident was forgotten. He was planning to go to college and she was already in the first year of junior high school. They were happy to be together and sat on the boxes, eating. Now suddenly someone began to shoot from the opposite apartment, from where once Mr. Kirby and then Clifford, the epileptic man, lived. Bullets kept piercing the window. T.S., her mother, and her stepfather were all on the floor, but B.P. was in the kitchen doing something. She remembers that she screamed. She remembers that her stepfather, who was covering her mom's body, shouted at B.P. not to come out. But B.P. left the kitchen as if nothing was happening. Was he coming toward her because she was screaming like crazy? Did he think that she was wounded and wanted to help? But then why was he not bending to protect himself? Why was he walking so upright, as if no one was shooting?

So this way, a bullet hit B.P. between his eyes and now all she remembers is glass shards and blood and red beans—God only knows where they had come from. She cannot remember B.P.'s face. It was covered with thick blood and she cannot remember anything after that, either.

Oftentimes in the dark night, under her blanket, after touching the blue revolver on her belly, she asks herself, what if she had not

screamed her lungs out, what if she had sealed her lips and re-
mained silent like on that dark night when they fled their country?
Would B.P. walk out of the kitchen? Would he get shot? Some-
times she feels as if she's choking on hard tears, tears that have
turned into stone in her throat. These are times when she confuses
the incidents; she thinks that it all happened on that Fourth of July.
She thinks that it was she, T.S., who killed her friend.

She can never remember how and when they moved to their
new house and how and when they changed her school from the
regular, crowded junior high to this school, to Dawn. She remem-
bers the past three years at Dawn. She remembers her sessions with
Dr. Middleton. She remembers her mom and stepdad and B.P.,
who is dead now, but she cannot remember anything else clearly.
Even the minefield and the bowl city and the grave just came out
today, because of this writing. Otherwise, they are always buried
in her head or somewhere deep and dark inside her body.

The young writer takes T.S.'s story out in the shady yard of Dawn,
sits on a bench, and reads it slowly. Now she lingers on the last
lines:

" . . . I remember when I was a weightless embryo floating
freely inside my mother; this was when I heard the bullets for the
first time. The father I would never see rolled in blood. Then I was
born and soon turned into a tree. I'm a tree now, growing thick
roots that force themselves out of me to pierce the hard earth. They

pull me down toward the dark depths of the ground, where I'll land one day. I'm as heavy as an old oak. I long for the day that I can float again like those blue, weightless particles in B.P.'s ocean water marbles. Float and float freely. Life feels so heavy on me."

What if all this happened? the young writer thinks. But then again, she knows that children have rich imaginations; they weave strange fantasies. This tall, heavy-set teenager with purple hair and many rings on her body is a natural writer, she thinks.

Could I ever make up such stories? The young writer sighs and steps out of Dawn's courtyard.

A PENGUIN READERS GUIDE TO

AGAINST GRAVITY

Farnoosh Moshiri

An Introduction to
Against Gravity

It is a few years after the Iranian revolution, a period of violent upheaval, the emergence of radical Islam, the onslaught of the AIDS epidemic, and bloody covert wars in Nicaragua and El Salvador. The lives of three remarkable people, each of whom is deeply caught in this historical moment, cross paths in *Against Gravity* and reveal the many ways history can shape us, destroy us, or prepare us for happiness.

Divided into three sections narrated by the three main characters, *Against Gravity* tells the intertwining stories of Madison, a young man who, after his father's sudden death, spirals downward into a life of aimless wandering, drug addiction, madness, and AIDS; Roya, an Iranian woman forced into exile after the revolution of 1979 whose husband has been killed in the Iran–Iraq war and who herself was imprisoned and tortured; and Ric, a social worker and former Marxist activist who devotes himself to helping others while his own family life falls apart.

These characters look back over the course of their lives to try to understand how they have come to be where they are and how they have come to know—and to love and hate—each other. Madison is in the advanced stages of AIDS when Roya moves in next door. He feverishly imagines her becoming his lover, who will nurse him through his final illness. But when Roya rejects his clumsy marriage proposal and offer to pay for graduate school, he vows to kill her. Having escaped prison and endured life as a refugee, Roya is hardly ready to care for a dying stranger. She is struggling to survive in America where, despite being highly educated and cultured, she must work menial jobs to pay her rent and care for her troubled daughter. She puts her plans for graduate study and a memoir of her time in prison and exile on hold. But when she falls in love with Ric Cardinal, the counselor Madison had recommended for her daughter, her life takes on a new focus and direction. The only problem is that Madison now has even more reason to want to kill her, or Ric, or perhaps both of them.

But *Against Gravity* is far more than a novel about a troubled love triangle and the pain that can lead to murder or suicide. It is a novel that brilliantly embodies the ways in which large historical forces play out in the personal lives of individuals. It maps the hidden territory where world history and personal history intersect. And in the end it shows us just how inseparable—and sometimes insurmountable—these two forces are.

A Conversation with
Farnoosh Moshiri

1. What inspired you to write about this particular group of characters, each of them deeply wounded in one way or another?

My own life and the life of the people I've known. Like any writer I imagined a hypothetical situation: What if these three people met? How would they affect each other's lives? Would these wounds heal or reopen? Would any kind of disaster happen?

2. Why did you decide to use three narrators to tell the story of Against Gravity?

Because their voices invaded me. I developed each character clearly in my mind and each had a distinct voice. They'd speak their words in my head as I drove to work. I'd write what they said on pieces of paper or record it while driving. This novel didn't want to be written in third-person narrative. It wouldn't work that way.

3. Why did you choose the quotes from Rumi, Whitman, and Rilke as the epigraph for Against Gravity? Why is Roya so drawn to Rumi and Whitman?

Rumi is, of course, an important part of my culture. I grew up hearing the verses everywhere. My father would recite for us; my uncle, who was a poet, would read Rumi in family gatherings. These are not easy verses; they have deep philosophical meaning.

But as a child I'd enjoy the language and the rhythm (which, of course, are lost in translation), until later that I grasped the meaning.

I became familiar with Walt Whitman when I was a graduate student. I became fascinated with this man as a human being and as a poet. I found amazing similarities between his poems (the philosophy—his Transcendentalism) and Rumi's Sufism. As you can see, the lines that I've chosen from both poets could be arranged in one single poem. The two poets become one. And why did I choose them as epigraph? They speak of freedom and lightness, of breaking down the doors and crossing boundaries, which the survivors of my novel do.

Rilke speaks of the heaviness of life. I have an immense love for Rilke's poetry and I think this short line contradicts the whole theory of lightness that the two older poets suggest. But Rilke is right too. Isn't life the heaviest thing?

4. *To what extent is Roya's story your own story?*

Roya has borrowed some of my life story and the locations I've lived in, but as a character she has a different psychology. When I experienced exile and lived in refugee camps, I was already a published writer and much older than Roya. I didn't have Roya's insecurities about writing. I'd been a feminist and a political activist in Iran and my views of the world were clear. Roya was never involved in politics but she had been jailed and tortured. I was involved but I had been able to escape. So Roya is not even my alter-ego, she is my creation, as Ric and Madison are. I've lent some of my life experiences to the male characters too. For example, I taught for eight years at a juvenile detention facility; Ric borrows this from me.

5. How does being an Iranian woman in America at this particular historical moment affect your writing and your view of the world?

It makes me bitter and cynical (more than I've ever been in my life). It definitely affects my writing. I keep writing about negative aspects of immigration, about displacement, uprootedness, the unhealable wound of exile. If I had remained in Iran (if I survived) I would've been a different writer; I would've written about different subjects.

My essential view of the world was shaped when I was very young. I grew up in a family of secular humanist intellectuals with a strong sense of social justice. These fundamental qualities drove me to political activity in my younger years and changed my life. If I had to live my life again, I'd pursue the same goals. I'd struggle for freedom and justice, even if that would bring about enormous pain.

Here, at this particular moment in America, what I feel is despair. Why is the ancient civilization of the Middle East (that has been the source of so much of the cultural and scientific achievements of the West) under such brutal attack? Who has created (or awoken) the ghoul of religious fundamentalism? Who has announced a "crusade" that could very well lead to the destruction of the world? I know the answers. And knowing them makes me despair.

6. How do you feel about the history of American involvement in Iran and the current situation there and in the Middle East generally?

The history of American involvement in Iran goes back to the CIA-directed coup d'etat of 1953 (under the code name of TP-AJAX—which became the blueprint for a succession of CIA plots to destabilize governments during the Cold War), the arrest of the elected Prime Minister Mossadeq (who wanted to nationalize Iran's oil), and restoration of the Shah's regime. I urge Americans to read the history of other countries (at least those under U.S. attack). By watching the selected daily news clips on TV, we only see distorted images that do not convey anything but pathological anger toward the West. Why did the Iranian Revolution happen? What if Prime Minister Mossadeq had not been removed by America and Iran had become a secular democracy in the 1950s? Would Ayatollah Khomeini have had a chance to take power? Why did the Shah exile Khomeini and anger him and his followers? Where is the source of all this?

My analysis of other American involvement in the Middle East is similar to my analysis of Iran's recent history. These are the questions that I ask: Who empowered Saddam? Who empowered Bin Ladin? Who financed, trained, and armed the Taliban fighters in Pakistan? Why did the September 11 incident happen? Would it still have happened if the Islamic fundamentalist ideology of the Bin Ladin type had not been encouraged by the United States in the 1980s?

7. How do your ideas for novels and stories come to you? Do you start with the characters and see where they take you, or do you have a fairly clear picture of the trajectory of the story when you begin?

I'm usually haunted by characters and they take me through the plot. But I never begin writing before I have a clear image of the whole universe of the novel. I must know the main map, the major incidents, and even the ending (although it may change later) to be able to begin. If I begin prematurely, the project might fail.

8. In your acknowledgments you thank your original publisher at Black Heron Press for supporting you when not many publishers were interested in serious literature from Iran. Why do you think you encountered this resistance or lack of interest in the United States?

In the mid-nineties, when I began marketing my first novel, *At the Wall of the Almighty*, the book market was not interested in literature from the Middle East. I received numerous rejection letters, almost all repeating the same refrain. They admired the novel, but didn't want to take a chance on it. I could understand. Why would American readers want to read a work of fiction about people, places, and incidents that didn't have anything to do with their own lives? What did it mean to them if an Iranian revolutionary was tortured because of his ideology? The situation is somewhat different now. The U.S. government has invaded Iraq. Iran has a new name now—it's part of the "axis of evil." People want to know where these mysterious places are and how these exotic and dangerous people live. Now that the East has been invaded there is a market for its literature. But unfortunately "Orientalism" (I'm referring to the term the late Edward Said used) is the source of most of the curiosity.

9. Are there plans to translate Against Gravity *into Farsi? How do you think Iranians would respond to your work?*

There are no such plans and I lack the genius and energy of Nabokov to be able to translate my own works. I'm not really sure what Iranian book readers (in Iran) would think about the book. Most probably, the subject matter wouldn't be as compelling to them as it may be to Iranian-Americans. People back home are dealing with different problems. Their issues and urgencies are of a different type.

10. What is your greatest ambition as a writer? What are you working on now?

My greatest ambition is to reach a literary level that invites serious readership. I wish myself sanity in this mad world and more time to think and write. I know that because of my lack of interest in the commercial market and "fame," I'll always need to work hard for my living, and this will contradict my writing plans, as has always been the case.

I'm working on a new novel. But it's too soon to talk about it. I have two works ready for publication. One is a long novel that was written before *Against Gravity* and rejected by almost all the major publishing houses in the nineties (some with words of praise). This novel is set in Iran; that might have been the reason for the rejections. And I have a novella that takes place in Houston. I have been alternately revising these two books for the past few years.

11. What other Iranian writers would you recommend to American readers?

It's fortunate that Sadeq Hedayat's *Blind Owl* has been translated into English. He is the father of modern literature in Iran and our Poe and Kafka in one. He wrote between the 1920s and 1940s and committed suicide in Paris in 1951. I also recommend Shahrnoush Parsipour's books. Some are translated into English. The anthology *A World Between: Poems, Short Stories, and Essays by Iranian-Americans* contains new voices. I recommend this and similar anthologies.

Questions for Discussion

1. Why has Farnoosh Moshiri chosen *Against Gravity* as her title? In what ways are the main characters weighed down? In what ways do they try to rise above the heaviness of their lives?

2. What effects does Moshiri create by using three narrators, telling these overlapping stories from three different points of view? How differently does each narrator view the same events?

3. Madison writes: "So the old bastard died and I died with him. Not because he died, but because of the way he died—so cheap, so ugly, so ungraceful" (p.14). Why is his father's death so devastating for Madison? How does it alter his life?

4. Why does Madison fall in love with Roya? What does he need from her? What drives him to want to kill her?

5. When she is forced to live in exile in India, Roya asks: "Who was punishing me? . . . Why did my country have mad leaders? Why had they taken my rights from me? Why couldn't I live in my own land? Had superpowers caused this dark destiny for our nation? If yes, then why? Who had given them the right to interfere in my country's affairs?" (p. 133). In what ways can Roya's fate be seen as a result of superpowers meddling in the affairs of Iran?

6. Ric tells Roya, "We're all refugees in a way. Many of us, many Americans live worse than refugees. This notion is wrong—this notion that we all prosper and we've all found that so-called American Dream" (p. 152). Which members of American society are forced to live in poverty, like refugees? How does America

appear when seen through the eyes of an Iranian immigrant, an AIDS patient, and a social worker?

7. Roya observes that "In America, almost everything is a deal. Even when you're receiving the kindness of your best friends you should never forget that one day you'll have to pay this back" (p. 175). Why does Roya feel this way? Do you think this is an accurate view of how people behave in America?

8. Why does Bobby try to kill himself? What is your opinion of what befalls him at the end of the novel?

9. At the end of the novel, Ric encourages Roya to finish her memoir. "Use your imagination," he tells her. "Who is interested in what really happened?" (p. 297). How are we to understand this final question? Aren't memoirs supposed to say what "really happened?" Do you think that Roya's memoir has become Moshiri's novel?

10. Both Roya and Ric are physically tortured, and Madison suffers emotional devastation and the painful physical deterioration of AIDS. What is it that enables Ric and Roya to transcend their pasts and to create a life together?

11. The events of *Against Gravity* take place primarily in the 1980s, but in what ways does the novel mirror and illuminate our current situation? To what degree are the problems the novel dramatizes still with us?

For more information about or to order other Penguin Readers Guides, please e-mail the Penguin Marketing Department at reading@us.penguingroup.com or write to us at:

Penguin Books Marketing Dept.
Readers Guides
375 Hudson Street
New York, NY 10014-3657

Please allow 4–6 weeks for delivery.
To access Penguin Readers Guides online, visit the Penguin Group (USA) Web site at www.penguin.com.

FOR THE BEST IN PAPERBACKS, LOOK FOR THE 🐧

In every corner of the world, on every subject under the sun, Penguin represents quality and variety—the very best in publishing today.

For complete information about books available from Penguin—including Penguin Classics, Penguin Compass, and Puffins—and how to order them, write to us at the appropriate address below. Please note that for copyright reasons the selection of books varies from country to country.

In the United States: Please write to *Penguin Group (USA), P.O. Box 12289 Dept. B, Newark, New Jersey 07101-5289* or call 1–800-788-6262.

In the United Kingdom: Please write to *Dept. EP, Penguin Books Ltd, Bath Road, Harmondsworth, West Drayton, Middlesex UB7 0DA.*

In Canada: Please write to *Penguin Books Canada Ltd, 90 Eglinton Avenue East, Suite 700, Toronto, Ontario M4P 2Y3.*

In Australia: Please write to *Penguin Books Australia Ltd, P.O. Box 257, Ringwood, Victoria 3134.*

In New Zealand: Please write to *Penguin Books (NZ) Ltd, Private Bag 102902, North Shore Mail Centre, Auckland 10.*

In India: Please write to *Penguin Books India Pvt Ltd, 11 Panchsheel Shopping Centre, Panchsheel Park, New Delhi 110 017.*

In the Netherlands: Please write to *Penguin Books Netherlands bv, Postbus 3507, NL-1001 AH Amsterdam.*

In Germany: Please write to *Penguin Books Deutschland GmbH, Metzlerstrasse 26, 60594 Frankfurt am Main.*

In Spain: Please write to *Penguin Books S. A., Bravo Murillo 19, 1° B, 28015 Madrid.*

In Italy: Please write to *Penguin Italia s.r.l., Via Benedetto Croce 2, 20094 Corsico, Milano.*

In France: Please write to *Penguin France, Le Carré Wilson, 62 rue Benjamin Baillaud, 31500 Toulouse.*

In Japan: Please write to *Penguin Books Japan Ltd, Kaneko Building, 2-3-25 Koraku, Bunkyo-Ku, Tokyo 112.*

In South Africa: Please write to *Penguin Books South Africa (Pty) Ltd, Private Bag X14, Parkview, 2122 Johannesburg.*